Dark Passage

By the same author

Dragon Wind Rising
Windstorm
Scarlet Wind

Dark Passage

Frances Burke

ROBERT HALE · LONDON

ISBN 978-0-7198-0667-4

Robert Hale Limited
Clerkenwell House
Clerkenwell Green
London EC1R 0HT

www.halebooks.com

2 4 6 8 10 9 7 5 3 1

In memory of a dear daughter,
Astelle

Typeset in 11/14½ Palatino
Printed in Great Britain by the MPG Books Group,
Bodmin and King's Lynn

CHAPTER ONE

NICOLA REDMOND STOOD at the balustrade, watching the waves forty feet below, sucking and receding from the rocks in the wash of a passing yacht. Beyond the steps tumbling down the cliff face the harbour spread, glistening in the sunlight, its magnificent foreshores buttressed in golden stone and scalloped in sand-rimmed bays.

'We own the best view in the whole of Sydney,' said a satisfied voice behind her.

Nicola turned and smiled. 'Why, Mother! Even better than Lake Maggiore? I thought the outlook from the prince's palace gardens was your absolute favourite.'

Millicent Redmond patted her shining coiffure and sighed. 'Ah, Maggiore, Como, nights at La Scala Opera. And Rome. How I miss the Via Veneto, the gardens, the galleries. Really, Nicola, it is not kind to remind me.'

Her daughter hid her impatience at this preference for a sophisticated European lifestyle over life in 'the colonies'. Nicola loved her home, a red-brick and stone mansion set high on a tree-lined point and almost surrounded by water. She loved the city, glimpsed a mile or two to the west, its sandstone buildings topped with coppered domes and spires that reflected the hot light peculiar to this great southern land. And she loved the relative freedom of a young and vibrant society where it was possible to escape the restrictions of the old world.

As Millicent stepped back through the long windows to rejoin her guests, sunlight was briefly trapped in the diamond bracelet at her wrist, her husband's gift to celebrate her recent return from their daughter's obligatory London season. Nicola blinked, momentarily blinded. Then her hand went to her throat, to the heart-shaped fire opal pendant that had been the expression of Papa's love for her.

Her reminiscent smile was tinged with worry. Papa didn't seem quite himself. At times he was quite distrait. But there could be no doubt of his joy in the reunion with his beloved wife and daughter. Just look at this magnificent party he'd thrown in honour of their return.

Snatches of conversation floated through the arched doorway from the salon, along with music and the clink of crystal as champagne flowed.

'I believe that recovery is in sight.' The booming tones of Arthur Claxton, insurance underwriter and prominent in the business community, were addressed to a colleague.

'Don't speak too soon,' was the retort. "Dollar Bill" Borbidge, whose nickname came from his habit of turning his money into American currency for investment, spoke with the dissatisfaction of a man whose system had lately let him down.

Of course, men could speak of nothing but finances these days, thought Nicola. In London, while reluctantly circling ballrooms and parading in The Row, she couldn't help hearing discussions of the mid 1890s crash and the Depression that had followed. British financiers who'd been caught up in Australia's disastrous bust were furiously disparaging. They tended to forget how eagerly they'd embraced the preceding boom.

Josephine Claxton's nasal voice cut across the conversation.

'Enough of such talk, Arthur. This is a party.' She strolled out to Nicola, trailing an aura of cologne and camphor that was peculiarly her own. 'My dear, what a wonderful trip you've had. All those exotic places; the opportunity to mix with *la crème de la crème.*'

Nicola hid a grin. Her favourite memory was of a scramble up a stony goat track in Greece to view the two-thousand-years old remains of a temple to Diana.

'And you were actually presented before Her Majesty.' Josephine sounded wistful. She enjoyed a relatively high position on the colonial social tree; but there was undoubtedly an extra cachet to acceptance into London's upper circles.

Nicola tried to look as if her presentation had been the highlight of her trip. But in fact she'd cheerfully have forgone the experience of tight lacing, of manoeuvring a three-foot train, along with fan, feathers and other useless furbelows, and the ultimate in anxiety: a full court curtsy. The wonder was that she hadn't toppled when rising from the difficult locked-knee position. It made her feel hot, just remembering it.

'Shall we go inside, Mrs Claxton? They're lighting the lamps, and I believe Papa is going to make a speech.'

Outside the sun was dropping beneath the horizon with the speed of the semi-tropics, and the evening star had risen above a pale crescent moon. All along the northern shore lights glimmered, reflecting in wine-dark waters. Nicola paused, held by the beauty of the tranquil evening.

At that moment her father brushed past her, walking as if in a dream. He crossed the marble paving to the balustrade and stood for a long moment, as though imprinting the scene on his mind. Then, as Nicola watched, frozen, not quite comprehending, he climbed to the railing and, without a backward glance, stepped into space.

CHAPTER TWO

NICOLA CLOSED THE door of her mother's bedroom softly, not wanting to disturb the waxen-faced woman lying drugged into merciful oblivion. With her friend Rose Basevi tiptoeing beside her she moved down the stairs and into the music room, her room, the one place which held no reminders of either her dead father or the mother who had retreated beyond the barrier of hysteria and subsequent exhaustion.

Nicola slumped on to the piano stool. 'What am I going to do, Rose? She's been like this for four days. I can't reach her although, God knows, I've tried in every way I could think of.' She pressed her palms to her throbbing temples, smoothing back a few loose strands of hair. Normally as vibrant as burnished copper, they were dull and stringy from lack of care. For the past few days she'd had neither the time nor the inclination to fuss over her appearance.

Rose crouched down and put an arm around her. 'Wait. It's all you can do. Doctor Freeman says she'll eventually recover.'

'Not if she doesn't eat. She wouldn't touch the pie you brought, or even Josh's tangerine oranges, which she normally adores.'

Rose pursed her lips. Palely blonde and reed slender, her bones seemingly too frail to support her, she'd always been seen as a foil to the statuesque Nicola. Although superficially unalike, and coming from entirely different backgrounds, they yet shared many things in common, and until Nicola's enforced departure on a Grand Tour they had been inseparable.

Now Rose's voice took on an edge. 'Yes – the oranges. The ones Master Josh is supposed to have bought with pennies earned at the market. I've my suspicions about that.'

'It was a kind thought. Don't enquire too deeply into the

provenance of the oranges.' Nicola managed a smile. 'You are lucky to have a young brother, you know.'

'I know. Nicola, what can I do to help? Is there someone seeing to your affairs? I'm afraid my father wouldn't be of much use. . . .'

Joseph Basevi's sacking from his position as supervisor in a tailoring establishment had brought his family to severely reduced circumstances, as Nicola knew. It had also changed him, severely undermining his status in his own eyes.

She said, 'Our affairs are in hand. I've an appointment with Mr Charlton Perry of Perry and Squires, solicitors, next Monday. He was always concerned with Papa's business.' Her face crumpled and tears slid silently down her cheeks. 'If only I'd known, I could have shared his worries, helped him find a way through. All that money spent on a stupid European tour . . . Oh Papa, Papa!'

Rose hugged her until she reached the sniffing stage and began to hunt for her handkerchief, then said, 'His pride and self-esteem were so bound up in his business. He just couldn't face the people who had depended upon him. I've seen how that can happen to a man.'

Nicola put away her handkerchief. 'Rose, he was a good man, but I can't help but think he abandoned his responsibility to the folk who trusted him and lost all they had in the world. He must have seen this coming for months.' She threw up her hands. 'Anyway, it's useless speculating. I must deal with the aftermath, with Mother's collapse and whatever else our dubious future holds. I expect Mr Charlton Perry will inform me of the details.'

Rose stood up. 'Nicola, I must go now, if I want to keep my place.' She paused. 'I so wish I'd been with you when it happened. I just couldn't afford to lose those hours of pay.'

'Of course.' Nicola hugged her. 'You came when you could. Rose, it's terrible that you must give up your own dreams and go to work in a factory. I'd no idea things were so bad back here, while I was off cavorting in London ballrooms.'

'And being bored beyond bearing, knowing you.' Rose smiled. 'Things will get better. Now, would you like Josh to come after school for company?'

'No, dear. You need him at home. I'll be perfectly all right alone.' Nicola glanced down at the piano keyboard, chequered in rainbow light from the Burne-Jones style windows, and felt her spirits lift. 'I still have my music, and it's a comfort.'

Minutes later the first notes of a Chopin nocturne followed Rose down the drive as Nicola sought her own brand of oblivion.

The family carriage having been put down, Nicola took the steam tram into the city for her appointment with the solicitor. Normally she would have enjoyed the novelty and the exhilarating sensation of speed. She didn't mind the cinders and grit. They were a small price to pay for the illusion of being part of the modern world, the scientific world racing them all into the next century. However, today her mind was on other matters.

Clutching her hat and averting her eyes from the few pseudo-holly-decorated doorways, incongruous in the heat of an Australian Christmas, she occupied herself with speculation on the news that Mr Charlton Perry would have for her. Might it be possible to salvage something from the ruin? Her mother received a small income derived from her own family property, so they wouldn't actually starve; yet, unless Papa had provided for them in some unspecified way, the future looked bleak.

She left the tram at the harbour terminus and hurried through the drab streets, aware that there was little sign of jollity to mark the season. There was no bunting or extra lights and only a minimum of stock displayed in storefront windows. Faces of passers-by were serious, and there were so many beggars. She felt her spirits sink.

The rooms occupied by Perry & Squires, Attorneys at Law, were pleasantly situated one block up from the Circular Quay, overlooking the busy shipping lanes. Nicola, being escorted to a seat opposite Mr Charlton Perry's desk, thought such a vista must be quite distracting for him. Perhaps he was too dedicated to his work for such diversion. His staid figure, in a frock coat of ancient cut, his creased cheeks outlined in mutton chop whiskers, were echoed on every wall, where a phalanx of strikingly similar faces hung, their collective frowning gaze confronting the room's occupants. It was all rather demoralizing.

Nicola sat with her hands clasped tightly in her lap. She'd taken care with her appearance, brushing her hair until it glowed like autumn beech leaves, before piling it high beneath a saucy little feathered hat. Her dress, in a dark-indigo shade which was the closest she came to mourning, was laced to the required hourglass silhouette, the shoulders raised and sleeves puffed to accentuate her narrow waist. Knowing how well she looked helped to give her confidence. With a glance at Mr Perry, she sat back and waited for him to open proceedings.

He surprised her by crossing to a side door and ushering in another man, much younger, taller and broader, and with a head of hair almost as startling as her own. Of a rich golden-brown shade, it waved thickly and was worn a good deal longer than fashion now decreed. His grey eyes rested on her with a steady, examining look.

Mr Perry cleared his throat. 'Miss Redmond, permit me to introduce Mr Andrew Dene.'

The newcomer bowed and took a chair opposite Nicola, while Mr Perry settled himself behind his desk and met her questioning gaze with the utmost blandness, saying,

'I have requested Mr Dene's attendance at this meeting since he is a beneficiary of your father's estate.'

Nicola's mouth opened and the lawyer waited politely while she sought for words. Eventually she said, 'Mr Perry, I understand that my father's estate has been bankrupted. My mother and I have little expectation, but whatever is left will surely be ours?'

'Hrrmph. I'm afraid that is not the case. It appears that many years ago your father borrowed a sum from Mr Dene's father, using your mother's dowry, an investment in a manufactury, as collateral. The money has never been repaid and the debt reverted to the late Mr Paul Dene's estate. Mr Andrew Dene has only recently made claim as the sole legatee.'

'I don't believe it. Papa wouldn't. . . .' Nicola choked, and stopped. Her gloved fingers gripped her purse tight enough for the seams to bite into her skin.

Andrew Dene leaned forward, searching her face. 'Your mother didn't tell you, Miss Redmond?'

'I don't suppose she knew.' Nicola controlled her voice with difficulty. She'd known things were bad, but losing her mother's property would leave them destitute. She turned to the lawyer.

11

'Can nothing be done? Surely the agreement can't be binding without my mother's permission.'

Mr Charlton Perry cleared his throat. 'Your mother would appear to have placed her affairs in your late father's hands. The agreement is perfectly legal, I assure you. I drew up the contract myself.'

'And Papa's estate? I know the bank has gone, but he owned houses in the inner city and had other interests in the press and in mining.' Under his strictly non-committal gaze her own didn't waver.

'It is regrettable, Miss Redmond, but your father's estate cannot cover his debts, let alone provide a residue for you and Mrs Redmond. However,' he nodded in Andrew Dene's direction, 'Mr Dene and I have come to an arrangement which I believe to be very generous on his part.'

She stiffened. 'What sort of an arrangement, Mr Perry?'

'One which I am sure you and Mrs Redmond will find satisfactory. I might add that there is absolutely no legal compulsion upon Mr Dene to offer any sort of assistance.' The solicitor's precise voice had cooled. The unspoken word: *ingratitude,* hung in the air.

Blood rushed to Nicola's cheeks. This man was her solicitor, but he acted more like a guardian. He simply had no right to be making arrangements for her future without consultation.

She said, 'Mr Perry, have I misunderstood, or are you actually proposing an act of charity by a perfect stranger?' Turning swiftly to Andrew Dene, she added, 'And you, sir. I've no doubt that your intentions are kindly, but they are also humiliating.' Her lips trembled with suppressed emotion, and she closed them firmly. The events of the past few days were having a delayed effect, but nothing would induce her to show weakness in front of these two men, not even this latest, shocking blow.

Andrew Dene said gently, 'Miss Redmond, you're quite mistaken, believe me.'

Mr Perry couldn't contain himself. 'My dear young lady, I can assure you that Mr Dene's offer is designed merely to redress what he sees as an injustice. Perhaps if I were to speak with Mrs Redmond . . .' The implication was all too clear: Nicola was a feather-headed innocent, not to be trusted with matters of business.

Mortified, Nicola rose with all the dignity she could command. 'Gentlemen, I can't possibly speak about this until I have discussed the matter with my mother. I shall be in touch with you, Mr Perry. Good day, Mr Dene.'

She moved swiftly to the door, but Andrew Dene was there before her, his voice concerned. 'Miss Redmond. Please believe that this situation has been a shock to me, also. I'm sure that a satisfactory arrangement can be reached after discussion.'

She nodded stonily, holding her purse to her bosom in an effort to contain the emotions threatening to boil over. Then she was through the door and out into the street.

Safe in the privacy of a cab, she waited for angry tears to flow. But she found they had turned into a solid lump of misery that wouldn't be moved. What could she say to her mother? How were they to survive? What had her papa been thinking of to leave them in such straits?

Her thoughts turned to the man who had, however unwittingly, filched her mother's last means of support. His benevolent offer, whatever it might be, was impossible. Helpless females, were they – she and her mother? Well, she'd show them all just what a woman was capable of when she put her mind to a problem. With youth and health and a reasonable intelligence, she could easily find work to support the two of them. One thing was certain: she'd starve before accepting charity from a stranger!

CHAPTER THREE

THE RECOUNTING OF her interview with the lawyer had been as painful as she had anticipated. Millicent Redmond, succumbing to hysterics, had kept to her bed, overcome by the horror of her new circumstances. She remained listless and unable to care for herself, bemoaning her forthcoming loss when her home and its contents would be sold up by creditors.

Her anguish when her gaze alighted on some cherished item about to be torn from her drew sympathy from her daughter. However, Nicola soon found there were limits to the number of times she could bear the tale of the long-case marquetry clock, a Restoration period treasure given as a wedding gift by Great Aunt Matilda; or the rather frightful Staffordshire dogs brought all the way from her grandparents' ancestral home to guard the Redmond dining room hearth.

Her awkward efforts to offer comfort were repelled by Millicent's emotional detachment, and Nicola now felt the full weight of responsibility while struggling with her own loss, her mother's dependency and the idea of home, security, permanence being things of the past. However, her natural resilience and a strong streak of independence helped her to face the challenge of the future. She told herself that it would be exciting to discover just how much she could accomplish using her wits, and without the interference of strangers.

When removal men arrived one morning Nicola watched dry-eyed as her beloved piano was loaded on to a dray, along with the marquetry clock, the Staffordshire dogs and other miscellaneous furnishings.

Beside her, ever-supportive Rose squeezed her hand comfortingly. 'You will get it all back one day, if I know you, Nicola.'

Nicola managed a grin. 'Everything but those revolting dogs! Now, Mother has a friend sitting with her, a Mrs Claxton, who is one of the few who have stayed loyal; and you did promise me a day for house-hunting. We'll take the tram into the land agents' office and see about premises to rent.'

When Rose hesitated, Nicola read her expression correctly. 'Don't worry, I have money for the fare. I sold some of my sheet music to Eliza Pettigrew. She always did envy my catalogues from England at Christmastime.'

'Oh, Nicola. You must have hated that.'

Nicola shrugged. 'After the first step, the others are easier. I know I'm not meant to dispose of anything, but the music was mine, not a part of "the estate". I'm beginning to hate those two words. Why should everything in our lives depend upon what Papa did or did not do? We're people, Mother and I, not chattels.'

'You are learning what the poor have always known: that you must live from one day to the next. Nicola, how are you going to afford rent?'

'I'll get a job of work.'

'What sort of work? You can't pin two pieces of fabric together, let alone sew; and I don't quite see you in service. Imagine you in a maid's cap tripping over the rug, dropping the best Sèvres cups, pouring tea on your mistress.' Rose stepped aside to avoid the rolled up carpet emerging like an anaconda through the front door.

Nicola laughed with her old carefree response to the ridiculous. 'What a shambles I'd make of such work. No, I shall offer my services as a teacher. New schools seem to be springing up all over the place in the wake of compulsory state education.'

'There is the small matter of training. It's at least a one-year course, even for infants' teachers.'

Nicola waved airily as she led the way indoors. 'It's not always essential. They still use the old pupil-teacher system in many denominational schools, so obviously they are not too particular about specialized training. I don't suppose that, with a good Anglo-Saxon name like Redmond, I can bluff my way into any Roman Catholic establishments. Maybe I should change it to Burke or O'Reilley.'

Rose shook her head. 'You're incorrigible. Where will you go for a reference?'

'To Mr Charlton Perry, of course. He'll give me a *character*, even though he's quite annoyed with me.' Turning her back on the dismal sight of a dining room denuded of all but its fireplace, she hurried her friend upstairs to gather hat, gloves and purse.

'I wonder how Mr Andrew Dene feels.' Rose peeped mischievously beneath her lashes and was rewarded with a snort.

'Guilty, I hope. He should.'

'Taking the bread from the mouths of widows and orphans? Still, it's not really his fault, Nicola. And he need not have offered to assist you and your mother.'

Nicola lengthened her stride, forcing Rose to break into a trot. 'Patronage!' she said. 'We can do without it.'

'That remains to be seen. After all, beggars can't. . . .' Rose caught Nicola's eye, and trailed off.

'Thank you. We haven't quite reached that stage. I know Mother would close with the offer instantly, but I just cannot. Something in me refuses to be beholden to a stranger.' A faint smile crept into her voice. 'Besides, he's so self assured. He irritates me. Now, let's run for the tram. Thank heaven for these new shorter skirts.'

Nicola returned home late, tired and dispirited, and glad to find her mother had gone early to bed. There would be no need to recount the day's refusals and civil snubs just yet. The man at the land sales office had been polite but unequivocal. Without a substantial down payment there could be no question of renting one of the salubrious cottages on any of the estates managed by his company. In fact, the rental figures mentioned had caused Nicola to swallow and apologize for wasting the agent's time. Clearly she would have to lower her sights.

Rose had gone back to earn her much needed pittance of twelve shillings per week. Jobs were getting scarce, as she had pointed out. Nicola should begin looking for one, immediately.

The following day turned out to be the most humbling. Nicola suffered a severe shock as interview after interview ended in her being informed that she was unsuitable, unqualified, inexperienced and entering a market where there were plenty of applicants. Her aspirations sank from teaching music and deportment to young ladies, to basic grammar and geography in primary school, to pothooks and counting-blocks in kindergarten.

Her ability to order and hostess a banquet for fifty people failed to impress; and no marks were given for native common sense, high energy and a wicked imagination. Nicola's real education had come from her father's library. She could produce no concrete evidence of her intelligence or capability.

What? No certificate demonstrating excellence in mathematics? A pity. The Chopin nocturne? Very nicely performed, but hardly useful in the science laboratory. Knowledge of the more exotic classics? Unusual, and hardly suitable reading for a young lady, if the comment might be pardoned.

Fuming, Nicola swallowed an astringent retort and took herself home, footsore and even more sore in spirit.

Her exhaustion turned to exasperation when she heard voices coming from the conservatory. A visitor, but not Mrs Claxton, she thought, as she turned wearily to the doorway at the end of the hall. She could not detect the odour of camphor and eau-de-cologne. Who, then?

She stepped into the humid hothouse atmosphere, pushing aside drooping palm leaves to encounter the grey eyes of Andrew Dene.

He rose, completely at ease. 'Good evening, Miss Redmond.'

Nicola was startled into forgetting her manners. 'What are you doing here?'

'As you see, I'm taking tea with your mother. I trust you are well?'

Nicola could feel her indignation swelling. Had he managed to win over her all too impressionable mother, already? She glanced anxiously at Millicent, hovering over the second best tea service. (Where and how had that been hidden from the creditors?)

Millicent said in a voice of smiling reproof, 'My dear! Do not keep Mr Dene standing. Sit down and have a cup of tea.'

Nicola obediently sank into the rattan chair vacated by the visitor. He drew up another beside her and hitched his trousers in what she decided was a vulgar manner. Also, the trousers were too self-consciously well cut, and his coat too modern, his hair too long, and . . . She caught herself up. This was unreasonable prejudice. She'd be far wiser to discover how far he had progressed with his campaign of interference.

Turning to him she said, composedly, 'You are fortunate to find us here, Mr Dene. We leave at the end of the week.'

'So I believe. I asked Mrs Redmond for her future address, but she tells me nothing is settled. I believe you are seeking lodgings?'

With the memory of the land agent's bare civility fresh in her mind, Nicola said in a hollow voice, 'Without any success, I'm afraid. But there's still tomorrow.'

'If I can be of any assistance, please call on me.'

It was only common courtesy, and yet. . . . Through her teeth she thanked him, while refusing the offer.

Millicent looked reproving. 'Nicola, do not be so quick to decline any help. Mr Dene has, in fact, devised a plan. It seems we are distantly connected by marriage, which naturally allows me to accept a proposal which I should otherwise—' Nicola's expression halted her.

So he'd gone behind her back. It was too much. 'Mother! You're not about to become this man's pensioner? You would not accept guilt money?'

Millicent's hand slipped and the teapot landed heavily on the tray. Nicola hardly noticed. She glared at Andrew, who said, 'Your mother sees the matter in a different light, Miss Redmond.'

'I'm not surprised. However, your tale of kinship doesn't impress me. Produce your family tree, Mr Dene, and show me where it joins mine.'

'Is that really necessary, Miss Redmond?'

'Mr Dene, shall we come to the point? My father is dead and I must take over his responsibility. Papa would expect it.' She turned to Millicent. 'Mother, I promise you that I'll do everything I can to make us a comfortable life together. What we do from now on is nobody's affair but ours.'

He tried once more, leaning forward earnestly. 'If you will only hear what I have to say—'

'No! Our way of life has been destroyed, but not our pride. We can take care of ourselves without interference from strangers. I must therefore, once and for all, decline your offer of assistance. I feel it would be better if you left now.'

He rose immediately, bowed to his hostess – who was now stunned into immobility – and left the conservatory. Nicola followed and closed the front door on him, then returned to face the music.

'All right, Mother. Out with it, before you explode. Or shall I say it for you? I was unpardonably rude to a guest and I've lost us the opportunity to be cared for and guided and told how to conduct our affairs. In short, I've maintained our pride and freed us from an unbearable obligation.'

Millicent pressed a handkerchief to her lips and spoke in a muffled voice. 'Unforgivable! You have shamed us both. How could you do it, Nicola? No. Do not speak. I find I can scarcely comprehend your reasoning these days. You are not the daughter I knew before … before … I don't know what I have done to deserve such treatment. Here we had an opportunity of saving ourselves and you have alienated a benefactor. Such a charming and personable man. So suitable.'

'Suitable for what, Mother?' Honestly bewildered, Nicola was struck dumb by her mother's answer.

'Why, as a prospective husband. He clearly admires you.'

After a few dazed seconds, Nicola went off into a gale of laughter. 'Admires me! He'd as soon embrace a wildcat. Mother, I think you'd better go to bed and recover. You are clearly overwrought.'

She cleared the tea things on to a tray and carried it out to the pantry. She would wash them in the morning before setting out on her search for work and for somewhere to live. Tonight she was too tired to bother.

The next three days reinforced for Nicola the difference between Miss Redmond of Mapleton House, Point Piper, with a cushion of wealth and privilege between her and hard reality, and Miss Redmond of nowhere, without prospects or a male relative of substance to stand surety for her. Yet the refusals she met only fed her determination to break through the walls of prejudice.

While resting for a few minutes on a wall in a shabby area below Darlinghurst gaol, Nicola faced the fact that she lacked the most basic training in the art of earning a living.

While idly watching children playing amongst the refuse in the gutter, she realized that a fight had developed. As shrill, tormented shrieks began issuing from the mêlée, she sprang up and, wielding her sunshade like a truncheon, joined in. A few strokes around grimy kneecaps broke up the huddle, along with the sunshade, and the attackers ran off, leaving a small boy snivelling and clutching a bundle of rags to his chest.

Surveying him for damage, Nicola began to wonder where the rags stopped and the boy's clothing began. She could see his thin ribs through the rents in his shirt, and his pants were almost indecent, patched and worn and flapping about skinny feet and ankles ingrained with dirt.

The boy peered up suspiciously through a thatch of dusty hair. He tried to scramble up, then fell back with a cry.

'Where are you hurt?' Nicola dropped to her haunches but didn't try to touch the boy.

'It's me leg,' was the surly reply.

'May I see? I promise not to hurt you.'

The boy searched her face, and nodded. 'Fanks for runnin' that lot off.'

Nicola grinned and began a gentle prodding of the grimy leg being favoured by the boy. Reassured that it wasn't broken, she sat back on her heels and offered her hand.

'My name's Nicola. What's yours?'

With a sudden odd formality, the boy took her hand and said, 'Benny. Pleased to meetcher.'

'What have you there, Benny?' Nicola pointed to the ragged bundle.

The boy's hand tightened protectively on his treasure. 'It's mine.'

'Certainly it's yours.' Nicola abandoned that line of conversation. 'Why aren't you in school, Benny? You must be at least nine years old, such a well-grown boy as you are.'

Benny's thin chest swelled. 'I'm seven, eight soon, though. I goes to the Ragged School down there – sometimes.' He pointed down the crazy, sloping street to a building like a warehouse, with no yard and nothing to indicate its purpose as an educational establishment. Benny grinned. 'Mr Murchison got took off to the 'ospital, real crook with a pain in 'is bread basket, and we got let out.'

Nicola gazed thoughtfully from Benny's pinched face to the building squatting in dingy squalor, and thought that this was her chance. A Mr Murchison admitted to hospital must surely remain off duty for a few weeks, perhaps even longer.

She grasped Benny's matchstick arm and helped him to his feet. 'Come on, laddie. Lean on me and I'll help you back home.'

'What about yer thingummy.' He pointed to the wreck of the sunshade.

Nicola shrugged. 'I'm not going to need such things in the future. We'll leave it with the other rubbish.'

They set off downhill, Benny clinging and hopping like a skinny frog, Nicola filled with hope and determination.

CHAPTER FOUR

'THOSE CLOTHES WON'T do.' Rose poked a scornful finger at Nicola, then lifted a flat iron from the hob and tested it against a piece of cloth. Satisfied that it wouldn't scorch, she set to work on the skirt spread before her on the table.

Nicola watched the busy hands, red and swollen from contact with caustic soap, and replied mildly, 'Why won't they do? They are neat and plain enough.'

'They'll be ruined in a week. Your pupils will be larrikins, running uncontrolled, dirtying everything they touch. Woolloomooloo is a filthy part of the docklands, worse even than here.' She placed the iron on a trivet while she rearranged the skirt, avoiding Nicola's gaze.

Nicola grinned. 'Are you trying to discourage me? Of course my pupils will be larrikins, half of them orphans off the street, mannerless and wild, and some most probably known to the police. I know what to expect. I also want to set an example, particularly to the girls. They need to see how a female should dress and conduct herself.'

'Deportment lessons, no less!' Rose thumped the iron as if teaching the skirt a lesson.

'Not deportment, self-pride. Those poor little bits of flotsam have washed up on the shores of charity. Their one chance of a decent life is getting an education. Few trained teachers want to take them on, especially in that part of the city, and I'm determined to do the best I can by them.'

Rose swapped her iron for another, hotter one off the stove, and kept on working. Sweat beaded her forehead and upper lip, but Nicola knew better than to offer to help. Instead, she lifted the boiling kettle with a cloth and filled the teapot, straining the water through old tea leaves preserved from an earlier occasion. Taking cups from the kitchen shelf, she noted the absence of Mrs Basevi's prized Wedgwood pieces. There were no biscuits and no flour to make any, only a tin of the cheaper sago.

'I'll take a cup of tea to your mother, Rose. Is your father at home?'

'No. He's out drowning his sorrow in spirits we can't afford, instead of seeking another position. Heaven knows if he'll be in any condition to do so by tomorrow.' Rose's tone was now more despairing than angry as she laid aside the iron and wiped her hot face. Nicola put down the teapot and rushed to comfort her.

'Oh, Rose, it was wicked of them to let you both go at once. They are a heartless lot at that factory.' She hugged her friend, then made her sit down and brought her a cup. 'Don't fret, my dear. Your father is an excellent tailor. He'll be taken on somewhere else, and your own stitching is so fine, I swear it looks done by fairies.'

Rose shook her head. 'Father's sight is not good now; and there seem to be so many women seeking work, with the men being laid off everywhere. I'll keep on trying, of course. Mama's piece-work is poorly paid, and I know it wearies her.'

To distract her, Nicola said, 'To return to your comment, what can be more serviceable than my perfectly ordinary skirt and blouse?'

'Canvas and calico and an iron hat. *They* might survive. Believe me, you won't want gloves and parasols in such a place.'

Nicola said ruefully, 'I've already killed off the parasol. Don't worry. The interviewing board left me in no doubt of the terrors in store.'

'Nicola Redmond! I do believe you are hoping for a challenge.'

'Yes, I am. I won't be an orthodox teacher and the curriculum will be stretched, not to say distorted, by reason of my deficiencies in some areas. Still, I mean to help these children the best way I can.' Nicola picked up the teapot. 'Now, I'll give your mother her tea and force that young minx, Daisy, to wash and change her pinafore, while you finish the ironing. Where is Josh, by the way?'

'He's gone to the brickworks for labouring work.' Rose looked defiant. 'I know he's supposed to stay at school until the age of fourteen. Well, for the poor it doesn't work that way, and we are now some of the poor.' She swept her arm in a circle. 'Do you think we live like this from choice?'

Nicola concentrated on pouring, knowing well enough how miserably cramped was this one living room with its gimcrack table and chairs, one shelf above a sink, and a pine food safe. A corner dresser held bits of cheap china, and the wedding-gift clock. But the floor was of tamped dirt, and the comforts and trimmings of a real home had gone, sold or pawned as the Basevi family sank lower on the social scale. The whole rat run area was a dumping ground for refuse, in dreadful contrast with their former address.

Rose sighed. 'I'm sorry, Nicola. You don't need to hear me whining. Please take Mama her tea. She'll be eager to see you.'

Nicola did as she was asked and spent the next half hour in cheerful conversation with the sick woman. Uncomplaining, always ready with a smile for a visitor, Jenny Basevi was the hub of her loving family. Not for the first time, Nicola envied Rose her mother.

Ready to leave, Nicola peered in the mirror set on the kitchen shelf and pinned on her hat at a jaunty angle, saying, 'I'm still not accustomed to my new home, Mrs Gardiner's Boarding Establishment, "clean rooms and cheap, only seven shillings the week with full dinner provided, not including Sundays." Mrs G. believes in keeping the Sabbath holy. Mother is being difficult, of course. She refuses to sit at table with persons of a lower order and has somehow bullied our landlady into giving us a corner of our own. You can imagine how well that sits with our neighbours.' She leaned to kiss Rose's cheek. 'I know you're worried, but I truly believe you will find something, as I did.'

From her dais Nicola surveyed the rows of expectant faces, attentive at the moment because she was an object of curiosity, the new teacher. Sunlight through barred windows of what had once been a mill, fell in strips across bench tops scratched and gouged by earlier generations. The air still seemed sifted with a residue of powdered grain, glinting and softening the building's grim brick walls. A cupboard stood beyond the teacher's desk and chair. The only other item of furniture, a blackboard, balanced on an easel to the right of the dais.

Left to fend for herself, following her introduction by a distracted head teacher, Nicola confronted the restless children.

'I expect we shall soon come to know each other well. Today I want to learn your names, so I'd ask you to call them out one at a time along each row, starting with this young man on my left in the front.'

The boy, of about eight years, glanced slyly from the corner of his eyes and muttered, 'Fred Horner, miss.' Like so many children in his age group, his growth had suddenly spurted beyond his clothes, and a ragged haircut added to his odd, scarecrow appearance.

'Well, Fred. Suppose we begin by you showing me what you have in your lap under the desk.'

The boy gaped. 'Nuthin', miss.'

'Oh. Then you won't object to standing and showing me your hands.'

Looking hunted, the boy slowly rose, stuffing an object into the pocket of his tattered pants.

Nicola strode forward and plucked the object from him. 'Well, now, a perfectly splendid shanghai. I can see why you would want to keep such a treasure with you, but it's not something that should be brought into class.' She eyed the wood-and-rubber implement with false enthusiasm, privately thinking, help! What this child could do with such a weapon! She gave him her best smile. 'What do you think, Fred?'

Fred's expression clearly said what he thought, but he muttered, 'Yes, miss. I mean, no, miss.'

'Then I think I'll just lock it away in the cupboard until it's time to go home. If you bring it to school again, I'll have to confiscate it. Do you know what that means?'

'You'll keep it for you.'

'No, Fred. I'll burn it.' Nicola turned her back while unlocking the cupboard, and heard behind her the rustle of a dozen pieces of clothing being adjusted. She faced the class again.

'I'm giving you all fair warning. Today is the last time you may bring with you forbidden playthings. Watch me write a list of these on the blackboard. I'll read each word and you can spell it out with me and copy it on to your slates. You may sit, Fred.'

Scowling, the boy slumped on to the bench. His neighbour grinned and dug him in the ribs, but the rest of the class of about twenty children looked thoughtful.

They worked their way through the list of offensive weapons, odorous materials and livestock, directing glances of surprised respect at the woman who seemed to know all the more mischievous ways of disruption and mayhem.

Nicola kept them at their slates, careless of spelling but determined to implant the lesson. When sure that it had taken root, she said conversationally, 'I should tell you that I was a particularly naughty and inventive pupil myself at your age, and I shouldn't be surprised to find I know more about giving trouble than you do. But I grew up and discovered how interesting lessons could be, and I stopped being troublesome – well, most of the time – because I wanted to know more about the world and how it works.' She gathered them in one by one with her roving glance. 'I'll make you all a promise. Each time you work hard and complete the set studies I give you, afterwards we'll do something fun and interesting.'

The joyful smiles rewarded her. These children's faces, in some ways as old as time, yet still naive, touched her. All at once she was glad to be unacceptable to the regular school system. Here, with these waifs whom no one else wanted she could be herself, try methods that would not be countenanced in the strict system that required learning by rote and lessons that were often tedious and lacking in intellectual demand. There was no shortage of intelligence in this room. On the contrary, she'd need all her wits to stay ahead and in control.

Elated rather than dismayed by the idea, she stood well back out of the stampede as the bell rang for recess and the classroom emptied like an unplugged cistern.

CHAPTER FIVE

TRUE TO HER promise, Nicola rewarded genuine effort with games or with stories of pirates and shipwreck and the derring-do of both men and women. Refusing to recognize the girls as weaker in any way, she treated all equally and, in return, received the tentative affection of these semi-wild ragamuffins.

Rose's prediction of damage to her clothes had proved true. Grubby hands pulled at Nicola's sleeve or skirt to draw attention, and she knelt on the floor for bobbins and ran with them between wickets set up in the dirty street, or joined in a boisterous game of rounders.

From her childhood treasure box she brought in interesting objects such as shells from the South Seas or a Swiss cowbell; and while books were in short supply, she substituted sketches of animals and remembered scenes from her travels, and wove tales around these. And in singing classes she tried to transmit something of her own passion for music.

By the end of the first fortnight she had conquered the discipline problem. The children were too interested in what they were doing and what might come next from this highly unusual teacher. She never had to send a child to be disciplined. No child was ever rude to her or offered any deliberate offence. She worked carefully on their crude manners and speech, and she got results. Arriving back at the boarding house each night, hot, tired and dishevelled, she felt satisfied. Her empty life had been filled, leaving her no time to brood.

It was otherwise with Millicent Redmond, who usually pounced on her daughter as soon as she appeared and poured out a litany of trivial complaints.

One evening as Nicola trudged uphill through the dusk

towards the better-lighted streets, she met her mother coming out of a chemist's shop. On seeing her daughter Millicent stopped, exhibiting a mixture of guilt and smugness. A brown-paper parcel was slipped into her purse and her expression dared Nicola to question as she said, airily, 'I have purchased one or two things of no consequence. How did you enjoy your day, Nicola?'

'Well, it followed much the usual pattern, if we discount one broken head from falling off a wall, one bilious attack with messy consequences and a small fire in the earth closet caused by a live cigar butt.'

Millicent shuddered. 'How can you bear it?' She tilted her head and stared measuringly at her daughter. 'I want you to do something for me, Nicola. We have been invited to tea on Sunday by an old friend and I'd like you to accompany me.'

Made suspicious by long experience, Nicola asked, 'Which old friend, Mother?'

'Josephine Claxton.' As Nicola said nothing, Millicent continued. 'I know you are not particularly fond of Josephine, but she is dear to me. I hope you will oblige me in this.'

Dressing up and wasting a precious free afternoon, Nicola thought. Yet her mother had few pleasures these days, and a little generosity cost nothing.

She said, 'I had intended to visit Rose on Sunday, but the next week will do. I'll be happy to pay a call on Mrs Claxton with you.'

'You understand that this is a tea party, Nicola. There will be several other guests and you will need to take particular care with your toilette.'

'Very well. I'll wear my indigo with the hundred and one buttons down the back.'

Millicent was repressive. 'I wish you would be accurate. There are thirty buttons on the gown. Also, it is unsuitable. You should wear black to show a proper respect for your father.' She touched gloved fingertips to her own black silk bodice.

Nicola shook her head. 'I loved Papa dearly, but I don't believe that dressing like a crow either denotes respect or would be what Papa would have wanted. He loved bright colours. What's more, it's the indigo or my schoolteacher's skirt and vest. I have no other black clothes. I don't like black.'

Her mother drew herself to her full height. 'You disappoint me, Nicola. Your year abroad in the most exclusive of company has been wasted, leaving me with an ungracious, vulgar miss who is happiest amongst the city's slum-bred guttersnipes.'

With a twisted smile, Nicola nodded her agreement. 'Do you still want me to come to the tea party?'

'Yes!' Millicent snapped, and turned away, leaving Nicola to follow as she willed.

It was extraordinary how reminiscent was the sense of smell, Nicola thought, releasing her short pelerine into the hands of the waiting maid and checking her hair in the hall mirror. As she tucked away two or three flaming wisps under her little hat, she inhaled the odour of wealth – a compound of flowers, ladies' toilet water and furniture wax. It brought back the past with brutal suddenness.

'Stop primping, Nicola, and come along.' Millicent swept ahead of her into the drawing room in all the glory of a jet-beaded silk afternoon dress. With her blond hair dressed into its usual crown, and gloves turned back to display her magnificent rings, she was reclaiming her position as one of society's leaders. The rings, thought Nicola, like the second-best tea set, had mysteriously survived the wholesale clearance of their belongings.

She followed her mother into the drawing room, resigned to being sociable with women who had no understanding of her new circumstances, and would be horrified if she enlightened them.

Her gaze took in the brocaded chairs stuffed within inches of bursting; the blood-red Turkey carpet; the massive tables and sideboards and chimney piece, all groaning under their own weight; and the forest of bric-a-brac and ornaments arranged without reference to pattern or taste. She'd been in this room several times, and it never failed to depress her with its overpowering display of indiscriminate riches.

However, tucked into an alcove at the end of the long room stood an object that made her tingle with lust. A piano, a magnificent Bechstein concert-size grand piano, kept tuned for the idle strumming of two spoiled children who would never have the application to be musicians.

Oblivious of others in the room, Nicola gazed at the object of her desire.

'You're positively salivating, Miss Redmond,' said Andrew Dene, his voice amused.

Nicola's chagrin at being caught in a passion of envy was only equalled by her indignation at her mother's deceitfulness.

Andrew said with a tinge of malice, 'You won't try to throw me out, will you? This is not your house. And you can't very well run away without greeting your hostess and drinking at least two cups of tea. That would never do.'

Nicola's voice was cool. 'Kindly leave me alone. I don't want to talk to you.' She moved forward to take Mrs Claxton's outstretched hand and kiss the air near her powdered cheek. The odour of camphor was eye-watering.

'My child, so good of you to come, when you are so busy nowadays. And your dear mother. So delightful to see my old friend again. You must allow me to introduce you to . . .' Josephine Claxton prattled on, towing Nicola around the room before settling her with a cup of tea on a seat designed for two people, and inviting Andrew Dene to join her young guest. 'You two have already met, but it's so nice to renew acquaintance, I think.' She glided off, oblivious to the atmosphere she left behind her.

'It's fate,' observed Andrew.

Nicola put down her teacup on a particularly horrible carved oriental table rioting with monkeys and palm leaves. 'I'm beginning to believe it is. Although I suspect my mother gave fate a helpful push this afternoon. What is your purpose, Mr Dene?'

'Well, it's certainly not to annoy you. I'd simply like to help you and your mother out of a situation for which I feel partly to blame.'

'You mean you would like to give us back the factory?'

Surprise sharpened his tone. 'No, I don't mean any such thing. What would two women lacking business experience do with a clothing manufactory, except lose it in the long run and throw several score people out of work?'

'I could learn. Until recently I didn't know how to teach

schoolchildren.'

'My dear girl – I beg your pardon – Miss Redmond, this is no time to be experimenting in the world of commerce. This city, this country has sunk into a business recession the like of which we've never known. It's taking everything we have to keep going. Your own father—'

'Let us leave my father out of this conversation, if you please. In fact, we'll change the subject altogether. I realize that Mother is vulnerable to your suggestions. She has always been cared for by men and sees them as natural protectors and providers.'

'And you do not?'

'No! I believe that, given the opportunity, a woman can make her own way in the world. We're not an inferior sub-species, you know.'

'But your mother is not like you. She's a hothouse flower and must be nurtured, or wither away.'

Nicola knew he was right, but continued to defend her position.

'I'm well able to care for my mother. I will not have her as your pensioner. You have given her money, haven't you? I caught her buying pretty soaps and talcum from a purse I knew to be empty. It's humiliating. Can't you see how I must feel?'

'Believe it or not, I do understand. I can see you mean to try to support the two of you, but you will fail. How much do you earn teaching at the Ragged School - thirty-five pounds the year? Forty? Two will starve on that.'

'My salary is none of your business, and we'll not starve. I budget carefully—'

'And go without any of the niceties of life. How long will your good gowns last, and how will you replace them? Can you sew? Will you be happy in something of poor cut and quality when you're accustomed to the best? How long is it since you had a day to yourself, just to watch the flowers grow?'

Quite suddenly he abandoned his lecture and smiled. 'I almost hesitate to ask but, would you be kind enough to delight us all with some music?'

Nicola stared longingly at the piano, and at that moment nothing else mattered. 'Yes. Oh, yes. I will.'

With Mrs Claxton's smiling permission, Andrew led the way, removing twenty assorted silver photograph frames and a silk shawl before the lid could be raised and propped in place. Nicola sat down at the keyboard, spread her skirts and flexed her fingers, and entered another world.

CHAPTER SIX

NICOLA HAD NEVER quite appreciated the meaning of 'Dickensian' until one particular cold winter's evening when Josh banged on her door to beg her help.

'Nicola, Ma's lying like a stone on the hearth, and Daisy's crying fit to bust. I tucked Ma up warm with a pillow under her head, but I didn't know what else to do.' His voice cracked and he dragged a sleeve across his eyes.

Nicola dragged on her coat and half an hour later she was assisting a tottery Jenny Basevi into bed, while Josh fed and comforted Daisy. The child seemed unkempt, thought Nicola, and her speech was larded with the argot of the streets, where she undoubtedly played when her mother couldn't supervise her. What a hopeless situation. Where was Joseph Basevi when he was needed? Josh didn't know and nor did his mother.

'You've got to fetch Rose home,' Nicola said.

Josh shook his head. "I daresn't go. Pa would make it hard on Rose if she lost her new place.'

Nicola thought this over. 'Shouldn't Rose be home soon, anyway? It's nearly six o'clock.'

'Nope. She's working sixteen-hour shifts for the extra money. Sometimes it's even longer.'

'What! I never heard of such a thing.' Nicola grimly retied her scarf. 'I'll fetch her myself, and stay on until your father comes home. Where is this slave compound where Rose works?'

Before she reached the narrow East Sydney street leading to Upton's upholstery establishment, it had grown quite dark. A bitter wind moaned around the corners of grimy brick-walled factories and warehouses, raising dust and papers from the gutters. Nicola wrapped her coat more tightly about her and registered the thinness of her boot soles. Another expense. When would she, like the Basevis, be reduced to pawning personal articles?

The streetlamps flared in the wind, dragging shadows along the walls, and she jumped when a dark feline shape sped across her path and hissed at her. Did Rose walk these streets every night alone?

Her nostrils wrinkled at the nauseous smell as she entered an alley and found Upton's sign swinging and clattering beneath a poorly lit doorway. The smell seemed to be coming from within the building. Hesitating only momentarily, she pushed open the door and stepped inside.

She reeled back against the wall, gagging and covering her mouth and nose. The place truly was straight out of Dickens. Her horrified gaze took in the rows of women and young girls bending to gather lumps from piles of unnameable material and stuffing them into the shapes of chairs, couches and mattresses, then stitching them into place. The din of machinery in the background, the flickering gaslight and, above all, the appalling smell swamped Nicola, making her giddy.

No one noticed her. The women worked like automatons plunging elbow-deep into the piles from which the disgusting smell seemed to arise. Nicola forced herself to move. A few steps brought her to a heap of a dark, prickly substance which she recognized as seaweed, slimy and rotten, but infinitely better than the filthy rags next to it that moved independently. Nicola's eyes were sending a message her brain was doing its best not to receive.

Maggots! she thought, unbelieving. The rags were alive with creepy-crawlies and the women were stuffing them into a new mattress.

Bile rose in her throat and she rushed to the doorway to drag fresh air into her lungs. Grasping the lintel, she struggled against a need to vomit. The hardest thing she had ever done was turn back into that hellish atmosphere. But she had to find Rose. She had to get her out of this place before she contracted some dreadful disease.

A man in shirtsleeves clattered down an iron stairway from a floor above, waving a journal and bellowing, 'No more. We're full up.'

Holding her handkerchief across her face, Nicola bellowed back at him through its folds. 'I have no intention of working in this disgraceful piggery. I've come to find Miss Rose Basevi. Can you point her out to me?'

The man's expression turned mean. Although he was short and weedy-looking, Nicola stepped back a pace. He said, 'She's on 'til ten o'clock, and not a minute earlier does she leave.'

'Surely the work can be made up later—'

His chopping motion with his hand stopped her. 'You're in the way. Get out of here or I'll have you put out. We know how to handle your sort.'

Nicola whisked past him to the nearest bench, calling to the woman standing at the end, 'Where is Rose Basevi working? Please, I must find her.'

The woman stared at her dully. It was doubtful whether she saw Nicola. Her eyes were half-closed, her skin running with sweat in the clammy atmosphere, wisps of hair were glued to her cheeks where they'd escaped the confining square of cotton wrapped about her head. She wore a mask across her lower face, but she still coughed as dust sifted through the air to settle on skin and clothing. Her hands were raw. Nicola couldn't bear to look at them.

Sinewy fingers closed on Nicola's arm, wrenching her backwards. The manager, or foreman, or whoever he was, had dropped his journal and prepared to take her other wrist.

'Release me at once!' Nicola twisted and broke his hold, raising her voice to a scream. 'Rose! Rose Basevi! It's Nicola. I need you, Rose.'

'Out, you!' Taking a firm grip around her waist, the man began dragging her to the doorway.

Nicola fought him, shouting Rose's name as she gave way inch by inch. With her fingers wrapped around the doorjamb, she hung on, seeing Rose come flying down an alleyway between benches, her face without a mask and as pasty as uncooked dough.

'Nicola! What is it? Why are you here?'

Nicola's captor turned to deal with this insubordination and she wrenched free once more.

'Rose, you must come home. Your mother has been taken ill.'

Rose threw off her filthy wrapper and addressed the man in

charge. 'Mr Simmons, I've got to leave, but I'll make up my time somehow, I promise you.'

Simmons angrily straightened his vest and glared at her. 'Get back to work. You're not leaving, but she is.' He lunged at her, just as Nicola stepped between them.

'Lay a finger on either of us and I'll have you arrested.' Nicola heard the virago note in her own voice and didn't care. Rose's pleading expression added to her fury.

Rose was begging. 'Please, Mr Simmons. My mother needs me. I'll work any shifts you like—'

Simmons turned on her. 'If you go now you don't come back. Choose quickly.'

'I can't. Oh, God help me, but I must go.'

'Then get out, slut. There's plenty more rats in the gutter.' He pushed her contemptuously towards the door, but kept his distance from Nicola, whose expression must have warned him to take care.

Rose deflated. Shoulders slumped, she shuffled out into the street, followed anxiously by Nicola. The door banged behind them and a bolt crashed into place. Closing her mind to the odour clinging to Rose, Nicola removed her coat, wrapped it around her shivering friend, and guided her home.

Inside, with the wind shut out and the stove heating, Nicola took stock. 'Rose, is it true? He really won't have you back?'

Rose shook her head. 'You heard him.'

Nicola said with forced lightness, 'There are other work places that could take your father, Rose. He's capable of bringing in a good wage. Then you may stay at home to care for your mother and Daisy, while Josh returns to school.'

'It's not as easy as that. Still, at least Mama is feeling better.'

After a thorough scrub in the washhouse, she set about preparing the evening meal, while Nicola laid the places and fed Daisy with a bowl of bread and milk, before putting her to bed. In the meantime Josh brought in wood and water and sheepishly obeyed his sister's admonition to scrub himself before eating.

Nicola put the plates on the hob to heat and stood back. 'Why is my solution not easy? Your father is a highly skilled tailor. There's always a place for good workmanship.'

'He was once skilled.' Rose's glance flashed to the front door as it opened. 'See for yourself what I mean.'

Joseph Basevi staggered in, giving a performance of a man too drunk to control his legs.

'Help him, Josh.' Rose returned to her stirring.

His expression mutinous, Josh helped his father to a seat and unlaced the man's boots. These were in bad repair, as were Joseph's clothes. He looked as though he'd been rolling in the gutter. His gaze shifted away from the others as he dragged a hand across his stubbled chin and demanded water. Josh brought him a mug, which he gulped down and almost immediately heaved up again all over himself.

Nicola stared at the ceiling and studiously counted the cracks.

Then, without warning, Rose broke. The ladle landed on the hearth with a clatter and she turned, hands on hips as she faced her father. 'So you've come home at last. Where were you when we needed you, when Mama needed you? With your head buried in a pint pot, I suppose, and quite happy. What sort of an excuse for a man are you? We're all doing our best to hold this family together and you desert us. You don't bring money, or food, or even caring into this house. You'd be better off gone entirely.'

Nicola and Josh stood open-mouthed, while Joseph Basevi seemed to crumble, shrinking away from this new, uncharacteristic Rose who wielded her tongue like a sword.

'Rose, my Rose,' quavered the man, his arms shielding his upper body as if he feared actual, physical attack. 'You've no right to speak to me like that. I'm your father.'

'More's the pity. I've watched you give up on your responsibilities and said nothing. I've seen you take the few pennies left in the house and spend it on drink, and I've tried to understand your need to have something for yourself. I've fed and cared for this family and done my best, hoping you'd recover and assume responsibility once more. But you haven't. You've let Josh take on jobs beyond his strength; you've let me exhaust myself running the home and putting in long hours in factories. See my hands? Pretty, aren't they? They've been buried in filthy rags crawling with maggots – all to pay for your dinner.' Her voice grew more strident and bitter.

Nicola went to her. 'Don't, Rose.'

Rose brushed her aside. 'I haven't finished. You're a weak man, Joseph Basevi. I'd have held my peace if you hadn't betrayed poor, sweet little Mama. . . .' Her voice broke.

Nicola exchanged a wild glance with Josh. What on earth had the man done? Then she looked at him, and saw guilt expressed in every line of his body. Weak tears gathered and overflowed, unchecked.

With a final contemptuous glance at her shattered father Rose turned back to the fire, picking up the ladle and stirring as if she'd dismissed him from her mind.

While Joseph sobbed and Josh shifted from foot to foot, Nicola contemplated retreat, knowing she couldn't leave matters like this. 'Rose . . .'

'There's nothing you can do, Nicola. We have reached our low point, I think. Doctor Freeman told him last time he was here that Mama could bear no more children. Well, she's three months gone, and it's going to kill her.'

Joseph Basevi left home early the following day without making any farewells. He did leave a note promising to write and send money when he'd found work up country.

Rose, who had reverted to her normal gentle nature, sobbed out her guilt on Nicola's shoulder, then set to on the piecework normally sewn by her mother. At least with the help of the Benevolent Society she could now remain at home to nurse her mother and curb Daisy's excesses, while Josh found a place at a printer's works.

Nicola called in as often as she could to bear Rose company, although she could ill afford the fare. Still, it saved her boots, which were now lined with pieces of cut out tin wrapped in newspaper – a trick she had been taught by her pupils.

While teaching claimed most of her energy, it also gave her joy, as she watched young minds expand before her eyes. Yet, in the early dark of winter evenings, while tidying up after class, melancholy took hold. Thoughts of Rose and her family's situation, and the terrible plight of all the women forced to work under intolerable conditions, surged up on a wave of compassionate fury. It was wrong. It was immoral.

Her own new lifestyle daily demonstrated the inequalities in society. She'd seen the faces of the hungry and the desperate, had her eyes opened to the greed of men like her father and the blindness of others like her mother and herself – and a certain unnamed usurper of other people's estates. As a pampered daughter of wealth she had unknowingly fed off the misery of the unfortunate men, women and children being destroyed by the economic machinery of society. Nicola felt accountable, and that there would be no peace for her until she did something about it.

CHAPTER SEVEN

Soon Nicola was faced with a major escalation in the ongoing tussle between herself and Millicent. The sheaf of requests for payment arriving by post one August morning did more to chill her than the east wind setting the casements of Mrs Gardiner's establishment rattling like badly fitting teeth. There were so *many* bills and for such frivolous items.

Nicola rushed to throw the pile of papers down on the bed where the widow reclined against pillows and sipped her morning tea.

'Do be careful, Nicola!' Millicent placed her cup on the side table and drew her dainty jacket close about her shoulders as if to shield herself from her daughter's vehemence.

'How could you, Mother? You know our circumstances. My salary will barely keep us, yet you've made all these purchases, all quite unnecessary.' She flicked the top paper. 'Toiletries: *Savon de Muguet, Crème Fraise*, Lavender Water. A satin bed pillow, for heaven's sake! What were you thinking of?'

If Millicent felt any remorse, she hid it well. 'You are shouting, Nicola. Please calm yourself.'

Lowering her voice, Nicola said, 'I can't meet these payments, you must have known it. Why did you do it?'

A slow flush mounted in Millicent's cheeks, and she looked away. Nicola waited. At last her mother said in a low, intense voice, 'I am accustomed to having nice things. I cannot live like this, Nicola. It is slowly killing me.'

Nicola sensed the old helplessness welling up in her. She had never been able to talk to her mother. Words seemed more like obstacles than a way of communicating. As for an emotional connection, how was it possible to cross the invisible but chilling barrier surrounding her?

'Mother, I know this year has been hard for you. I understand how much you miss the old life, and Papa.'

'You have no understanding. You do not appear to regret our previous life at all.'

Nicola couldn't speak. Not regret the loss of Papa, of her music, of so many, many things? Eventually she said, 'It's no use repining. That life is over and we must make a new one. It may not be to our liking—'

Millicent held up a hand. 'What you do is your concern. Speaking for myself, I find this . . . this mere existence intolerable. I feel I have been cast adrift, and there is no place that I recognize as my own.'

Hearing a note of panic in her mother's voice, Nicola took a step towards her, then stopped, repelled by the emotional protection that Millicent wore like armour – had always worn. Papa, alone, had supplied the cuddles and kisses in Nicola's childhood, and named her his dove. She quivered inwardly at the memory.

Then her gaze returned to the bills. She picked them up and waited for Millicent to regain her poise, before saying, 'My lack of understanding won't alter things. Who will meet these bills?'

Millicent's eyes held a spark of defiance. 'Andrew Dene would.'

'So that's it. You've deliberately forced my hand.'

'You drove me to it. You have become entirely too managing, Nicola, and I will not stand for it. If I choose to accept assistance from a gentleman connection—'

Nicola exploded. 'Andrew Dene is no more connected to our family than the Prince of Wales. But if you must deceive yourself, so be it. I can't meet your debts and I must therefore seek the only help available, from Andrew Dene. It will be a humiliating experience for me, but that will not concern you.' She stuffed the bills in her skirt pocket and made for the door. 'We'll go together this evening, after school finishes.'

She needed all her concentration to teach that day. By the time she had climbed uphill to the boarding house with the wind tugging her hair from under her hat, she was tired, cold and hungry, and in no mood for what lay ahead. She stayed only to wash her face and put on tomorrow's clean shirtwaist. Andrew

Dene would have to take her as she was.

Without regard to expense, they set off in a hansom cab, travelling in silence, with Nicola planning her approach, and still too angry with her mother for polite conversation. Millicent, wrapped in hauteur, paid her no attention.

The cab entered through pillared iron gates and followed a driveway curving up to an old stone house standing foursquare and solid against a backdrop of trees and sunset sky. A veranda in iron lacework ran the length of the upper level, and light spilled out in welcome from every floor-length window. It shone through the bevelled glass of the fanlight above double entrance doors heavy enough to repel cannon shot and furnished with solid brass knobs.

Nicola sighed with appreciation. Having grown used to grimy streets and rows of congested terraces, she only now realized how much her spirit craved a home surrounded with the green freshness of lawns and gardens. Many of the trees were bare, their naked arms etched against a sky banked in mountainous cloud. Others, thickly foliaged, swayed in the wind with a voice she well remembered, heralding a coming storm. She stood at the front steps, breathing in the heavy air, the smell of mown grass mingled with winter jasmine somewhere amongst the shrubs. Reluctantly she pressed the bell.

A housekeeper, round and pleasant, ushered them into a reception room furnished with the taste only made possible with money, as well as a sense of style. Millicent nodded approvingly as she sank into the depths of a buttoned velvet sofa and absorbed the atmosphere that was her natural milieu.

Nicola, stepping gingerly on to a pale Chinese rug, had the wry thought that it sneered at her boots. She, too, approved the mixture of comfort and elegant restraint, and wondered whether it could possibly be a reflection of Andrew Dene's taste. With his flamboyant hair and the modern cut of his clothes, she'd guessed him to be something of an exhibitionist. She knew he frequented clubs and gambling-houses, and possibly worse. There had been no shortage of gossip at Mrs Josephine Claxton's tea party; and Nicola had heard him exchanging banter with the other men on the subject of racehorses; she concluded that he continued to survive the current economic crisis without much difficulty. It only reinforced her opinion of him as a spoilt member of a class into which she no longer fitted, or wished to.

Now, standing in Andrew Dene's drawing room as a supplicant, she longed to puncture his self-esteem. Her mirror image over the fireplace showed a scowling, redheaded termagant, and she hastily rearranged her expression as he entered the room.

He was in full evening dress, and Millicent apologized for disturbing him. He waved this aside to greet Nicola gravely, with a lurking twinkle that set her hackles up. She gave him no chance to pre-empt her speech.

'Mr Dene, we have come to accept your offer of help, your financial help. We . . . unfortunately we have incurred debts which we are unable to meet.' She choked, and saw him repress a smile. Her good resolutions flew out of the window. 'You've given my mother money and encouraged her to spend. You knew she would never be able to restrain herself. I'm sure you must be very pleased with the result of your stratagem.'

'I'm pleased to be able to assist you,' he said, carefully. 'What is the sum of money owed?'

Nicola fished in her purse and produced the bills, giving them to him with a trembling hand. 'Almost six pounds.'

He inclined his head. 'I shall be delighted to discharge these for you.' He bowed again to Millicent, who grandly thanked him in a manner suggesting the favour was hers.

'It's fortunate that you didn't come a day earlier,' he continued. 'I've been out of town for a week and only returned this morning.'

Nicola ignored this gambit, although her mother immediately enquired as to whether Andrew had enjoyed his trip.

'Very much. It was most stimulating.' His eye caught Nicola's disdainful look and he laughed. He then begged them to be seated and sent for refreshments.

Over a glass of wine and some biscuits Nicola heard her mother agreeing to become Andrew's pensioner on a regular monthly basis. She had known the outcome was inevitable, although she still found it hard to accept with a good grace. And when at last they rose to leave, she learned that her trial had not yet ended.

The gathering storm had broken, whipping rain against the

windowpanes, and Andrew Dene insisted upon accompanying the ladies home. Nicola found herself being tenderly assisted into the carriage by a manservant holding an umbrella overhead while expertly arranging a rug across her knees. If she hadn't been forced to listen to her mother flattering her host and playing the *grande dame*, she'd have been delighted with the unaccustomed comfort of the journey.

A few days later she received an envelope addressed in shaky script on vellum paper, with the name 'Dene' printed on the back. Opening it in the privacy of her room, she learnt to her surprise that a Mrs Eleanor Dene begged the pleasure of Nicola's company the following Sunday afternoon to take tea.

So, he had a wife, was her first thought, and was surprised to feel a stab of – certainly not disappointment. No, surprise was more like it. For some reason he hadn't seemed like a married man.

She read on: *I was disappointed that we did not meet when you called last week. Sadly, I am now almost entirely confined to my rooms, but it would give me great pleasure to receive you there, if the date is suitable.*

An invalid. The poor woman, with a husband who left her alone while he enjoyed the social whirl. But what had Nicola Redmond, a poor schoolmistress, in common with the wife of her antagonist? The invitation intrigued her. Did she want social contact with the Denes? Was there any point in trying to straddle two social levels?

She puzzled for a while, and in the end her curiosity won. She would take tea with Mrs Eleanor Dene and then she would retire gracefully and permanently, leaving Mother to maintain the connection. Nicola had no intention of being drawn back into the artificial world that had once been hers.

CHAPTER EIGHT

NICOLA ARRIVED ON the appointed date, full of curiosity and slightly wary of her reception. However, her pleasure in revisiting this beautiful home was real. She followed the housekeeper up the curved cedar staircase to a balcony running the length of the upper floor, contrasting its cool airiness with the dim and ugly congestion of her landlady's house. Tinted sunlight fell through the glass-domed roof. The only sound to be heard was the song of a canary in one of the rooms and, more distantly, a man's whistling as he worked in the grounds.

The canary's warbling crescendoed as the housekeeper opened a door and a woman seated in the window alcove turned and spoke in a sweet, clear voice.

'Come in, Miss Redmond. You will forgive my not rising to greet you. I have this stupid affliction which ties me to my chair.'

Nicola hesitated, seeing her mistake. Not Andrew Dene's wife, but his mother, a smiling lady who held out her hand in welcome. Nicola crossed the polished floor rapidly and bent to touch fingers that had once been long and tapering, but were now twisted aside as if broken and badly reset. She looked into a face furrowed with pain, yet still beautiful beneath a crown of plaited hair, thick and snowy white. Eyes as blue as lakes in summer sparkled with a youthful spirit transcending time. Nicola felt an immediate rapport.

'It was kind of you to invite me to tea, Mrs Dene. I fear I've fallen in love with your beautiful house.'

'Many people are kind enough to admire it. Sit down, my dear, and let me look at you.'

Nicola took the woven cane chair opposite and faced the light, only too happy to gaze out over the sweep of lawn and trees. Great pots stood on the veranda just outside the shutters, overflowing with early spring flowers, and the aroma of cut grass wafted through the windows.

By current standards, the room was shamefully bare. Furniture had been kept at a minimum, consisting of a grouping of couches at one end around a pink-veined marble fireplace, bookshelves and a writing desk; watercolour paintings lined the walls, which were painted rich yellow, like sunlight. Two bright rugs, a lamp on a drum table and several cushioned basket-weave chairs with side tables completed the furnishings. The canary sang on his gilded perch, the air smelled of lavender polish, the fire burning on the hearth was cheerful, if unneeded. Nicola sighed with pleasure.

She turned her head to see her hostess eyeing her with satisfaction.

'I know how fortunate I am, believe me.' When Nicola glanced at her legs, wrapped in a pale fleecy blanket, she added, 'My difficulty in moving about is greatly compensated by my surroundings and by the companionship of good friends; while my son spoils me disgracefully.'

Nicola's polite agreement made her laugh.

'You know, my dear, you have a revealing face. Your opinion of Andrew is no secret. Yet as a mother I must enter a plea for him. Whatever faults he displays, he is most loving towards his family.'

Nicola blushed. 'I don't doubt it, ma'am. Please don't think me rude. . . .' She stopped, unable to think of a tactful way of telling Andrew's mother that she considered him to be an interfering controller.

'But? You find him opinionated and lacking in tact. I'm afraid Andrew has always believed that he knows best. Has he tried to run your life?'

The sympathetic yet rueful tone touched Nicola. Smiling, she said, 'Yes, indeed. We are at loggerheads whenever we meet. He has succeeded in winning my mother over, but I stand on my independence.'

'How frustrating for him. It will do him good, of course.' Andrew's mother reached for a small hand-bell on the table. 'My dear, I'm so grateful that you could find time in your busy life to visit an old woman. I know how you earn your keep, and let me say how much I admire your spirit.'

'Well, I always wanted to know more about life beyond the proper existence of a young lady on the hunt for a husband.' Nicola's eyes twinkled. 'I could have wished for something a little less drastic than penury. They do say we should be careful what we wish for in case it's granted.'

Mrs Dene made a vexed sound. 'In our society, young women from well-to-do families are simply not taught survival skills. It's well enough to know how to adorn, to entertain, to supervise a staff, but how many have a professional skill to help them in adversity? The working class girls are at least taught the domestic sciences: cookery; laundering; sewing. If circumstances deal them a blow such as yours, they have a way of earning money.'

She struck the arm of her chair in frustration, and stifled a gasp of pain. 'Education! It's the answer for everyone. Not the padded existence that is nothing but a cage for heart and mind.'

Nicola had a sense of delighted discovery. Here was a woman who understood the drive towards knowledge of a wider world. She waited impatiently for a tea trolley to be wheeled in and deposited beside her hostess's chair, noting that the maid and not the mistress, poured the tea.

The girl had barely left before Nicola burst out, 'That's exactly how I feel. I longed to enter the University, but my father wouldn't hear of it. Often I wished I were a son, with the freedom granted to males.'

'Oh, my dear, you mirror my desire when I was a girl.' Mrs Dene gestured for Nicola to take her cup. Rings glinted on her poor twisted fingers, drawing attention to their deformity.

These hands were a tragedy, Nicola thought, recalling the fine heirloom rings still displayed on her mother's elegant fingers, regardless of the inappropriate circumstances.

Her hostess continued, 'I was fortunate in my father, who finally resigned himself to the fact that I was a single child and treated me as the son he never had. He taught me to question, to seek out answers, to make decisions based upon my own experience. I have blessed his memory for such a gift.'

Her face softened. 'I can hear his rumbling Scottish voice now: "Eleanor, my lass, the world doesn't owe you a thing. You have to get out there and fight for what you want." And I did. How I fought – and won. Which is why I have such a respect for others of my sex who do something for themselves instead of waiting to be supported by some man.'

'Eleanor. Eleanor,' Nicola muttered. Her cup landed on the side table with a rattle. 'Of course! You're Matron Eleanor Ballard, founder of the Nursing Training College. You're nothing short of a living legend!'

Eleanor Dene laughed. 'An exaggeration, but thank you for the compliment. It's many a year, alas, since I had anything to do with nursing. A carriage accident ended my useful career, I'm afraid. However, the work has been carried on most ably by others.'

With a feeling of awe, Nicola realized that she was in the presence of a woman almost unique in her time, one who had dared to take on the establishment and create a now honoured profession, liberating her sex and giving them a choice beyond domesticity. She said, respectfully, 'It's an honour to meet you, Matron Ballard.'

'No, my dear. Elly Ballard is long gone. I'm now Eleanor Dene, twice widowed, and mother of Andrew, the thorn in your pretty flesh.'

'You know a good deal about me. Has your son talked so much about us, my mother and me?'

'Do you mind? Andrew and I discuss most things. We are very close. I asked you here because I knew of your circumstances and because I felt sure that we should be *en rapport*.'

Nicola nodded agreement. She accepted a biscuit absent-mindedly and considered the conundrum of Andrew Dene. According to his mother, naturally biased in his favour, yet not blind to his faults, the man had another, less authoritative side to his nature.

She said, 'I grant him a sense of humour, although I've never yet been in the frame of mind to appreciate it. He frets me like chalk on a slate. Why must he try to take over people?'

Eleanor looked apologetic. 'I fear Andrew inherits his managing disposition from me. His instinct to protect is strong and can take him too far.'

'Well, he may have cozened my mother, but I stand on my own two feet, battered as the boots may be.' She stared down at them and laughed. 'I may have to beg my mother's aid after all if I'm not to display bare toes in public.'

She and her hostess drifted into other subjects of interest to them both and it surprised Nicola to find the afternoon had passed so quickly and enjoyably. When she rose to go, Eleanor Dene drew a parcel from beneath her rug. 'This small gift is more of a return. It's something I feel you should have. I hope you will accept it.'

Wondering, Nicola undid the wrapping to display a blazing heart of fire. It was the opal pendant that had been her father's gift to her on her return from London. With trembling fingers she turned it over and read the inscription on the mount – 'For my dove, with my heart.'

Nicola sank back into her chair and cried as if her real heart would break. At last she said, between great gulping sobs, 'I thought it had gone for ever. They said it was part of the estate and I couldn't keep it. Oh Papa, Papa!'

Eleanor Dene patted the girl's knee. 'It's iniquitous to take a keepsake. When I heard what was happening I commissioned Andrew to buy it, hoping to one day find an opportunity to return it to you.'

Mopping her face, Nicola replaced the heart in its wrapping. 'Mrs Dene, this is the kindest . . . You don't know how much . . . I'm sorry. Please don't be offended, but I can't accept your gift.'

'Why not?' Eleanor's voice was gentle. 'Is it because of its monetary value? Or perhaps you dislike the association with this family?'

Nicola hung her head. 'I can't . . . It *is* too valuable.'

'Ah, but think of the intrinsic value. This is your last link with the father who loved you. His words of love are inscribed on it. How can you refuse?'

Fingers curled tightly about the jewel, Nicola was stabbed with shame. What a curse money was, or the lack of it. It shrivelled gratitude and placed a market value on the acceptance of another's kindness.

She slipped down beside Eleanor's chair and kissed the cheek of a woman she had known for two hours. 'Please forgive me. And thank you, thank you.'

'Wear it under your gown, always. It would not be wise to

display such a piece in your present circumstances. But these will change. I know you will not rest until you've made a good life for yourself.'

Nicola went back to her bleak room, comforted by the beginnings of a friendship and by the token of her father's love nestling in her bosom.

In bed that night, musing over the day's happenings, she knew that she had Andrew Dene to thank for her treasured opal. He had taken the trouble to investigate and realize its intrinsic value to Nicola, and he had purchased it so that his mother might return it to her. Which certainly cast a different light upon the man. Perhaps she had been a little too sweeping in her judgement of him.

But he was still an interfering, overbearing male.

CHAPTER NINE

When Rose asked Nicola to accompany her one morning to retrieve Joseph Basevi's second best coat for the rapidly growing Josh, Nicola discovered another, important part of the world to which the family had sunk. Mr Montague Pritchard's establishment for the temporarily embarrassed impecunious (according to discreet newspaper advertisements) was situated in the warren of laneways running behind Lower George Street, otherwise known as Chinatown.

The two women hurried past doorways occupied by impassive sloe-eyed gentlemen smoking pipes. There were cabinetmakers' shops, fireworks shops and others with tables piled with unnameable vegetables and fruits. Out in the open, dark slabs of meat and naked birds hung from hooks, and the air was thick with strange, exotic smells. Rose laughed at Nicola's reaction to a tank crammed with plum-coloured lobsters all treading over one another, their antennae bumping along the sides, stalk-eyes swivelling as they sought a way out.

'Here we are. This is Mr Monte's.' Rose had stopped under the three balls sign before a dusty window crammed with unlikely bedfellows: smoothing irons hung with strings of jet beads; a tin bath filled with battered toys; someone's best straw Dunstable bonnet atop a baby carriage, and most incongruous of all, a rusting ploughshare supporting a gentleman's silk waistcoat that was embroidered and buttoned in diamante and sporting a perfect round hole above the heart.

Inside the dark little store with its jingling doorbell, Nicola had to duck her head to avoid hitting the objects strung from the ceiling. Sidling around a battered watering can that threatened her hat, she followed Rose to the counter. There presided a bald-headed giant with rimless glasses and a belly which kept him at a distance from his wares. What Nicola could see of his face behind a brobdingnagian moustache glowed and glistened like a polished red apple.

'Good afternoon, miss,' he boomed, and the tin goods hanging from the rafters shivered. 'What may I have the pleasure of doing for you?'

Rose rested her basket on the counter. 'I've brought our mantel clock, Mr Monte, and I wish to redeem the coat I left with you last month.' She handed him a pink ticket with a number on it in small print.

The giant tugged at his moustache and pondered.

Nicola watched, astonished, as customer and proprietor entered into a spirited argument over relevant values of clock and coat, with Rose's bargaining skills displayed. When eventually Mr Monte retreated, miming despair, Rose turned to Nicola, grinning in triumph.

Heading home again, Nicola questioned Rose about the need to pawn the clock, receiving an evasive answer. Nicola saw why when she entered the Basevi home, now almost bare of furniture. She turned to Rose and said grimly, 'Why didn't you tell me you were reduced to such straits?'

'Because you have no more money than I.'

'I could have borrowed from Mother.'

'Oh, yes? Then all three of us would be pensioners of your Andrew Dene. Thank you, but we're not yet reduced to beggary. Nicola, don't let's argue. I so look forward to your visits.' Rose took off her hat and went to see to her mother, and to release the volatile Daisy who had been tied to a chair for the period of her sister's absence.

Nicola declined a cup of tea, having surreptitiously investigated the caddy and found it empty. The food allowance and rent assistance distributed each Wednesday at the Pitt Street rooms of the Benevolent Society had clearly been exhausted, and the week had just begun. Despite Rose's brave assertion, she and her mother had indeed joined the band of hundreds of the aged, widows and deserted wives supported by the society and categorized as objects of charity.

That night, as she prepared for bed with a heavy heart, Nicola paused at her window, then knelt down to watch the lamplighter at his work on the corner. Using the hook on his rod to thrust open the trap, he then pushed up the lighted end and the lamp bloomed like a small moon, throwing shadows against the walls. The sight never failed to comfort her. It took her back to a time when life was kind. The lamp-lighting was a form of magic, after all – something to be observed with childlike wonder and tucked away in the memory.

The newspapers kept Nicola abreast of more than world and local happenings. She could hardly avoid seeing Andrew Dene's name in connection with any gala event taking place in town. He seemed to be in everything: sporting fixtures; civic balls; Government House soirées. People spoke of him as one of the wealthy property owners who rode the wave-crest far above ordinary mortals swamped by the Depression.

He hadn't worked for his money, Nicola thought. It was inherited wealth, and he was just a spoilt man-of-the-town who liked to get himself talked about. It must sadden Eleanor Dene, who might have expected any son of hers to take an interest in matters beyond the gambling table and racecourse.

Over the next few weeks Nicola paid several more visits to Andrew's mother, each time strengthening the bond existing between them.

'This country needs strong women who will fight for their rights,' Eleanor told her. 'The men have made a mess of things long enough. It's time women had a say.'

Nicola agreed, instancing the number of women going on to a university education and the professions, many of them choosing to hand on their knowledge as teachers of girls avid for the same training. There were, she knew, many good schools available at secondary level – not the likes of her own alma mater, the Jephson Academy. To amuse Eleanor she recited her so-called 'Accomplishments Curriculum', strutting affectedly across the room, hand to breast and nose elevated, while claiming to be '. . . a social preserver of morality and the embodiment of culture, refinement, good manners and etiquette.'

The redoubtable Eleanor had laughed, then snorted. 'Poor girl, did you actually suffer such an education? Callisthenics. Watercolour painting. Flute. Pah!' With each word she stabbed the air with her walking-stick. 'Nicola, what are your plans?' she asked. 'You will not be content to remain at the Ragged School for ever. I see the light of ambition in you.'

'Yes, I have plans. But for the present I must earn my keep and at least give the impression of supporting my mother. One day I'll continue my own education, and there are other things . . .' Her ideas for the betterment of women's place in society were still unformed. She wasn't yet ready to bring these into the light of discussion.

There was a certain awkwardness in meeting Andrew Dene in the front entry, just as she was leaving. However he dismissed her attempt to thank him for the opal, attributing it entirely to his mother's kind nature.

When he learned that Nicola intended to walk home, he insisted on her using his carriage. 'It's far too hot to go on foot for such a distance. You have even come without your parasol.'

Nicola couldn't help laughing. When he demanded an explanation, she told him the story of her parasol's demise, which led to talk of her children at the Ragged School, her favourite subject of conversation. It was some time before she realized that she had been led on a gentle parade of the flower-beds while by some surreptitious means Andrew had sent for his carriage.

Irritated, yet amused, she said, 'It would have been good for your nature to be a pupil at a ragged school, Andrew Dene. You would have learned that you cannot always have your way.'

'Ha! You should consult my old nanny. She lives in my memory as the greatest thwarter known to childhood.' His reminiscent smile was full of mischief and, yes, tenderness.

He must have been an engaging little boy, Nicola thought, then pulled herself up. The years beyond the nursery had clearly allowed full rein to the child who had become virtually lord of all he surveyed. She had no intention of becoming another member of his entourage.

She turned and walked back to the front steps, saying primly, 'I accept your kind offer – for today. But in future, when I visit your mother I shall make my own travel arrangements.'

'I understand. Allow me to assist you.'

His face was perfectly straight as he handed her into the carriage, but she just knew he was secretly laughing.

His hand on the door, he met her gaze. The grey eyes sparkled.

'Nicola, when next you call you will find an assortment of parasols to choose from.' Stepping back, he nodded to the driver, and the horses sprang forward, leaving Nicola no chance to respond.

At home there was a message to say there had been an accident at the printers. Josh had fallen between the gears of the printing machinery and been badly injured.

Nicola was filled with fury when she heard the truth. 'Sheer negligence! It's abominable that anyone should work in such dangerous conditions.'

Rose looked at her, helplessly. 'I know. But you've seen for yourself the callousness of employers. How can we fight them?'

Nicola made up her mind. Rose already carried too heavy a burden. If something were to be done, she, Nicola must do it.

CHAPTER TEN

THE END OF term, with all the uproar of the Christmas play, left Nicola exhausted. It was a somewhat depleted warrior who set out, on her first free day, on her warpath to MacGregor's Printers.

A fleeting thought that Andrew Dene might intervene on Josh's behalf had been summarily dismissed. He was an employer, like any other, and could have no interest in an accident to an unknown boy.

Remembering her reception at Upton's Upholstery, she approached the main entrance of MacGregor's warily. However, this time she carried ammunition. Clutching a copy of the Employers' Liability Act, she rang the big brass bell beside the door, and when it opened, stepped boldly inside. The noise was appalling. The building reverberated with the sound of pistons, rollers, giant flywheels and cogs driven by steam engines. The very air shivered with sound waves. Nicola's senses felt battered by the barely restrained power thundering so close to her. How could anyone bear to work under such conditions?

The boy who admitted her stood dumbly waiting for direction. Pale and stooped, he looked half-witted, as if stunned by his surroundings into mindlessness. When Nicola mouthed 'manager?' the lad pointed a fishbone finger at a doorway to the far left. Nicola nodded her thanks and watched him disappear into the mechanical maelstrom, ducking and weaving along an impossible pathway between ravening monsters seemingly determined to crush and grind him to extinction. With Josh's injuries still fresh in her mind, Nicola turned away, unable to watch.

Beyond the door the roar of the presses was muted. The floor still vibrated beneath Nicola's feet but it was possible to converse, as she found when angry voices reached her from a room beyond.

'You get the hell out of here before I throw you out!' The speaker sounded almost incoherent.

Another, younger voice with a jibing undertone answered him. 'I'll go when I'm ready, when I've told you what I think of you and your methods, and when I've spoken to the poor devils slaving under your roof.'

His voice was beautiful, Nicola thought, despite his inflammatory words. It had a lilt, almost a singing quality. She paused in the doorway, unnoticed for the moment, and examined the antagonists.

One, middle-aged, balding, running to fat, leaned forward to support himself on the desk, belligerence in every taut muscle. In his shirtsleeves, with collar undone, his snarling lips exposing teeth yellowed by nicotine, he did not make a prepossessing figure. The younger man facing him was stocky and muscular, dressed in a workman's clothes. His chin jutted menacingly, and he held his hands clenched by his sides, as though he had trouble keeping them under control.

Detecting movement behind him, he spun around and took one springing step towards Nicola, but halted immediately.

'What are you doing here?' the lilting voice asked. Beneath a forest of black brows the man's eyes were surprising – dark sherry-coloured, fringed like a doe's but hard as agate.

Nicola pulled herself together and answered, 'I'm here to see the manager in charge of the machines.'

Those hard eyes were turned back on the older man.

'I *will* have your workers join the union. The end is coming for vermin like you. There'll be an end to exploitation and the beginning of a new day for the men you've ground almost out of existence. You're lower than a snake's belly, Wade, do you know that?'

'Get out of my office. Get out of this building!' Wade's voice shook, and blood rushed to his face. He glanced at Nicola and added, 'You can hop it, too. I'm not seeing anyone today.'

'Are you the manager of MacGregor's?' she asked, standing her ground. 'Because if you are, I've come to tell you that Joshua Basevi is very seriously injured. He . . . may not walk again.'

Wade stared at her uncomprehendingly. 'Who. . . ? Oh, the brat who stopped the run. What of it? It was his own fault. He should've been watching what he was doing.'

Nicola began to tremble. 'Is that all you can say? A boy in your employ – and he's under age and should never have been taken on – this boy has a horrifying accident and you don't even bother to discover how he fares.'

Wade shrugged. 'He's not employed here. Never has been.'

'Of course he was!'

'Prove it.' He spat deliberately into a cuspidor.

Nicola felt a hand on her arm, supportive but also warning. The younger man spoke in a deceptively mild tone.

'This lady has more to say to you, Wade. I suggest you listen politely.' The next moment he had whipped around the desk and forced Wade into his chair, pinning him there and saying over his shoulder, 'Madam, say what you will. I guarantee Wade will hear you.'

She didn't hesitate. 'What kind of monster are you to let children amongst dangerous machinery? I'm sure there are laws saying you must provide such safety measures as guard rails.'

Wade ignored her, but his captor nodded grimly. 'There are such laws, but they're flouted regularly. The inspectors are paid by the council, whose members are all local businessmen. If the matter ever does come to court, who do you think sits on the magistrates' benches but the manufacturers and pit and foundry owners themselves?'

'Well, then, what about the law governing an employer's liability in case of accident?'

'It's as useless as any other. Your Joshua would have to prove negligence on the part of the employer, or faulty machinery.'

'But he can prove negligence. Grease had dripped on the floor from a can used to oil the machines. He didn't see it in time and he slipped and fell . . .' She faltered. 'He fell against a giant wheel. His leg snapped instantly.'

Wade smirked, and Nicola itched to slap his face. She turned again to his captor. 'Is that law useless, too?'

'I'm afraid so. Whoever dripped the grease, it was not the manager. He's therefore not held accountable, and neither is the company.'

'So there's nothing I can do to compensate Josh, or see his employers charged?'

The younger man nodded, and released Wade, who bounced upright, ready for battle.

'Give it up, Owen. You'll not get the men here to join your union. They're afraid for their places. There are a hundred I could call on tomorrow, and they know it.'

'They're not all afraid; many of them are fed up with the treatment you and your sort hand out. The bad times will pass, Wade, and one morning you'll wake up to find your slaves have acquired bargaining power. Unionism is rising. It's already too late to stop it. Remember the maritime strike? Next time it'll be even bigger and more costly. It might even cost lives.'

The musical voice had taken on a power that was both thrilling and frightening. Nicola had listened to oratory before, but she'd never heard anyone so instantly capable of reaching down inside the listener and grabbing him. She could quite easily believe in the coming conflict, and saw by Wade's face that he did, too.

Owen turned to Nicola. 'Come, let's leave this den. We can't do any more for the present.'

Disappointed, and furious at her helplessness to bring Wade to book, she accompanied the young man out into the laneway, trying to place him. A workman with a command of language that declared an education was highly unusual.

He held out his hand. 'I'm Hugh Owen, firebrand at large.'

She smiled and clasped his hand briefly. 'Nicola Redmond, schoolmistress. I've never before met a firebrand, and I know little about unions and the battle for fair treatment in the work place. I'd very much like to know more.'

His gaze was searching. 'Would you? Then come with me to the nearest café and I'll enlighten you.'

Unconventional, thought Nicola. Yet, why not? She might learn what was being done for women like Rose and those poor creatures at Upton's.

She said, 'There's nothing I'd like more. Pray lead the way, Mr Owen.'

Speeding across town a few nights later, in answer to a plea from

Rose, Nicola felt history repeating itself. Last Christmas had been horrible; now it looked as though this year it would be as bad. Frail Jenny Basevi's tenuous grip on life was slipping. She would fight to stay alive until the child within her had a chance to be born. Afterwards. . . ? Nicola's heart contracted at the thought of that small family losing the gentle presence that was their core.

Where was the husband and father who was desperately needed?

Remembering her own father, her throat tightened. Had he not failed her and her mother in the end? While the path remained smooth and well-paved, he'd been strong; but when disaster struck he'd buckled, deserting them when they most needed him. Weak! However physically superior, all the men she had known were weak in spirit.

Take Andrew Dene, a hedonist, sipping the wine of life without a care, living on the proceeds of other men's work – and women's and children's. She despised him.

A desperate Rose met Nicola at the door. 'It's been twenty-four hours. Something is wrong. I know Mother needs expert help, but I can't afford the doctor. I've sold or pawned everything of any value. There's nothing left.'

Nicola took off her hat and looked fruitlessly for somewhere to lay it. 'Let me see Jenny.'

A few minutes later she was putting her hat on again. She'd never conceived of such agony as she'd witnessed in that cramped little room where a new life was struggling to be born. Jaw set, she said, 'Send for the doctor. Tell him that I guarantee the payment. He knows me and he knows I keep my bond.'

'Oh, Nicola. I shouldn't accept, but I must.' Rose went off to find a street urchin willing to run her errand, bribed with heaven knew what from the bare house.

It was dark when Nicola arrived in Chinatown, but the streets were gay with red lanterns all ready for the Chinese New Year. Strings of fireworks hung in doorways, and shop fronts were decorated with masks and vivid paper dragons. The joss house had been newly painted in scarlet and gold and wisps of incense trailed in the air. It all looked bright and Christmassy to her, which made the contrast with her misery so great.

She banged on the door of the pawnshop until a woman nearly as large as the proprietor himself opened it. Nicola couldn't see her clearly against the lamplight, but she must have read the trouble in Nicola's face, for she beckoned her in and closed the door behind her.

'My man is eating of his supper. What is it you want, miss?' Now she could be seen to have a pleasant face, wide-mouthed and heavily freckled. Masses of sandy hair piled up with tortoiseshell combs made her appear even taller than in actual fact.

Nicola said, 'I'm sorry to disturb you so late, but I must see Mr Monte tonight. I . . . it could mean someone's life.'

Mrs Pritchard put a massive hand on her arm and led her into the family dining room. 'Montague, leave your supper and help the lady. I'll put it on the hob to keep warm.'

Fork raised, Mr Monte watched his plate whisked away. He wiped his moustache with resignation and lumbered to his feet.

'Do you remember me coming here with Miss Basevi?' Nicola asked.

'I remember,' he rumbled. He led the way into his shop. 'What can I do for you?'

'I want to sell you . . . this.' Nicola plunged her hand beneath her collar and drew out the fire opal on its chain. She heard his breath hiss in. She removed the chain and held it in her palm, adding, 'My father had the piece valued at five hundred pounds.'

His gaze riveted to the heart, he said, 'It's not the sort of thing I handle. There's not much call—'

'Please. Make me an offer, Mr Monte.'

She saw the cupidity in his face and felt badly placed to bargain, but she had no choice. The doctor must be paid. This was the only way.

'I'll give you thirty pounds.'

'No. It's worth more than ten times the amount.'

'How do I know its worth? I don't know about opals.'

'If my word is not good enough, Mrs Eleanor Dene will vouch for the piece. She bought it recently at auction.' She could hardly bear to think, not only of parting with her father's love token, but also of the insult to Eleanor's generosity.

'Mrs Eleanor Dene isn't here, and you want the money now,

right?' His eyes had narrowed into slits, his nostrils indented with greedy excitement. All the same, he fetched a loupe from his drawer and examined the heart carefully. He snorted. 'Thirty-five, no more. I'm not running a charity.'

'Mr Monte, this money is needed for a sick woman.' Nicola put a stranglehold on her pride and continued, 'I beg you, be generous. I'll give you this ring as well.' She pulled off the signet ring that was all the other jewellery she possessed, and held it out to him.

He grasped it, turned it over and threw it on the table. 'I've got two dozen like this. My price stands.'

'Montague!' His wife sailed into the room, her plain face wrathful, her freckles standing out like polka dots.

'Yes, Abigail, my love?' Her husband looked sideways and sucked in his lower lip.

'Montague, I've been listening. How could you try to profit by such distress? I'm ashamed of you.'

'This is just business, my love.' He sounded plaintive.

'I understand business just as well as you do but, Lord love a duck, there's such a thing as common decency. Eighty pounds is fair, and we'll hold the jewel in pawn so the lass has got some chance of getting it back.'

Nicola let out her breath in a sigh. Eighty pounds. It wasn't anything like what she had hoped for, but at least it more than doubled the first offer. She blessed the wife who had her husband firmly where she wanted him, and waited while Mr Monte opened his safe and counted out the money with an ill grace.

His wife watched, dangling the heart from her fingers.

'It's a pretty thing,' she said to Nicola. 'I don't know as I'd care to wear it. Gewgaws don't suit a face like mine.'

'You have a lovely face. It matches your kind heart.' Nicola took Abigail's hand and pressed it. 'Thank you. You don't know what this means to me.'

'Ah, get along with you. It'd be a nice thing if I couldn't please myself in my own house. Now, Montague, give the lady her ticket and you'll have your supper back again.'

Mr Monte's sullen face brightened. He wrote out the details of the transaction in his journal as fast as he could, slapped a pink ticket into Nicola's hand and hurried her to the door, his mind clearly on beef pie with onion sauce.

Nicola tucked the notes inside her bodice and fled.

Back in Upper Kent Street the first thing she noticed was the quiet. Rose knelt by the bed with her hands clasped beneath her chin. Nicola breathed in deeply. The room smelt different, of lavender water and crisp, clean linen. The blood and pain and sweat had been wiped away as if they had never been.

Jenny lay at peace, her faded brown hair brushed into wings over her shoulders, her lined face now smooth, her eyes closed. She looked like a sleeping child. In the crook of her arm lay a doll with pouting rosebud mouth and winged moth brows. Its eyelids were satin fringed with cobweb and one cheek was crumpled like tissue. And like a doll, it had no life.

Nicola felt leaden. Dropping to her knees beside Rose, she put her arms around her and just held her.

CHAPTER ELEVEN

NICOLA DIDN'T MEET Rose again until the end of the month. Then she found her evasive, bustling over household chores, too busy to chat. Nicola visited Eleanor Dene more frequently, and was introduced to the heady world of feminism, devouring the books loaned to her and discussing them with her friend. The writings of local women astounded her, dealing as they did with such daring subjects as marriage seen as an institution which prostituted a woman to a man; or the question of how a woman could fulfil herself if she was expected to devote her life to the service of her husband's career.

Rose was still mysteriously busy, although she and Nicola met once or twice across a table in one of Quong Tart's teashops, several of which were dotted about the city. Then, at one of these meetings over tea and scones Rose shyly displayed a pretty little ring set with seed pearls and slivers of opal, and announced that she was engaged to be married.

Nicola had to search for words. 'You didn't tell me! You've kept this a secret for weeks!'

'I know, and I'm sorry, dear Nicola. I wanted to tell you, but it was all so uncertain. I didn't know whether he truly cared. I couldn't be sure, until now.' She gently twisted the ring, smiling at her thoughts. 'He gave it to me this week.'

'It's beautiful. But, who is *he*? Why all the intrigue?' Nicola floundered, not quite able to believe that Rose would keep such a momentous event secret from her.

'I can't tell you yet. He's an important man and is engaged in an extremely delicate operation that takes all his time. We plan to make an announcement soon.' Rose's smile turned mischievous. 'I promise you will be the first person to meet him. Will you be maid of honour at my wedding, Nicola?'

'Need you ask? Oh, Rose, you know I'm happy for you. I just wish . . .'

'You wish you could meet my love and satisfy yourself that he's good enough for me. You will like him. Nicola. He's wonderful, so tender, so loving. I wish I could put into words what I feel for him.'

Nicola took her friend's hands. 'You don't have to. It's written in your face. You are positively luminous.' She kissed Rose's cheek and released her. 'Then you will introduce us soon?'

'Soon. I promise.'

Nicola put aside her misgivings and allowed herself to fall into a reminiscent mood, recalling various pranks and pitfalls of their school years. When Rose had to go, she left Nicola sitting over a cooling teacup, her head filled with girlhood memories. There was no question that the strong link going back to childhood was important. Rose mattered in a way that no one else ever could.

But as she gathered up her purse to leave, Nicola's misgivings over this strange betrothal returned in a floodtide. Rose might be deeply in love, yet how far could a man be trusted who kept his identity secret, for whatever reason? *Why* must no one know of their liaison? Was he ashamed of Rose; or was there some other, darker, reason?

The more she thought about it, the more alarmed Nicola became. She determined to visit Rose before nightfall and use all her powers of persuasion to extract some satisfactory answers.

But when she got there the house was dark and no one answered her knock.

Then, with no previous warning, Nicola was informed that a new government school was to open in her area and the Ragged School would close at Christmas.

After a session with the board of management, she returned to her classroom and sat numbly trying to come to terms with her situation. She had always known that her position was temporary; and she had to be happy that the children would now be well taught and prepared for high school. Their chances of escaping the poverty trap would be greatly increased. But these children had become hers and she did not want to part with them. She would miss them terribly. She would miss their love.

Saddened and surprised at the strength of her feelings, Nicola would have liked to talk to Rose. Why hadn't she responded to the messages left pinned to the front door? What was happening about the wedding announcement? Josh couldn't say. Nowadays he appeared unkempt, and larded his speech with cant terms; his eyes shifted away from hers when she questioned him. Their old camaraderie seemed to have vanished. She was losing Josh as well as Rose.

One summer's evening, after visiting Eleanor, Nicola waited in growing darkness for her tram, watching lights blink against a backdrop of trees in Hyde Park. A sharp, unseasonable wind blew and the few people about didn't linger. She noticed a woman standing in a doorway, shivering in an inadequate dress and shawl. A tart, she thought, noting the rouged cheeks and lips. Yet, something struck her as familiar behind all the paint.

The woman looked up and their eyes met.

'Lizzie! Lizzie Perkins. What are you doing here?'

The woman's red mouth twisted. 'What do you think I'm doing? Waiting for me golden carriage with six white horses, a'course.' She spoke jeeringly, but there was a haunted look about her that struck Nicola to the heart.

'Oh, Lizzie. Is this the only way you can make a living?'

The woman shrugged thin shoulders.

Nicola thought about the lateness of the hour and about the last tram. She also remembered the day a maidservant had been dismissed by Millicent for carelessness, and without a thought for her future.

'I'd like a cup of tea, Lizzie. Do you know where we can get one at this time on a Sunday evening?'

Lizzie said with alacrity, 'Yus. There's a pie cart down the end o'the park.'

'Come along, then. We'll freeze, standing in this wind.'

With two cups of milky tea in her, plus some additive from a bottle in her pocket, Lizzie became jaunty and off-hand, inclined to view Nicola as an innocent who knew nothing of the world's ways.

'Who'd a'thought it, eh? You and me together here, just like ladies.' She leered confidentially. 'Only there's some has taken the wrong turning, for all they was eddicated in a fine school and rubbed shoulders with their betters.' She nodded portentously and the broken feather in her hat flopped forward.

Nicola realized that the woman had been imbibing before they met, and the extra added to the tea had tipped the balance. Poor Lizzie looked rather like a half-plucked fowl, with her silly cockscomb bonnet and flapping shawl.

'I'll have to go, Lizzie, if I'm to catch the tram.' Nicola finished the last drops of tea and put the mug back on the cart.

Lizzie took umbrage. 'Oh, the likes o'me's not good enough for your ladyship to talk to, is that it? Well there's some like you what've taken a right tumble, and now they're not so proud. What about your friend, then? What about her, what does the job in any lane if the man won't pay for a room?'

'What ever do you mean?' Nicola was more mystified than annoyed.

Lizzie smirked and picked a tea leaf out of her teeth with a broken nail. 'I mean Miss Rose Basevi, for all her fancy ways, is just like me. She's on the game, she is, and right popular, I hear.'

'What absolute rubbish! How dare you say such a thing!'

Lizzie's expression was a silent jeer.

Suddenly, Nicola could stand her no longer. She turned and hurried off up the street, blind to the sparse traffic, to people, to obstacles in her path, with Lizzie's malicious words resounding in her head, making her sick with disgust. She'd have to be stopped. Rose should be warned, and the police asked to take a hand, if necessary. Raging inwardly, Nicola took the tram back to her room and a night of broken sleep.

CHAPTER TWELVE

OF COURSE LIZZIE Perkins's lies were nothing but malicious fabrication – laughable if they were not so hurtful. However, Rose had clearly disappeared. Why?

Nicola was still seeking an answer when the end of term loomed. The long hot days leading up to Christmas were filled with last-minute preparations for the school break-up, and for Nicola's departure. On the Saturday before the end of term she cleared out her desk and carried home some of her books, closing her mind to the thought of the coming separation. She felt tired, hot and unhappy, and in no mood to be met with her mother's bald announcement that she was leaving Australia and returning to her family home in England.

Nicola let the books slide out of her arms on to the floor. She stared at her mother's pale, composed face. 'You're leaving me,' she half-whispered.

'Would you want to come?'

'No. This is my home.'

'Well, it has never truly been mine.' Millicent shivered. 'Only for your father's sake could I have born this harsh country and its rudimentary society. You may think me selfish. In fact, I know you do. I can admire your strength of purpose without in the least envying it. Your roots are in this land, and your spirit. But I was made for a different life, and I miss it, desperately.'

'I'm sorry, Mother.'

Millicent's smile was bitter. 'You tried to help me. I simply cannot reconcile myself to what amounts to a living death. So I am returning to my own milieu, where I shall be supported and understood. I may even marry again.'

Nicola choked back a hasty response.

'Oh, Nicola, you do not know very much about love, do you? I did care very much for your father – enough to know that he would put my happiness before all else.'

'I . . . expect so.' Nicola couldn't imagine any man taking Papa's place. A practical thought occurred to her. 'How can you afford a passage, Mother? You didn't . . . you couldn't ask Andrew Dene for such a sum!'

This time Millicent's smile was triumphant. 'I sold the diamond bracelet.'

For the second time that day, Nicola was bereft of speech. Papa's final gift to his wife, on the day of his death. Well, Mother had never been sentimental. And she had other mementos, no doubt.

Nicola thought about that, and laughed without much joy. 'I see. The second-best teacups again.' At her mother's puzzled expression, she explained: 'When our goods and chattels were being sold up, you hid the second best tea set. Apparently, you also hid the bracelet.'

Millicent said frostily, 'Those people had no right to it, or to anything else of a personal nature.'

'What else did you secrete away, Mother?'

'Oh, very little. Only what could be tucked into my corset. However, I kept the diamonds for a real emergency.'

An emergency escape, Nicola thought. She knew that she was not important in her mother's schemes. They'd never been close, so why be surprised that the parting had now come? 'When do you leave, Mother?'

'I sail on Monday.'

'Monday! In two days' time!'

'There was no point in telling you earlier. I prefer to make the break as swift and painless as possible.'

Unspeakably wounded, Nicola turned away. 'Then I'll leave you to pack.'

She went straight to Eleanor for comfort. Unfortunately she was resting after a painful night, and it was Andrew who met Nicola and somehow manoeuvred her into his book room for a talk.

Still rigid with the pain of her mother's rejection, she scarcely glanced at the elegant proportions of the room with its comfortably deep leather chairs, the walls of volumes broken only by windows and fireplace, the rich carpet beneath a workmanlike desk.

'I've been expecting you,' Andrew said.

'Ah! I might have supposed you would have a hand in breaking up what remained of our family.'

He tried to lead her to a chair, but she stepped away from his touch. She was brittle with emotion and unsure of where it would lead her.

Andrew said, gently, 'Sit down, Nicola, before you fall down.'

Feeling suddenly light-headed, she sank into one of the leather chairs, but ignored the wineglass he set beside her.

He poured himself some sherry. His eyes were watchful, as if unsure of her reaction.

'Please look at me, Nicola.'

A mix of misery and defiance warred in her, goading her to speak unwisely, but she struggled to contain the words.

Andrew either did not see, or chose not to. He said, 'You are always honest with yourself, so you should admit that, from the beginning, your relationship with your mother has been hopelessly flawed. It didn't need an outsider to cause the break.'

'My relationship with my mother is no business of yours.' She paused. 'Very well, I will admit to there being problems; but we managed to hold things together until you interfered.'

'Untrue. The breakdown came with your father's death and the collapse of your fortune. Your mother is constitutionally unable to cope without strong emotional and financial support.'

'Are you saying I failed to give Mother the love she needed?' It was true. Yet that chilly barrier between them had not been of her making.

Andrew picked up the wineglass and folded her stiff fingers around the stem. 'I wish you would drink this, Nicola, and let me say what you've already acknowledged in your heart.'

To conquer her light-headedness she drank, feeling the liquid fire run down her throat to warm her stomach.

Andrew now leaned back against the desk, watching her.

'Nicola, it's obvious to everyone but you, that Millicent Redmond can only be happy when she reigns in her social circle. Her marriage and move to Australia cut her off from the cultural interests that were her background, and there was little else for her to do but assume a butterfly existence, until your father's death brought that world crashing down. Yet, as a sophisticated woman, she was never truly happy in a society that she viewed as provincial. My dear, you can't support your mother in any way that would be meaningful for her, so let her go to those who can.'

She kept a blank face while she dealt with this. Various emotions chased one another through her mind – astonishment, rage, humiliation and, finally, acceptance. She hated admitting it, but Andrew Dene had seen to the heart of her relationship with her mother. Yet, to confess it openly was galling.

Feeling disadvantaged with him standing over her, she set down the wineglass with a snap and rose. 'You are a clever psychologist, Andrew Dene. I can't deny your interpretation. Obviously Mother will be much happier back in the bosom of her lordly family. All the same, you shouldn't have meddled. It was your constant offer of financial support that kept her unsettled.' She knew that, in the long run, his interference would not have affected the outcome, but she was wounded. She didn't care if she was being unfair.

For the first time Andrew lost his composure. 'That sticks in your throat, doesn't it? It's not a matter of money at all. It's the control. You need to be the one to make the decisions.'

Outraged, Nicola found her voice stuck in her throat. She took a deep breath. 'The thing I most dislike about you, Andrew Dene, is your assumption that you have all the answers. Men are the ones who need to feel in control, and woe betide any woman who tries to think for herself.'

'I thought we'd come to that eventually. Do you say your rebellious creed to yourself night and morning? How does it go: All men are power-hungry monsters; all women are downtrodden slaves?'

They glared at one another across a deepening gulf of misunderstanding. Nicola didn't know how she might have responded but for a sudden, loud interruption. The hall door swung back with a crash and Josh stood there panting, the housekeeper pulling at his coat while apologizing to her employer.

Nicola read the boy's face, and turned pale. 'Josh. What are you doing here? Where have you been?'

After a quick frowning glance at Nicola, Andrew nodded to the housekeeper. 'It's all right, Mrs Peck. Let the lad come in.'

She retired doubtfully, while Josh bounded forward to grasp Nicola's arm.

'Oh, Nicola, you've got to help me! I don't know what to do. Rose has disappeared. I've searched everywhere I can think of. I'm afraid, Nicola. What'll I do?'

He didn't pause for an answer, and Nicola listened in numb disbelief as the boy's sorry tale of pain and degradation gushed from him like a river that had broken its banks.

At first it was a complaint of loneliness and loss of independence. 'I didn't know for a long time, Nicola. I just thought she was out at night with her fancy man.' He looked up, shamefaced.

Nicola said gently, 'You resented being left behind to mind Daisy. You wanted a little fun of your own.'

'That's right. Because Rose seemed so happy, you see.' Josh gulped.

Andrew's voice was equally gentle but it had authority. 'Go on. Tell us what happened, lad.' He led the boy to a chair and made him sit.

'She started going out earlier and not coming home until light. She stopped doing the cooking and washing, and I had to do everything. I thought she was just skiving off, you know.' He brushed a sleeve across his eyes. 'She got thinner and more and more cross and prickly. It's terrible, Nicola. She just wasn't like our Rose at all.' He took another gulping breath. 'I didn't know, you see.'

When he seemed to have come to a halt, Nicola wanted to shake the words out of him. She said, in the calmest voice she could manage, 'What didn't you know, Josh?'

'I didn't know it was the stuff doing it to her. *He* gave it to her. She didn't know what it was. She wouldn't, would she? It must've been him. If could find him I'd kill him! I'd ... I'd ...' His voice cracked.

Nicola knelt beside the chair and put her arms around him.

But Andrew persisted. 'Go on, lad. What was the *stuff*?'

'Cocaine.'

Nicola's gasp drowned in Andrew's next question.

'How do you know it was cocaine?'

'Rose told me. She looked so awful one day; I wanted her to go to the doctor. I went on and on at her about it until she told me to shut me up.'

'Did you ask her where she obtained it?'

Josh shrugged miserably. 'She just laughed. But she didn't sound happy. Then I asked her why she went out so much at night and left me to do all the work, and . . . and. . . .' He floundered to a halt.

Andrew was inexorable. 'What was her answer? Come on, lad. Tell us.'

'Andrew, don't.' Nicola still held Josh. 'You know what he'll say. There's no need to force it out of him.' She took a deep breath. 'Josh, Rose has gone on the streets, hasn't she?'

Josh nodded. He didn't meet her gaze.

They fell silent. The clock ticking sounded like a drumbeat to Nicola. Its monotony was maddening. She whispered, 'Someone told me, but I didn't believe her. Oh, Rose. My poor, dear Rose.'

Andrew poured another glass of wine, putting it in Josh's hand and bringing it up to his mouth. When the boy jibbed, Andrew forced him to drink. Nicola, seeing the colour come back into Josh's face, let him go. Her mind seemed blank. She knew there were more questions, but she couldn't seem to formulate them.

Andrew did it for her. 'You said a man introduced your sister to the drug. Was it he whom she went to meet each night – at least in the beginning?'

Josh nodded. 'I think so.'

'Rose told me about him weeks ago,' Nicola interjected. 'She loved him, you see. That's how he trapped her.'

'The bastard!' Josh sprang up, almost oversetting his glass.

Andrew laid a restraining hand on his shoulder and pressed him to sit down again. 'You've no idea who this man could be? Your sister never mentioned any names?'

When Josh shook his head, Nicola said fiercely, 'She told me he needed to remain incognito for some reason to do with his standing or business venture, or some such thing. It sounded hollow to me at the time, but I didn't want to upset Rose. She was so very happy.' She stifled a sob. 'I wish to God I'd said something then. Somehow we never really spoke again on such an intimate level. She had someone else to confide in – someone who took all her love and trust and destroyed her!'

CHAPTER THIRTEEN

A SEARCH WAS mounted immediately, headed by Andrew Dene. Nicola welcomed his help. He could command forces that were beyond her reach, including the police, who, without Andrew's pressure, would undoubtedly have shown little interest in the disappearance of a prostitute. There was no hiding Rose's true employment if there was to be any hope of tracing her.

Nicola wanted nothing more than to rush out and ransack the streets, herself. Instead, she went back to Mrs Gardiner's and took over the care of Daisy until, with daylight, she could join in the search, enlisting the aid of 'her' children who knew the back streets and alleys of their part of town as animals know their own territory. She was still out when her mother's hired coach came to pick up her trunks and she boarded the Peninsula and Orient Line's crack liner *Britannia*, ready to sail at dawn.

That night the main body of searchers met at the central location of the Dene clothing factory in Redfern. Nicola sat in the manager's office with Josh close beside her for comfort. Andrew and some of the men he had co-opted crowded in to compare notes, and more men arrived every few minutes. On the floor below them machines crashed and whined non-stop in an atonal symphony that Nicola grew to hate, her hopes diminishing as the negative reports came in.

Then, with the midnight change of shift, voices rose above the clamour of the machinery. Someone screamed, and Nicola sprang up as the office door was wrenched open. A woman in a work pinafore hung on to the jamb to fetch her breath, her face red and excited.

'Murder!' she gasped and pointed dramatically down the stairs.

'Where?' snapped Andrew.

'Down in the alley.' The woman clutched at her heart. 'It's some tart lying in the dirt. Oh, I think I'm going ter faint.'

Andrew brushed past her, grabbing one of the searcher's lanterns as he went, and took the stairs in a few bounds, with Nicola close behind him

The alley was only a narrow drain dividing the factory from the yard next door, a weed-grown area behind a deserted foundry. Workers arriving for the new shift at Dene's via the back entrance must have literally tripped over the body in the dark. The lantern quivered in Andrew's hands, revealing smudged foot marks on a tumble of skirts, and a black straw hat, its jaunty feather buckled in jet. Nicola knew the search had ended.

Rose's face was dark and engorged, her tongue protruding. Her eyes, filmed over, seemed to stare at Nicola – until Andrew strode forward and flung his handkerchief over the awful face.

Josh, after one terrible cry, had gone silent, hanging from his crutches like something pegged out to dry.

Nicola staggered, and might have fallen if Andrew's arm had not supported her.

'Come away, my dear. There's nothing you can do for her.'

She shook her head. 'Look at her bodice. There's blood. She's been cut.'

He leaned forward, then drew back sharply. 'It's the letter 'W', carved on her breast.'

Trapped in a mist of horror, Nicola was barely aware of onlookers crowding behind her, of heads cramming the window above, voices commenting, theorizing. All her senses were concentrated on the heap of ragged clothing with two stockinged legs protruding. The hat buckle drew her attention. It gleamed like a small, dark star, keeping her from seeing the blood.

She said in a voice quite unlike her own, '"W" for "whore", of course. It's a message from her killer.' She began to laugh hysterically. 'Of course she's a whore. He made her one, and then blamed her for it.' Her voice cracked. 'Oh, Rose. I'm so sorry. I should have searched harder for you. I should have made you talk to me. My dear, dear Rose!'

'Come away, Nicola. You and young Josh shouldn't be alone tonight,' said Andrew, urging them both inside.

Nicola didn't respond. The words made no impact. They simply passed straight out of her mind.

'Nicola?' Andrew watched her intently.

She nodded brightly at him.

Josh tightened his grasp on her arm. 'I'll stay with Nicola,' he said.

Andrew was insistent. 'I want you both to come home with me for what remains of the night. My mother has been anxious for you.' Urging them back up to the office, he said, 'Wait here. I won't be long.'

Made obedient through shock, they waited there, separated from the scene of the investigation and protected from curious eyes. Nicola sat with her hands clasped and head bowed, her mind curiously numb. Down in the alley there was activity as police searched the surrounding area, and the police surgeon carried out his preliminary observations under the eyes of Detective First Class Robert Carrington.

Nicola continued to stare through Andrew when he returned to report all this. It was as though, if she tried hard enough, she could penetrate the wall behind him and see down into that horrible alley. She wished Andrew and Josh would be quiet. Their voices distracted her from concentrating, from visualizing what was happening down there. They'd be handling Rose's poor little body, examining it for traces left by her murderer. Traces, indeed, she thought bitterly, with the marks of his fingers on his victim's throat and the knife cuts labelling her so cruelly.

She felt hands on her shoulders, shaking her.

'You're not hearing me, Nicola.'

She looked sideways at those hands, first one, then the other – broad hands, muscular and strong, quite capable of. . . . With a cry, she tore herself free, her eyes wild as she fended Andrew off.

Immediately he stood back, hands dropping to his sides. 'I'm sorry. That was stupid of me.'

'No . . . I apologize. I wasn't thinking.' As her thundering heart-beats eased, Nicola felt her normal senses returning, and with them the tearing pain of loss. Somehow she managed to speak rationally. 'Please thank your mother for her kindness, but I'd rather be alone, except for Josh. I'll go back to his house.'

'I wish you would reconsider,' said Andrew, with obvious restraint. 'You've both been terribly shocked. Even that cold fish of a detective recognizes it, and has postponed your interview until tomorrow.'

'I need to be away from other people. Please, understand.'

He sighed. 'Very well. I may call for you and take you to the police station in the morning?'

'Thank you. We'd be grateful.' All this politeness, thought Nicola, drearily. Yet the formality helped to hold her together until she was alone and could afford to release the lock on her emotions.

Detective Carrington eventually joined them, his manner detached and respectful. But Nicola didn't quite believe in it. This man was a bloodhound. His educated English voice added to his air of capability and command, and the constables, and even the surgeon, responded to it like lower ranks in the army. He could be just the man to track down the killer.

Having briefly expressed his condolences, the detective reminded all three that he expected to see them in his office in No.109 Pitt Street at ten o'clock in the morning. They gave him their assurances and were then allowed to leave.

Andrew drove them to the down-at-heel tenement that had been Rose's most recent refuge. His grim-faced reaction to it made no impression on Nicola. She thanked him and hurried inside with Josh. Then, at last, she could throw herself down on Rose's narrow bed and abandon herself to her grief.

The detective branch of the police had its headquarters in an ordinary-looking building with a cast-iron-railed veranda on both levels. Nicola was led to a cubbyhole office where she took her seat on a utilitarian chair and faced the detective seated behind his desk.

Last night she'd been aware of the man's force, but only peripherally. Today, Robert Carrington, tall, slim, muscular, gave the impression of coiled energy held in reserve.

She answered his questions as fully as she could, yet as the interview progressed she had no sense of real communication with her interrogator and felt alienated by his detachment. Added to this was her physical discomfort. Her eyes, red and puffy, itched as if they'd had sand blown in them, her nose was stuffy and she had a headache.

She was disappointed. The detective's attitude from the start had been almost perfunctory, his questions quick and the answers barely noted before the next question was fired. He was not bringing his bloodhound abilities to this case. Possibly he considered it beneath his dignity and senior rank. Whatever the reason, it didn't suit Nicola.

When at last the questions ceased, she said, 'Have I now leave to add some further information of my own, Inspector?'

Carrington laid down his pencil carefully in the groove of his notebook and examined her face. 'Of course, if it will aid our discussion, Miss Redmond.'

'Our discussion seems to me to be more a one-sided interrogation, but yes, there is something. Rose was betrayed by a man who pretended to love her and dragged her down to the gutter.'

'Who was the man?'

'I don't know. She had been meeting him for some time before she told me that she . . . she had a lover. Afterwards, she avoided me. I'll always regret not pressing her for more information. I should have known there was something strange about such a hole-in-corner relationship.'

'Just so. And she gave absolutely no indication of his identity?'

'Beyond the fact that he claimed to be a man of affairs, none at all.'

His sceptical expression enraged her. She sat and simmered as he sent for Josh and Andrew Dene to be brought in.

Andrew moved swiftly to her side. 'Nicola, are you unwell? You look pale.' He turned to Carrington. 'This lady still suffers from severe shock. You might have postponed your interrogation until she had recovered.'

Carrington's rigid mouth quivered. 'Indeed!' He gave his full attention to Andrew. 'Don't you find it strange, Mr Dene, that the victim should be discovered virtually at your back door? Did you know her when she was alive?'

The veiled imputation that he might have 'known' Rose in the way of sexual commerce was not lost on Andrew, as Nicola saw, but only a fractional narrowing of his eyes betrayed it.

'Actually,' he said, 'the back door gives entrance to a place of business situated in an area noted for its roughness after dark. Presumably Miss Basevi chose to offer her wares there in the local taverns, of which there are many. She may even have accompanied her client to the alley, as a place suitably dark and deserted.'

'You haven't answered my second question. Did you know the deceased?'

'I met Miss Basevi once, briefly, at Miss Redmond's home, about two years ago. We didn't speak.'

Carrington's brows rose, but he passed smoothly on to Josh whom, from the beginning, he'd treated with blunt kindness. 'Did your sister never confide in you, lad? Can you tell me anything at all about where she went, whom she met? Did she ever say she was afraid of anyone in particular?'

Josh stared at him mutely. He seemed unable to collect his thoughts this morning, despite Nicola's efforts to prepare him for the interview. The boy's unexpressed misery transferred itself to her, and she responded protectively.

'Josh can't tell you anything you don't already know. Rose tried to keep the reality of her life from touching him or Daisy.'

'Was she robbed?' Andrew asked.

'Oh, yes. The lobes of her ears were torn where earrings had been wrenched out.'

Nicola felt sick.

Andrew went on remorselessly. 'Had they bled?'

'Not greatly. It was done after death, as I see you appreciate.'

Forcing herself, Nicola asked, 'Was she wearing a small pearl and opal ring? I . . . I forgot to look.'

Carrington showed interest.'No ring was found. It does appear to be robbery, with a little social comment thrown in.' When Nicola's gaze widened, he amended, 'I mean, the slashes upon the victim's breast need not have been made in anger. The murderer was making a statement, of course; but many men who frequent women of the night profess to despise what they crave.'

Not you, though, Nicola thought. You're too bloodless to allow yourself cravings. She had a brutal headache developing, the waves of pain building in a crescendo, to crash down on her, leaving her almost reeling with their force. Yet she couldn't leave without knowing what would be done for Rose.

'Detective Carrington, are you saying this was simply a robbery assault – that Rose was killed for her few bits of jewellery?'

'It does look that way, Miss Redmond.'

'I don't believe it! It was the man, the brute who betrayed her. I'm sure I'm right.'

'We have no evidence to support your assumption.' He rose, indicating that the interview had ended.

'But you haven't achieved anything,' Nicola protested. 'What will you do to find the killer? You can't just leave matters like this.'

'I don't intend to, Miss Redmond. I can assure you that I will do everything in my power to apprehend this villain. The machinery has been set in motion—'

'Don't insult me with clichéd phrases, Detective Carrington. I insist that you tell me your plans.' Sick with pain, she clutched the back of the chair for support.

Andrew quickly intervened. 'Nicola, police regulations will not allow it. Look, this is too much for you at present. Let me discuss the whole thing privately with the detective. You may rely on me to do my utmost to help you and Josh.'

She put a hand to her splitting head. 'I can't let . . . Oh, very well.' Perhaps, just this once. 'Do whatever you think best. I'll talk to you later. Come, Josh. We must fetch Daisy home before Mrs Gardiner decides we have fled the country.'

'I shall escort you—'

'No! No thank you. Please talk to Detective Carrington now.' She hurried Josh out the door before Andrew could protest.

Sitting in the tram, with its jangling noise covering any low-voiced conversation, Josh broke his silence. He stared down at his work-roughened hands and said to Nicola, 'He doesn't look like a copper-man. Do you think he knows what he's doing?'

Nicola sighed. 'I think he knows. Whether he will make the effort is another thing. Detectives don't wear a uniform, Josh, although I'll grant you this one seems more like a glass of fashion than an employee of the state.'

She had wondered what brought a man of Carrington's obvious education and upbringing to join a colonial police force. Was he a remittance man? Maybe he'd lost all his money and needed to earn a living. Did she really care enough to speculate any further?

Closing her eyes, she sat quietly, longing for the journey to finish and for the peace of her own room.

It was not to be. Daisy, left in the hands of strangers for too long, had passed from the stage of noisy tantrums to destructive hysteria, and Mrs Gardiner had had enough.

'Locked her in the laundry room, I have, where she can try kicking the mangle to pieces with my blessing. She'll only hurt her own toes.' Mrs Gardiner took a quick breath and continued, 'I'm not one to be disobliging, miss, as you well know, but take responsibility for that young limb I will not. You'll have to leave her at the orphanage. It's the place for her.'

'Oh, no!' The instinctive cry rose from both Nicola and Josh, who stared at one another in consternation.

Josh said, 'I'll watch after Daisy. She'll mind me.' Distant howls and the sounds of a door being kicked made them all wince.

'You can't, Josh.' Nicola's voice had dwindled to a thread under the renewed assault of the headache. 'You're not yet able to earn your living; and when you do get work, you can't leave a little girl alone in the house – particularly in such an area. I can't take her. I must work, too.' She looked helplessly at him. 'I'm afraid there's no help for it. Daisy has to go into care.'

'No! I won't let you do it.' Josh pushed past her and hobbled down the passage to unbar the door of the laundry room.

Daisy emerged like a thunderbolt, her hair streaming wildly around her shoulders, her face scarlet and wet with tears.

Nicola glanced instinctively at the child's boots, and saw the toes were worn almost through. Compassion welled up in her. The poor mite was only expressing her misery and loss, after all. First her mother, then her sister. It was too much for any child. She knelt down in the passageway. 'Daisy, come here to me, darling.'

The sincerity in her voice reached the girl, who paused in her noisy lamentations to look her over. When Nicola held out her arms, Daisy barrelled into them, almost knocking her over. While her shoulders heaved with dry sobs, Nicola held her. They stayed like that for a long time until she calmed. Then Nicola led her away to wash her face and persuade her to rest on Nicola's own bed. She knew precisely where to go for help.

Nicola paid a visit to the Dene home the following morning, accompanied by a suspicious Josh, wary of his luxurious surroundings and the crippled older woman who presided over them. However, Eleanor's genuine liking for children soon won him over, and with the arrival of teacakes and scones he capitulated entirely.

Soon he had agreed to Daisy being placed as a foster child with a family whose kindness was matched by the ability to discipline their own tribe of children. Nicola went home that afternoon profoundly relieved. Josh had hobbled off in a burst of male independence, and she let him go without protest, thinking he might need time on his own.

Nicola went back to Mrs Gardiner's to pack. The life she had carefully constructed for herself when thrown on her own resources had collapsed. Another had to be built away from reminders of the old one, especially from memories of all the people she had lost. All but Rose. She would never know real ease until the mystery of Rose's death had been solved.

CHAPTER FOURTEEN

ONCE HAVING ESTABLISHED herself in a neat cottage conveniently situated in Strawberry Hills, Nicola was ready to pursue
her quest to find Rose's killer. She called at the detective bureau
on a dry and windy day guaranteed to try the temper. Sydney
was experiencing an unusually hot spell of weather for April, and
people kept indoors if they could, or hurried through the streets
head down, shielding themselves from flying grit.

Nicola paused just inside the doorway to remove her protective
veil and brush the dust clinging like brown velvet to her sleeves.

Carrington came out to meet her, his attitude considerably
warmer than at their first meeting. In fact, his gaze was distinctly
admiring. Nicola couldn't help the thought that she might turn this
to her advantage. Any weapon, any tool was valid in her cause.

Ushering her to a seat opposite his desk, he said, 'Miss
Redmond, I should tell you that we have made a little progress,
but not as much as I could wish. Frankly, we don't have the men
to spare for it.' When Nicola flashed a glance at him, he hastily
amended, 'Not because your friend's death is less important than
any other, believe me. We're simply short-handed.' He paused.

'I will be honest. There is very little to be done in this case.
We've found no one who will admit to having seen the victim that
night, and no indication that she had acquired a client. There is
nothing on the body to identify her killer, no skin or blood under
the fingernails where she might have scratched him while fighting
for her life, no fabric or buttons clutched in her fist. The wounds
on her breast were made with a seaman's knife, but it has proved
a useless clue. The alley has afforded none, although we believe
that the victim died elsewhere and her body was later thrown
over the wall, to be discovered later, rather than sooner. In short,

there's nothing to go by.'

Nicola pressed her handkerchief to her mouth and sagged in the chair. The picture created in her mind by Carrington seemed hardly bearable. All too clearly she could see Rose struggling with her assailant, her cries muffled by the big hands about her throat. She could feel Rose's agony and terror as she sensed her life slipping away. Had she seen the knife? Had that added to her terror? And then to be tossed like garbage over a wall to lie in a rat-infested alley, without even dignity left to her.

Carrington leapt up and covered the distance between them in two strides. His hands supported her elbows, easing her against the chair back.

'What a damned idiot I am to speak so plainly. Forgive me.'

He loomed close. She could almost have counted the hairs of his silky moustache. She closed her eyes.

'Could I have some water, please?'

'Immediately!' He hesitated. 'You won't swoon?'

Nicola stiffened her spine. 'Of course not. I felt a momentary faintness, that's all.'

When he hastened back with the water, she thanked him and sipped it, feeling the blood returning to her head.

'Detective Carrington, you must think me a fool. I beg for information, and when I get it I behave like a schoolgirl.'

Hovering still, frowning, he shook his head. 'It was entirely my stupidity in relating details that must affect any lady. My one excuse is that the females I see during the course of my work are mainly of a quite different order, hardened to crime and indecency. I wish you would not concern yourself with the conduct of the case. It's not fitting.'

Well, now, thought Nicola. The detective is vulnerable after all. Despite his air of tough cynicism, he still believes in the gentility and fragility of the 'lady'.

She smiled bravely. 'I can't desert Rose. She has no one else to fight for her.'

'I will fight for her.' The words *for your sake* hung in the air, unspoken, and Nicola took unblushing advantage.

'Would you? May I rely upon you?'

'Yes, Miss Redmond, you may.' Carrington's eyes had lost

their habitual coolness; they blazed like beacons in his pale face. However, he stepped back from her, easing the tension of the moment.

Nicola knew it was time to leave. But the events of the morning were not quite over. There were sounds of a row brewing beyond the door, and when Carrington excused himself and opened it, Nicola could see a man with manacled hands being dragged unwillingly to the sergeant's desk by three uniformed police.

'What's going on? Carrington demanded. 'This isn't a watch house. Why are you bringing a prisoner here?'

Panting from his exertions, one of the police constables managed a salute. 'Sir, the prisoner, being of a troublesome disposition, refused to come any further. We had enough bother getting him this far.' He scowled at his captive.

Carrington was sarcastic. 'So three of you could barely manhandle the one. Where's the police wagon, you dolt!'

While the constable and his two battered companions tried to explain the loss of their wagon and the extreme difficulty of conveying a prisoner on foot in the midst of a crowd threatening to overwhelm the custodians of Her Majesty's law, Nicola regarded the prisoner. Dishevelled, with blood seeping through the tight, dark curls, he was still unbowed, still the feisty firebrand, Hugh Owen.

'Mr Owen! Whatever has happened to you?'

He grinned jauntily. 'You'd best ask these poll-crackers that question. Wasn't I minding my own business, talking to a few friends, when they upped and dragged me away. I naturally took exception to this, and you see the result. When they've come to their senses, I'll probably charge them with common assault.'

Carrington looked disapproving. With jutting jaw he demanded a clearer explanation from the nearest constable, who sprang to attention.

'Sir. The prisoner was apprehended as causing a breach of the peace. When he refused to go quietly, he was forcibly manacled, at which time he assaulted us three officers of the law.'

'In the course of our duty,' chorused the trio.

Hugh Owen snorted. 'Since when is it a duty to arrest a man talking to his friends?'

Carrington had been studying him. Now he said, 'I know you. You're the unionist rabble-rouser causing disruption in factories and warehouses. Didn't they run you out of Melbourne two years ago?'

Hugh Owen merely smiled.

'Where did you pick him up?' Carrington demanded.

'Sir, in the Domain, shouting from a soapbox. He was encouraging strike action among the workers.'

'I was talking to friends, merely deploring the recent regrettable maritime strike.' Hugh Owen shrugged. 'And tell me when it became illegal for a man to stand on a box and give aloud his personal opinions?'

'Not if it was seditious talk,' Carrington retorted.

Nicola said quickly, 'I'm willing to vouch for this gentleman. He is a friend, and I'm quite sure he would not spread seditious talk.'

A chorus rose against her, but Carrington, now as stiff as a ramrod, held up his hand.

'I can't help but think this affair has been mismanaged from the start. You three,' he nodded at the constables, 'have no proof of seditious intent on the part of this man, who was exercising a legal right to address citizens in the Domain. You have lost a valuable police wagon, which will by now have vanished into the fastnesses of a thieves' den; the state of your uniforms is a disgrace; you even brought your prisoner to the wrong station.'

The three constables stiffened to strict attention.

'Release this man and get out of here before I decide on a disciplinary action.'

When he turned to Nicola he was as cool as to a stranger. 'Good day, Miss Redmond. Our agreement still stands, and I promise to keep you informed.' He walked off towards his own office.

Released, Hugh came to her, rubbing his wrists and smiling wryly. 'I suspect that I have your charm to thank for my speedy release, rather than any good-heartedness on the part of the law.'

Nicola flushed. 'How ridiculous. You were wrongfully arrested, and Detective Carrington knew it.'

Hugh shook his head. 'Nevertheless, I feel that a celebration is called for.' He waved to the scowling constables, offered an arm to Nicola, and carried her with him out through the door.

CHAPTER FIFTEEN

THE HOT WIND hit them, driving them back against the wall. Nicola hastily pulled down her hat-brim and veil and Hugh hailed a hansom, almost lifting Nicola inside.

'How much money have you with you?' he asked.

Surprised, Nicola replied, 'Almost none.'

His rueful expression reminded her of the ragged, impish Benny caught out in a misdemeanour. 'My pockets are equally to let. We'd better leave this cab at the next corner.'

Nicola laughed. 'And you wanted a celebration. I'd have settled for a cup of tea in this heat. You'd better come home with me. I can raid my savings to travel in comfort.' She gave directions to the cabbie and sank back with relief out of the wind.

The unconventionality of riding alone with a man in a hansom cab was as nothing to the notion of inviting him back to her house, unchaperoned. But Nicola, happily aware of cocking a snook at convention, felt herself to be one of the new women, ready to take a stand against society's restrictions. Besides, she was a good judge of character, and while the Welshman might not share Detective Carrington's belief in the fragility of a lady, he certainly held women in respect. In previous encounters with him she'd noted and approved his attitude. Hugh Owen was no predator.

Back in Viola Terrace, Nicola flung back the shutters on her parlour window and bade Hugh sit down while she boiled water for tea and fetched the hydrogen peroxide to attend to his cut scalp.

While she worked she questioned him. 'Why do you do it, Mr Owen?'

'Hugh. Call me Hugh. Anyone who patches my wounds is entitled to fraternal and sisterly rights. Do you mean: why do I stand on a box and harangue the crowds about unionism?'

'I mean all of it. You go out of your way to meet trouble. There are other men fighting for change, politically and socially, and they don't seem to be always at risk.'

Hugh shrugged, then winced as she dabbed at his scalp. 'I told you, I'm a rebel at heart. I can't stand to be tied in by restrictions. Let others try to change the laws. I'll cheer when they enforce shorter hours and decent wages and conditions. But they won't do it all above board. The big men have too much to lose. They don't fight fair, and neither should we.'

'You mean factory and mill owners like Andrew Dene?'

'He's one of the more decent ones. Go into any of his workshops and you'll find reasonable conditions and payment of a living wage. Still, for every boss like Dene you'll find twenty using sweated labour in unhealthy and dangerous surroundings.

Nicola hid her surprise. But it was something to be thought about later.

Hugh went on, his mild voice a contrast to the misery he spoke of. 'There are still children employed in tanneries, standing up to their waists in offal and acid chemicals; women who make waterproof clothing fall down in a dead faint through inhaling naphtha fumes; lads and lasses less than ten years old are employed at starvation wages in tobacco factories – never mind the laws on juvenile labour – and are deliberately addicted to smoking and chewing to keep them there. Have you ever seen those children, sallow, lardy-skinned, running about like rats in unventilated workrooms in an atmosphere of heat and stench that would put a navigator under?'

Nicola shook her head. 'I never have. But I've seen the upholstery factory where Rose worked. Many of the children I taught at the Ragged School had been rescued from such conditions.' She added, fiercely, 'That wicked man at the printing works didn't care at all about Josh almost losing his leg in unguarded machinery.'

'He knew there were plenty more lads to replace him.' Hugh's shoulders seemed to sag under the weight of his knowledge. 'So, there's the answer to your question. I do what I do because I can't live with the unfairness in our society.'

Nicola touched his arm, before gathering up her bowl and lint and the bottle of peroxide. 'You're a good man, Hugh Owen. I'm glad I met you.'

They drank their tea in the cool parlour and Hugh listened to Nicola talk about her hopes for the future, her need to be a part of the fight for the rights of women and children. He agreed with her that women workers should have union representation, but dismissed this as an issue to be addressed when unionism had been firmly established. The men should first secure jobs in order to support their families. They did not need women and children taking positions away from family men.

Nicola could not believe that Hugh supported this attitude. An argument brewed.

He did deplore the recent attacks on women staff at the printing works producing *The Dawn* magazine, a vociferous supporter of women's rights. But he added, 'All the same, the women were taking up jobs that would normally belong to men who are now out of work.'

'Perhaps so. However, in most cases women are relegated to the kind of poorly paid work that men won't take on – the unskilled trades like service and food and clothing. These trades seem to be of little concern to the trade union movement. Women need the opportunity to train for skilled work.'

'Why? Someone has to perform the unskilled jobs. If women want to enter the paid workforce they had better stay where they're needed, and not take work from the traditional breadwinners.'

Nicola was aghast. 'How can you say that? You must know how many families are now without their breadwinners, the husbands and fathers having left home to seek work in the country, or simply run off to avoid responsibility. What about the men who spend their wages on drink and let their families starve? What about widows and orphans?'

Hugh looked uncomfortable. 'There are charities. . . .'

'I know about charities. I've seen what depths a family must sink to before being considered "deserving" of five shillings a week towards rent and a little tea and sugar and flour. I've seen old women who have walked two or three miles in heat or storm to collect their food and carry it all the way home, only to have to do it again a few days later. Besides, the philanthropists can touch but a fraction of the people in need.'

'Hey, I should lend you my soapbox. You'd do well in the Domain.'

Nicola didn't smile. 'I may end up there yet. I intend to involve myself with the women's organizations in any way I can.' She began to clear the tea things on to a tray.

Hugh also rose. 'I see it's time I left. Nicola, we can still remain friends, can't we? We are technically on the same side in this battle.'

'I suppose we are. Yes, of course we are friends. But I warn you, I'll keep trying to convert you to my way of thinking.'

Hugh nodded. 'Good. That will keep me on my toes.' He stood up to leave, then hesitating, said, 'Nicola, will you tell me why you were at the detective bureau? You may say I'm interfering in your private life but, if you're in any trouble, I'd like to help.'

'Oh, Hugh. Thank you. I forgot that you didn't know about Rose.'

He looked enquiring.

'She is . . . she was my dearest friend, and she was murdered. I saw her body, lying in an alley.'

Hugh's face froze. 'You saw. . . .' He seemed unable to continue.

Taking a firm grip on her feelings, she said, 'Sit down, Hugh, and I'll tell you about it. I'm sorry I shocked you.'

White-faced, Hugh sank into a chair. 'You actually found her body yourself? My God!'

By the time Nicola had finished her tale it had occurred to her that Hugh might be in a position to help with the investigation. She put the idea to him straightforwardly.

'What do you think, Hugh? There must be places you can go and people you can talk to who would never be available to Detective Carrington.'

He shrugged ruefully. 'Are you suggesting that I inhabit some dark underworld, Nicola?'

'Something of the sort,' she admitted. 'Have I offended you?'

'No. In a way you're right. There is such an underworld in our society, and in the course of my work I do talk to men and women who would disappear at the first sight of a police uniform.' He shook his head. 'It's just too terrible a crime to contemplate. That poor young girl.'

He still seemed shaken, and Nicola warmed to him for his compassion. She didn't protest when he leaned forward to take her hands and draw her nearer. Gazing into the steady dark eyes she felt comforted.

'Nicola, I swear to do everything in my power to bring this villain to book.'

'Thank you, Hugh. No friend could do more.'

CHAPTER SIXTEEN

'WHAT UTTER RUBBISH!' Louisa Lawson, owner and editor of *The Dawn*, stood by her press, hands on hips, frowning at Nicola. They had been introduced by Eleanor through her membership of the Women's Literary Society – which was much more like a political club devoted to changing society's treatment of the female sex. And Nicola had plunged into the feminist world with the eagerness of a puppy after a bone.

Today Louisa's scorn was directed, not at Nicola herself, but at her report on Hugh Owen's opinion of women taking the jobs meant for men. 'These unionists are so simplistic. They see women forced to go out to work, they see their own work disappearing, and they equate the two as cause and effect. The truth is that mechanization of manufacturing has everything to do with the diminishing work pool. Craftsmen are no longer needed as the machines take over the processes.

'And, of course, there's the slump in the building trade and in the call for consumer goods. We're not just talking about skilled trades, but about labouring, which is where many men found their work. Don't tell me women have taken over there!'

Nicola sighed. 'I wish I'd known all this when I needed to rebut Hugh's argument.'

'If it's ammunition you want, I can supply it. Still, I'd be surprised if your Mr Owen didn't have the figures in his own head. Now we must go, or we'll be late for the meeting.'

The air was loud with the sound of fifty women chattering and greeting one another. Curtains had been drawn over the windows, and the brightly lit stage was set with a table holding water jug and glasses, and a row of chairs facing the audience. The women all appeared to Nicola to be well dressed, some exceedingly fashionably, and in total contrast to her own shabbiness.

But all thought of such mundane matters soon fled. Nicola was never to forget the main speech given that day by a Mrs Rose Scott, a well-known lobbyist. Already excited at associating with such dedicated women, Nicola was totally stunned by the opening words describing the marital bedroom as, in many cases, 'the chamber of horrors'.

'The entire situation of a wife dependent on marriage for livelihood, identity and respectability is sexually coercive,' Scott declaimed, ignoring the gasps of shock from some amongst her audience. 'The wrongs of men during the strikes were loudly vented by public speakers. Yet who speaks for women enduring wrongs in their homes in seclusion? Let me read to you from Frances Power Cobbe's article published in 1878. It is titled *Wife Torture in England,* and was instrumental in the establishment of judicial separation under English law on the basis of cruelty and violence.'

Listening, Nicola felt the hairs rise on the back of her neck. Louisa Lawson, beside her, kept muttering interjections.

'Women have always been weak and unorganized.' And later, 'If only they weren't so isolated, and so silent through embarrassment or fear of social stigma. The new divorce laws have extended the grounds to include habitual cruelty or extreme sexual crimes, but these must be proved publicly and beyond doubt. Moreover, society will continue to discriminate against the divorced woman.'

Scott continued, calmly ignoring the hasty departure of some of her weaker-stomached audience. Those who remained heard about her own battle to raise the age of consent for girls, quoting the numbers of child prostitutes known to practise in the colony.

'She won't win that one,' Louisa whispered to Nicola. 'Too many wives here today actually profit by their husbands' ability to stray.'

'What. . . ? How. . . ?'

'If the men are out philandering elsewhere, they're not making demands on their wives, of course. It's why society condones prostitution as a so-called necessary service that protects virtuous women.' She added angrily, 'And the younger the female, the less likely she is to carry disease. It accounts for the premium on virginity.'

Nicola absorbed this, along with other pieces of feminine wisdom new to her, and went home thoroughly confused. Clearly Louisa Lawson had little time for men, and yet she enjoyed the verbal interchanges with them at every opportunity; while Rose Scott, having just vilified men from the platform, remained the confidante of politicians and worked with them to change conditions for the underprivileged. Were these women two-faced, or merely pragmatic?

Eleanor Dene, when appealed to, showed sympathy tempered with common sense.

'So, you have had your first dip in the feminist pool and found yourself beyond your depth.' She beckoned Nicola to take a biscuit with her tea, and sat back, waiting for her to gather her thoughts.

The harbour breeze penetrated the French doors on to the veranda, bellying the curtains and carrying the scent of climbing roses twined about the veranda posts. It was a blue and gold day, one of summer's best, and Nicola lay back in her wicker chair and felt at peace for the first time for weeks. Whether it was her physical surroundings or simply the harmonious atmosphere created by Eleanor, Nicola couldn't say. She only knew that to her it meant a haven in an unpredictable world.

'That speech did rather shock me,' she admitted. 'Miss Scott looks demure, but she can use words like hammer blows. She's by no means crude, yet her choice of subject in public forum staggered me.'

'I imagine it propelled some of her audience right out of the door.' Eleanor smiled.

'It certainly did. Yet it also demonstrated a passionate care for others. If the half of what Miss Scott said is true, she's right to ask women to fight such debasement. I know Mrs Lawson agreed with her.'

Eleanor sighed. 'I do admire them both. Yet, I believe that they are putting the cart before the horse. A good start has been made with public education, which will help women to become economically independent. But real change will only come with political power in the hands of women. They will never get needed laws passed until they have suffrage. It all hangs on that.'

Both women sipped their tea thoughtfully. Eventually Nicola broke the peaceful silence.

'Eleanor, must we hate men? I felt sure I did when I saw the terrible things done to Rose; but later, when I could think clearly, I reasoned that in part she had invited trouble. I don't mean that her degradation and her death can in any way be justified...' She tailed off.

'Your Rose was an innocent, my dear, whatever her experiences in the streets. What was done to her was a vile betrayal of woman-hood. Yet, not all men are brutes, just as not all women are sluts.'

Nicola still struggled to put her dilemma into words. 'I suppose my own small experience of men has led me to be wary. My father, whom I thought I knew, revealed a fundamental weakness that betrayed him and his family. Rose's father is the same.' She paused for thought, and continued.

'One man I know is a dedicated fighter for his fellows, yet can't see that women have the same need for support. There's another who has been born to wealth and, while carelessly kind, he ... No, I'm not being fair. He can be thoughtful of others. Yet he fritters away his life in idle pursuits, instead of using his wealth honourably.'

She shrugged. 'At the other end of the spectrum is the working-class lout who fathers children regardless, drinks the money that should be spent on them and beats them as a regular exercise until they run away.'

Eleanor carefully replaced her teacup. 'I know, my dear. I know. But you're seeing from only one viewpoint at present. This will change. Become involved in the women's movement; use your intelligence and strength on behalf of others; understand that many of us started from where you stand. I don't believe that you would allow yourself to be distorted by hatred of anyone.'

Nicola stayed another half-hour, then, just as she was about to leave, Eleanor said, 'Nicola, the indolent, hedonistic man you spoke of earlier was Andrew. Am I right?'

Nicola's silence was answer enough.

'My dear, I have to agree with you to an extent. But you don't know my son as I do. How could you? He is many different men beneath the face he shows the world.'

Nicola hastily agreed. 'I had no right to say what I did. Your son has been very kind to my mother – and to me.' She had to smile. 'He'd like to take over our lives. I really think, Eleanor, that most men have this in-built need to be in charge, to run things, whether or not the matter is any concern of theirs.'

'It's called power, my dear. Men run the world to suit themselves. It comes as a rude shock to find a woman who is in charge of her own life and knows exactly where she's going. It took my late husband and me years to learn the meaning of compromise. Andrew has yet to do this.'

Nicola sobered quickly. 'There's one area where he could help more. I hate to say it, but, since that first effort, little seems to have been done to find the man who killed my dear Rose. The police have as good as said that they've reached a dead end. Now no one seems to be doing anything. No one but me seems to care.' A sudden pain in her fingers made her look down and hastily unlock them. All the tension dissipated over the past two hours had returned, and she felt like an overwound watch spring.

Eleanor drew Nicola to her and kissed her cheek. 'My dear, justice is often slow in coming, but I believe this cruel man will be found in time. Suppress your pride, and go to Andrew and ask him to increase his efforts. He has a good deal of influence in all sorts of odd places.'

Close to tears, Nicola thought, why not? The avenging of Rose was all that mattered, not her own reluctance to ask Andrew Dene for help. She said, 'Where is the best place to find Andrew at this time of day?'

Andrew Dene could not be found at the clothing factory, nor yet at the building yards. In fact, he was not at any of his usual places of business. Nicola sent a message via the haughty doorman of the Australia Club, with the same lack of success. Frustrated, she set off for home.

It was just chance that she should be passing on the opposite side of the street when the doors of the Nelson's Victory opened and Andrew appeared with a woman on each arm. Their faces branded them immediately for what they were, and Andrew was smiling broadly as he escorted them to a waiting cab.

Nicola stood rooted, her mind and body momentarily frozen. Seconds later she felt the blood rushing to her head, along with a devastating sense of disappointment. So, he was like all the rest of them. She'd been a fool to think he might be different. Even worse, she couldn't ask him for help, knowing now that he had a foot in the enemy camp. Rose had been killed by a man who frequented harlots. He and Andrew were joined in spirit – not perhaps as murderers, but as men without respect for women.

Nicola took herself home in a mood as desolate as any she had ever known.

CHAPTER SEVENTEEN

A s a new member of the Women's Literary Society, Nicola found herself in congenial company. She enjoyed the cultural meetings where she resumed acquaintance with many old friends between the pages of books, and was introduced to works that would never have been permitted across the threshold of Miss Jephson's educational establishment. Many of the ideas promulgated would have had that rigidly proper lady flat on the floor.

Such notions as provision of contraceptive information to unwed girls, rather than have them pitchforked into marriage, ignorant and unprepared, were as startling as Rose Scott's stance on rape in marriage. However, Nicola's real interest lay in the improvement of wages and work conditions for women. Her Rose would not have died had she not been trapped in the sweated labour market. So Nicola offered her services and was sent out with an unofficial woman inspector to record what she saw and heard and report back to the committee.

Her first case was a woman making bags from old canvas pulled off packing cases and covered with tar. At threepence-halfpenny a dozen, she had to make four dozen to earn a shilling and twopence per day. The poverty of this home appalled Nicola, with mattresses on the dirt floor and a packing-case for a table. The woman herself was a skeleton in a dress of patches, and her children looked no better.

Exclaiming over some of the most wretched conditions, Nicola met with little sympathy from the inspector.

'There are worse things. There are the women who try to earn more by going into the factories and take their babies with them. The children are dosed with cough syrup to keep them quiet, with the amount increasing as they develop a tolerance to opium, the main component. Often enough they become addicted and die.' The inspector's face had set hard, denying any weakening compassion.

Nicola could understand the need for detachment, and tried to hide her reactions. She faithfully wrote up her reports and the committee received them with thanks and passed on the information to the members. Those with influence wrote to their political acquaintances; others wrote to the newspapers. Nicola sought out Hugh Owen.

Despite their early disagreement, it set her back to discover that, while expressing some sympathy, he had no desire to take action over her findings.

'You know my thinking, Nicola. We can't afford to spread ourselves thin; our efforts must be concentrated. When we have the power, then we can examine your women's problems.'

'They're not *my women* and what you call problems are no less than life-threatening situations,' she flared. 'I know we've had this argument before; but given the severity of the cases I've outlined to you—'

'They are not my concern.'

'How can you be so one-eyed, Hugh?'

'It's called focus.'

'I'd rather term it sexist mule-headedness.' Nicola stomped off to confide in Eleanor.

She found her friend seated on her veranda, swathed in shawls against the cold, and supervising the efforts of her gardener.

'Look, Nicola.' Eleanor pointed to the round bed set in the middle of the drive. 'From here I can watch my tulips opening a little more each day.'

Nicola, who had swept by the bed unseeing, too frustrated to notice her surroundings, now gazed down on the tapestry of green pinpointed with bright colour. Tomorrow those points would be spearheads, the next day globes, then finally cups of wildly flaring reds and oranges and golds. Like the uninhibited product of a child's paintbox, she thought, or the deceptive brush-strokes of a Van Gogh. She stopped frowning and breathed in deeply, feeling the chill air strike her lungs, inhaling the pungent smell of leaves burning on the gardener's pile.

'I came to complain and, as usual, you've diverted me into a pleasant pathway. That's your genius, Eleanor.' She dropped a swift kiss on the white head.

Eleanor searched her face. 'I think I'll go inside now. The sun has dipped behind the trees.'

Gently led to unburden herself once more over tea with sympathy, Nicola stayed late. She was discomfited when Andrew put his head in to enquire about his mother's day, and seated himself, prepared to help entertain her guest. His dancing eyes dared her to leave, vanquished.

On an impulse she challenged him. 'I've joined the Women's Literary Society. We are working towards laws governing the hours and working conditions of women in factories, particularly in the clothing industry.'

He grinned. 'What splendid news. Miss Scott and her associates do good work.'

Nicola stared at him. 'Don't you mind? I know Hugh Owen says your workers are treated reasonably well; but we want far more than someone like you would be prepared to give.'

'How do you know what I'm prepared to give? I like Owen, even if his ideas are a touch more radical than those of Miss Scott. He follows his convictions.'

'You know Hugh? You approve of unionism?'

'Let's say that I sympathize with his aims, but not his methods. I don't want to see lawlessness and people being hurt.'

Nicola thought for a moment, and concluded that this translated as 'I don't want trouble. Let's keep things running smoothly.' She wanted to puncture his complacency, but her usual feeling of antagonism towards him had melted away some time ago.

Before that scene outside the tavern she had been in a fair way to liking him very much. His kindness to her, his earlier efforts on behalf of Rose, all the pleasant things she had heard said about him had gradually worn away her resistance, leaving room for the meeting of minds. He could have been her friend.

Not that she was affected by his obvious charm. She was not so shallow.

Sighing inwardly, she picked up her gloves and bag just as Andrew said, 'Please stay a moment. I have a matter to discuss with you. Will you excuse us, Mother, if we go down to my book room?'

Left with little choice, Nicola kissed Eleanor and preceded Andrew down the curved staircase. Ushered into his book-lined study she refused to be seated. 'I must go soon. It's dark early and my little part of Sydney is not too salubrious at night.'

'I'll take you home in my carriage – with your permission,' he added, as she stiffened. 'If you will give me a few minutes, I'm awaiting two visitors whom I think you will want to see.' He sounded so positive and businesslike that Nicola's interest was caught.

'Who are the visitors? What is it you want to discuss with me?'

'One moment. First, let me thank you for being a companion to my mother. She's extremely fond of you, and the time you spend with her helps to alleviate what must be hours of tedium. I know she occupies herself mentally but her frailty restricts her physically, as you know. You might not realize how much pain she suffers. She's reticent about it.'

Nicola softened. 'I love your mother dearly. And, yes, there are days when I see the lines in her face have deepened and she has put aside her books. Sometimes she goes to lift her cup, then decides against having tea that afternoon. I don't comment because I respect her privacy.'

'You're very understanding.' He straightened his shoulders, as if shifting a burden. 'Eleanor Ballard was a great hospital admin-istrator and the most caring of the patients in her charge. Those days are long over. The wasting disease of the muscles has all but paralysed her, and there's only her indomitable spirit left housed in an all-but-useless body.'

Nicola said softly, 'It's heartbreaking. Yet her staunch spirit is a wonderful example to others. She's a fighter, and she makes others want to fight as well.'

'You two are in the same mould. It's why I like you.'

'Thank you.' For the life of her, Nicola couldn't return the compliment. Aware of her inconsistency, she still could not equate the man she had thought him to be with the one she had seen enjoying the attentions of street women. She could tally all his kind acts, admit his charm, enjoy his humour and admire his skill in slipping gracefully through verbal minefields without disturbance. But she couldn't respect him; and for her, respect was everything.

The sound of wheels on the drive saved her further awkwardness. Andrew went into the hall to greet his guest and usher him into the book room. Nicola greeted him with surprise.

'Detective Carrington!'

Robert Carrington's habitually severe expression relaxed. 'Good evening, Miss Redmond. I'm delighted to meet you again.'

She glanced questioningly at Andrew, who shook his head. 'Be patient for just a few minutes longer. I hear someone else arriving.'

Hugh Owen's entry came as an even greater surprise to Nicola. She turned to Andrew.

'I sense a conspiracy here. What are you plotting?'

'Nothing but good, I assure you. Nicola, I know you've been disappointed over the investigation into Rose Basevi's death. So we three, with Detective Carrington's permission, have decided to join our efforts, to attack the problem in individual ways, but to pool the results.'

Robert Carrington interjected, 'We wanted you to know that your friend has not been forgotten and the case filed away.'

For a moment Nicola could not speak. 'How kind you all are. I'll admit that lately I have despaired over the lack of results. But Hugh, you never met Rose.'

His rich Welsh voice was soothing. 'She was your friend, Nicola. As you said before, because of the, er, circles I move in, I hear many things that the police could never know. I can call in favours, use the ring of informants who report to me.'

Robert Carrington glanced at the unionist and interjected in a voice sharpened with dislike. 'My own position allows me to officially demand information, as well as to use my detective force to enter premises closed to others. And I, too, have my informants.' His lip curled. 'I also have an extensive knowledge of the habits and loyalties of the criminal classes, and of the street-walkers who would have been Rose Basevi's companions.'

Nicola winced, and Andrew said hastily, 'I actually tried consorting with a few such ladies, but not only had they no information to give, but they wanted to drink themselves under the table as quickly as possible at my expense. Perhaps in future I might leave such interrogations in official hands.'

'You would be wiser to do so,' Robert's tone was repressive.

Disconcerted by Andrew's revelation, Nicola could only ask him what part he now intended playing in the investigation.

'A minor one, at this stage, I'm afraid. Aside from acting as coordinator of our little committee and providing the venue for meetings, I merely propose to offer a reward for information. This will be well publicized and, we must hope, will tempt someone with useful knowledge to come to us.'

When Nicola learned the size of the reward to be offered, she was astounded. Two hundred pounds! She could only stammer her thanks and wonder at the oddity of the situation. These men would normally have little in common. Now it seemed she was the link – a difficult position, fraught with possible misunderstanding. She quailed at the thought of possible entanglements. But this was for Rose, she reminded herself. Anything was worthwhile for her sake.

With strategies outlined, the meeting broke up. Andrew was quick to offer to escort Nicola back to Viola Terrace, to the obvious chagrin of Robert Carrington and apparent amusement on Hugh's part. However, when the two men had gone Andrew invited Nicola to stay to dine.

'It's quite proper, you know, with my mother upstairs and Mrs Peck in charge. I'll have you home at a reasonable hour.'

Out of habit, Nicola sought an excuse, then realized that she had none. She was under great obligation to Andrew, and had badly misjudged him. There was every reason for her to accede to his request.

'Thank you. I'll be happy to dine with you.' Surprisingly, it turned out to be true.

CHAPTER EIGHTEEN

A smiling Mrs Peck led Nicola to a guest room to wash her hands and tidy her hair. Nicola took time, also, to pull herself together mentally and emotionally.

Because she was always honest with herself, she now faced the disturbing knowledge that she had been hiding behind excuses. It was a shock suddenly to realize that her relationship with Andrew was, in fact, quite different from what she had imagined. He attracted her physically; secretly he had always done so. But circumstances had helped her to disguise this sexual tug. She had built a wall between them, based upon their differences, and upon her own rejection of the life she had once led.

Brick by brick she had added to this wall, citing his moneyed lifestyle; her 'stolen' inheritance, which had not been anything of the sort; his well-meant pampering of her mother and his irritating habit of trying to take control. Then, to make quite certain that he was ineligible as a friend, she had jumped to an unwarranted conclusion that he consorted with the degraded women of the streets – women like Rose.

Then, brick by brick, he had unknowingly brought down that wall. Andrew was kind. He was generous. His factories were well and fairly run; he was understanding with Josh; he had done all he could on that terrible night of the murder, and afterwards. His mother had said that there were facets of his nature that Nicola had not yet seen and appreciated. Well, tonight he had excelled himself in generosity and support. The wall was down at last and Nicola was exposed – to herself.

How was she to face him with this new self-knowledge? Because there was an important capstone to her deconstructed wall – the certainty that she could not bear to return to an idle, self-indulgent life at the top end of society. She had just begun to spread her wings and soar into the heady atmosphere of freedom. The world was changing, and so was she. Andrew's feelings for her were still at an early stage. He was attracted, as any man is attracted to a personable woman, but he could be headed off. He must be. She couldn't afford to let him stop her.

As for her own feelings, well, she was learning just how strong she was. She would pay the price of freedom and survive.

Twenty minutes later she faced him across a yard of damask, with firelight and candlelight creating an ambience far too intimate for her liking. Seeking a neutral topic, she examined the portrait hanging on the half-panelled wall opposite.

'Is that your late father, Andrew?' His name slipped out naturally, without thought.

'Yes. It's a good likeness, done before he fell ill. My mother swears I'm in his image.' He waited for a maid to serve the soup and leave the room before resuming. 'Mother can't bear to see the portrait, so it stays downstairs, out of her view.'

'Because she loved him deeply and misses him so much?' Nicola couldn't help sounding wistful.

'They were inseparable for years, until the carriage accident that crippled her and the onset of the wasting disease that followed.' His tone seemed to warn her off, and Nicola dipped into her soup and kept silent for a time. Then curiosity got the better of her.

'Such a terrible event would surely draw two loving hearts closer. Why did their relationship change?'

Andrew sighed and put down his spoon with finality, his appetite apparently gone.

'I've never truly understood it. What child knows the bonds linking his parents? But I believe Father blamed himself for ruining his beloved wife's life. No matter how she reassured him and demonstrated her own affection, he couldn't forgive himself. He retreated from us, mentally and emotionally. It was as if I had no father, and Mother had no husband. I think she found it far harder to bear than any physical injury.'

A lump had risen in Nicola's throat, obstructing the soup. She, too, replaced her spoon.

Sharp-eyed, Andrew said, 'You're over-empathetic, Nicola. You will have your heart cut to ribbons if you don't learn to guard it.'

'It's better than having no heart to hurt.'

'Is that what you think of me, that I have no heart?'

'Why, no,' Nicola said, surprised. 'I referred to no one in particular.'

'Oh. Well, take care not to invest too much of yourself in your new ventures. It takes a stout suit of armour to protect a woman who leaves her milieu to do battle in the public forum.'

Nicola's eyes sparkled. 'Thank you for the warning. I believe I know what I'm doing.'

Nodding in assent, Andrew rang for the almost untouched soup dishes to be removed. With the fish course he steered the conversation into innocuous channels, and Nicola smothered the emotions stirred by his anecdote. Her swift empathy with Eleanor and her disturbed husband had been heightened by the thought of their young son, trapped in an adult situation he couldn't understand, virtually deserted by a once-loving father and a mother who was an invalid.

'Tell me about *your* father, Nicola. What kind of man was he?'

She'd rather have avoided this, but he had allowed her to delve into *his* privacy. After a moment's hesitation she said, 'Mother and I knew him as a loving husband and a doting father. That was partly his problem. He could refuse us nothing. Many times he gave to us before we could even think to ask. He was believed to be a clever businessman, but events proved otherwise.' She pointedly picked up her spoon and dug it into her custard and jam roll, which she did not want.

Andrew would not be put off. 'He must have had some business acumen to build up his many resources in the first place.'

'I expect it comes down to poor judgement in the end. Just look how many men who were considered solid citizens have gone under in this terrible depression.' Nicola's tone was final. She couldn't go on discussing Papa. She pictured him bustling to and from his bank, happily looking ahead to the newest venture. That was the way to remember him.

Andrew remarked, 'It was too easy in the boom times of the eighties, with money pouring in from Britain and *expansion* the catchcry for everything from railways to gasworks. A lot of other people fell into the same trap, you know.'

Nicola nodded, her heart full. If only he would change the subject.

He leaned towards her, his expression so understanding that she had difficulty in swallowing the lump that had risen again.

'Nicola, he was an ordinary man with weaknesses. The shock of finding he was responsible for ruining the people who had trusted him would be enough to push any man off balance. The really sad part is that he didn't confide in his family. You might have helped him over the crisis into a state of acceptance.'

Nicola dropped her spoon with a clatter and clasped her hands in her lap. 'I know it. Do you think I haven't gone over and over that moment in my mind, wondering if I had only realized what was happening. If he'd talked to Mother. If we could somehow have induced him to speak of his troubles. . . .'

Enough was enough. She must get off this seesaw of emotion. Laying down her napkin she made ready to rise. 'I should like to go home now, please. Will you call for the carriage?'

Andrew came around the table and put a hand on her shoulder. A jolt like an electric spark ran through her.

'Forgive me for upsetting you. I simply wanted to know more about you and your family. Please stay a little longer. I don't want to feel that I've driven you away.'

Had he felt that jolt? Nicola freed herself with a wriggle and dredged up an embarrassed denial. She said, with an attempt at diversion, 'You know, it's hardly fair of you to talk of my family, yet avoid discussing your own history.'

It was a successful ploy. Andrew drew up a chair beside her, saying, 'What do you want to know?'

Hesitating, she recalled that Andrew had only learned of the Redmond connection when taking up his inheritance late. Why late? There was some mystery there. Perhaps it stemmed from Eleanor's accident.

'Tell me about the change in your life when your mother suffered her accident.'

He regarded her for a long moment. 'Very well. When she failed to recover, my father sent her to Switzerland for treatment at a clinic specializing in her illness. She was the only bearable thing in my life and I couldn't stay in the same house as my father without her. I ran away.'

'But surely you must have been just a boy!'

'I was fifteen.' Andrew's sombre expression lightened. 'You mustn't think of me as suffering. I got myself taken on at a cattle station in Queensland, soon advanced from general roustabout to mustering hand, then head stockman. In general, I led a good hardening life for a young man.'

Incredulous, Nicola glanced down at his well-kept hands, at the fine cut of his coat, then met his amused gaze.

'It's the truth, I swear it. Until five years ago I knew nothing of the bright lights and city diversions. I was a bumpkin.'

'Never! I'd sooner believe you'd wangled your way into the squatter's home and probably courted his daughter.'

Andrew's laughter rang out. 'You have a wonderful opinion of my abilities. Admittedly, my upbringing and my father's name – he was a noted member of parliament in his day – helped me along; but the boss was a hard man and extracted his last ounce of work for pay and privileges. In the end I owed him nothing except respect for his honesty. I might even have stayed on and run the property for him if it hadn't been for one thing.'

'Your father died?'

'Oh, I already knew that. What I hadn't known, until the lawyers wrote again much later, was that my mother had become incapacitated. She hadn't wanted me to know. She didn't want me to return out of a sense of filial duty, and her letters were full of cheer.'

'Then you had known about your inheritance?'

He shrugged. 'I had no feeling for my father and I wanted nothing of his.'

'But you eventually came back and accepted it. Because of Eleanor?'

'Yes. The years of separation melted away when we met again. As an adult, I understood that she hadn't abandoned me at all; she'd had no choice. And now she needed me. It simply meant changing my mode of living.'

It certainly had been a change, Nicola thought, viewing another

entirely new aspect of Andrew. It required a stretch of the imagination to envisage him booted and spurred, sweating and shouting
as he chased cattle at the gallop through clouds of dust. From that
life to this had been a real sacrifice. Or had it been one? He seemed
to have embraced city excitements and entertainments with joy.

As if following her thoughts, Andrew's smile twisted. 'Now
I wonder shall I regret telling you such a tale? Has it made you
dislike me?'

'Of course not.'

'Then we are friends. Good friends.' He held out his hand
and Nicola felt obliged to place hers in his, feeling the muscular
strength beneath the well-kept skin. He retained his grip, turning
her hand palm upwards to study it. 'It's never wise to rush one's
fences, but the field has widened lately. These pretty fingers would
be the better for a ring to set them off.'

Nicola tugged free and stood up, saying rather breathlessly, 'I'm
not particularly fond of jewellery, and it's inappropriate to my new
station in life. Mother had beautiful rings, which she promised
to me, but I don't suppose I'll see them again. Do you know she's
considering remarrying? The gentleman has two daughters, I
believe. I hope Mother finds them to be more in the mould she
wished for.'

On and on she chattered, scarcely knowing what she said, but
determined to head Andrew off from any more personal discussion. She kept it up in the carriage and by the time it drew up at
Viola Terrace she had grown tired of the sound of her own voice.
Bidding Andrew a quick goodnight on her doorstep she thankfully retreated into her haven with a good deal to ponder.

The question foremost in her mind was how on earth to forestall
a declaration from Andrew? She was certain that he was not yet
in love with her. Perhaps he found her a challenge. Her spikiness,
and her determination to stand on her own feet, had provoked a
situation which he'd completely misread.

As if she didn't have enough to contend with. Andrew plus two
more admirers – none of whom could she afford to alienate while
they worked to avenge Rose.

CHAPTER NINETEEN

JOSH PROVED ANNOYINGLY elusive. Busy with her meetings and her investigative forays into workshops and homes, Nicola had little time to spare. And Josh was never at home when she called.

However, he did reappear one winter's morning, and in unhappy circumstances. Nicola returned from a trip to the vegetable market to find Robert Carrington on her doorstep, with a scowling Josh in his grip. She invited them in and, over refreshments, Carrington told Josh's tale.

'I brought the lad to you because he seems to know no other responsible citizen, and I'd like to stop him going down the road he's on.' He glanced at the surly boy now seated in Nicola's best wing chair with his hands wrapped around a mug of cocoa and his gaze fixed on the strip of Turkey carpet.

'Josh?' At Nicola's questioning tone he looked up.

She was dismayed at his expression, compounded of cocky defiance and misery. 'What have you been up to, Josh?'

'Nothing.' He went back to studying the carpet.

Carrington said, 'A patrol picked him up on the docks as part of a gang of ruffians who've been rolling seamen – the kind who get roaring drunk within two hours of leaving their ship. Easy pickings, if there are enough of you.' His derisory tone stung the boy into speech.

'I wasn't one o'them. I just tagged along, like.'

'Skirmishing around the fringes and hoping to be admitted to the gang, I suppose.' Carrington added mildly, 'Did you know their victims often die of their bludgeoning, of the cold, of choking on their own vomit because they're lying insensible in some gutter?'

Josh paled and put down the cocoa. But he remained defiant.

'We were just on the rantan. You know. Having a spree.'

'This time, yes. Your pals usually wait until dark before marking a victim. Daytime is for checking the steel in their boot caps and polishing up the knuckle-dusters. Lucky for you, my lad, that you weren't carrying the razor.'

'Josh!' Nicola's exclamation brought Josh's head around to her.

'I never, Nicola. I wouldn't. Honest. I was just hanging about outside the Man O' War having a spit and drag with the boys, and along came these rozzers and jumped on us. I give the one twisting my arm a toother and he knocked me down flat.' He pointed to the swelling on one side of his jaw.

Nicola's lips tightened. 'Detective Carrington, Josh is only a child, and half-crippled to boot. Yet one of your men attacked him like a bully.'

Carrington still responded mildly. 'He was not one of my men. But he was outnumbered by as nice a little crew of cutthroats as you could meet in this city. I happened to see the boy brought in at Central and I enquired into the matter and decided he'd be better away from such company. I might add that I had to compromise the truth quite drastically to free him from a charge.'

Her anger turned to gratitude, but before she could express it Josh broke in.

'I'm not a child! I'm fourteen years old.'

Nicola hardened her heart. 'Old enough to know better than to consort with ruffians who'll get you into real trouble. Josh, I thought you had more sense.'

'I have . . . I mean, I am . . . I just want to be left alone!'

The cry, with its underlying pathos, touched Nicola deeply. It held all the loneliness and pain following on the loss of family, home and familiar things. It was no wonder the boy sought belonging of a kind, even if it had to be with the scum of the waterfront. She wanted to take him in her arms but she knew she must not. A boy of fourteen was perilously close to being a man, with all a man's pride and need to present a good face to the world. Instead, she drew on her skills learnt in the handling of a class full of rebels and survivors of the streets.

'Josh, we're both on our own. We've both suffered a terrible loss and are trying to make sense of our lives. I need someone with me whom I can trust. It's not wise for a woman to live alone. Would you . . . could you bring yourself to help me?'

Bright eyes peered suspiciously at her from beneath the fringe of more than usually scruffy hair.

'You're just saying that. You're not afraid of anything.'

'Not afraid, just nervous and rather lonely.' Nicola glanced at Carrington, silently begging him to keep quiet. Any threat of reformatories or prisons as an inevitable alternative if Josh continued in his ways would drive the boy deeper into retreat.

However, the detective seemed content to let her lead the conversation. He sat quietly, watching Nicola. It made her uncomfortable, but she concentrated on reaching Josh, on connecting with the fledgling male, so wary, yet so much in need.

'I'm no good!' he suddenly burst out. 'I can't get work with this leg, so I can't earn any money. I'm not even allowed to look after Daisy. They're all gone. There's only me left. Nobody wants a stupid, useless cripple.'

'You're not stupid, or useless, or a cripple. Your leg is a lot stronger, as I can see. One day you *will* be able to work, Josh, but at something much more interesting than oiling a machine or shifting bricks. Come and keep me company, help me with my work, and I'll teach you. I'll have you passing examinations to fit you for a real education, at upper school and university. Do you realize what that means, Josh? One day you will be in a position to help people like Rose, ordinary people who have been destroyed by the system. You will be a man of power. Wouldn't that be a thing to aim for?'

His eyes flickered. She saw the dawning hope, and held her breath.

'No catches? No rules hedging a fellow in?'

'No catches. And my only rules are of decent behaviour and honesty between friends. Oh, and hard work catching up on the lessons you've missed.'

Josh got up, stretched and glanced across at the detective who gazed impassively back. The boy turned to Nicola.

'That'll suit me. My hand on it.'

She gravely shook his hand. 'Thank you, Josh. You may move in as soon as you like. There's a small room upstairs all ready for occupation. Do you have much to bring with you?'

'Not much. Just a few clothes and bits.'

'I'll come and help you pack.'

There was a twin chorus of male 'Noes' and Nicola hid a smile as Josh declared his current address an unsuitable place for her to visit. He'd conveniently forgotten her earlier calls.

When Carrington announced that *he* would go with Josh, the boy scowled, and Carrington hastily denied any wish to interfere in his affairs.

Nicola had just one more question. 'Josh, tell me, what's a "spit and drag"?'

He grinned. 'A fag. Don't worry. I've give it up from today. I don't like it much, anyhow.'

While Josh investigated the contents of the larder, at Nicola's invitation, the conversation in the parlour languished. She was all too conscious of her other visitor's interest in her and searched rather desperately for a new topic. With Josh close by and in his present mood she didn't want to discuss Rose's murder.

Carrington examined the scantily furnished room, his glance alighting on her desk under the front windows. Stacked with books and papers, it was revealing.

'This is a work room,' he commented.

'Yes. I've enrolled as an evening student at the university. I hope to be a teacher one day. However, it will be a while before I can complete the course.'

Carrington's eyebrows rose. 'This, as well as your daytime work with the women's organizations? You're diligent indeed.' His admiring tone warned her as much as the way he hitched his seat forward, bringing himself closer.

She quickly said, 'Tell me about *your* work. I know very little beyond what I saw in the police station.'

His pleased expression showed that she'd struck the right note.

'As it happens, I've been involved in a particularly interesting case of coining. The men who do it are known in the business as "smashers" and the ones passing the bad coins are "snide pitchers". There's a whole new language in the thieves' world.'

Nicola no longer had to feign interest. 'How can you tell a base coin from a true one?'

'By biting it. The base coin leaves a gritty sensation on the teeth.'

'Hmm. I don't fancy putting coins in my mouth. Tell me how the "smashers" make the coins.'

'They obtain the base, pewter, by stealing pots from public houses and melting them down. Plaster of Paris moulds are made with the impressions taken from true coins, slightly worn, and the metal poured in the sides. When cold, they're milled carefully with a knife and file, which is a delicate operation, then placed in a rack and silvered in a battery. A scratch brush is rubbed over them to dull them and they're coated with lampblack and grease, then washed. And there you have it.'

'It sounds easy enough. How do the counterfeiters pass the coins? Do they pay bills with them, or buy household goods?'

Carrington laughed. 'Hardly. A fellow caught passing a coin and in possession of another will be convicted. So he has an accomplice holding the stock and handing them one by one to the 'pitcher'.'

'How interesting.' Nicola *was* interested, but she hoped that Josh would soon have eaten his fill and be ready to leave.

Carrington patted his pocket. 'Look, if you would care to read it, I'll leave you a copy of my *Police Gazette.*'

'I'd like that.'

Josh appeared in the doorway, looking replete. He said, 'I'm ready now, Nicola. Your pork pie was good.'

Carrington rose reluctantly. 'We'd best be off. Come along, lad.'

Nicola liked the way he clapped the boy on the shoulder and teased him about his appetite. Josh's wariness of the police seemed forgotten as he responded with a remark about moustaches as food traps. Nicola saw the two off, bickering more like contemporaries, and shook her head over the amazing transformation of the hard-edged detective. It seemed he had a soft spot indeed for youngsters, despite his rigidity with adult offenders.

She was not conceited enough to think that he had rescued Josh merely to curry favour with her, although it certainly hadn't harmed him in her regard. There was a deal more to Robert Carrington than she had at first supposed. And since she had recently been forced to say the same about Andrew Dene, it now only remained for her to discover untold depths in Hugh Owen's character. Which would be a lesson to her in making quick judgements.

CHAPTER TWENTY

NICOLA HAD THE opportunity to complete her assessment of the three men when Hugh Owen asked her to attend a secret union meeting with him. Having limited her visits to Eleanor, in order to avoid Andrew, and needing a break from her evening studies, Nicola agreed. She was eager to extend her knowledge of both the man and of the union movement, which seemed to her an exciting indicator of the future.

That evening they travelled in a closed carriage to an area of wool stores where the narrow streets were blank-faced and ill lit, the high meshed windows barely visible from the footway. Upon entering the building from a side lane too narrow for a vehicle, they were scrutinized by a doorkeeper. This secretiveness would have amused Nicola, but for the cold examination of the watchmen guarding the entrance and, for that matter, the general air of her present company. It would have been an exaggeration to call it menacing, but she was glad of Hugh's presence beside her.

The men gathering in the empty warehouse were purposeful and oddly silent. Nicola mentally contrasted their manner with the meetings of the women's groups where the preliminary noise was more deafening than a cage full of lorikeets.

In the light of a few weak gas flares Hugh found her a place on a bench well to the side, although most people sat on the floor or crowded against the dirty brick walls. There had been no preparation made for them, no comforts provided. The air was already oppressive with the smell of sweat and dirt. Many had obviously come from their work, with no time to wash or change their clothes, had they been so inclined. A few wore suits, but most were in the workman's uniform of hard wearing trousers, patched shirts and threadbare jackets, and boots often broken beyond repair. The few women present were equally poorly clad. Their faces had the lined, weary expression familiar to Nicola from her visits to homes and factories.

Early speakers urged the need for change to the laws governing work practice and the enforcement of those statutes already in place – laws meant to benefit the workers, but usually ignored by management. Much of what was said made good sense to Nicola. She found herself applauding with the audience a proposal for regulation of work hours to no more than eleven for boys under sixteen years.

Someone spoke of the dangerous conditions in many factories. Accidents were cited, some so appalling that Nicola was sickened, and at the same time grateful that Josh had got off comparatively lightly.

As time passed the mood of the gathering changed. The crowd had begun by giving quiet attention to the speakers, but as various ones rose, had their say, then returned to their places, a ripple of increasing excitement ran through the hall. Hugh stiffened, then bent to whisper in Nicola's ear.

'This is what I came for.'

Nicola craned to see a small, nondescript man move forward to the front, parting the crowd like a reaper through a field crop. He mounted the speaker's box and faced his audience, and Nicola found herself trapped in the fiery gaze of a committed evangelist. A powerful voice issued from his small frame, capturing whatever part of the crowd had remained impervious to his glance, and he began his tale.

It started on the London docks where the flotsam and jetsam of the waterside slept in the fo'c'sles of empty ships while waiting for employment, subsisting on scraps of mouldy biscuits left over by their crews. The brutal sub-contractors set them to work with rotten plant and defective machinery. However, with the frantic competition for freights, they could scarcely count on more than two days' continuous work at starvation wages, and they scrambled for these. Accidents were common, leaving limbs mangled and useless, and their owners to perish in crippled destitution.

Then these poorest of the poor, without hope or training, somehow found the courage to band together in their thousands and go on strike. Their demands were unheard of – that their labour should be hired at not less than four hours at a time and at a uniform rate of sixpence an hour. The dock-owners, relying on the poverty and disorganization of the poor derelicts they exploited, tried to starve them into submission.

For two months they held out, cheered on by men who had come forward as leaders – by the speaker himself, Ben Tillett, who knew they had the sympathy of the public and a growing socialist movement. And they'd won. Not only were the terms agreed by the dock-owners, but also a great union of unskilled labour, the Dock Wharf and Riverside Labourers' Union, had been founded.

The roar from a hundred throats that greeted this tale of victory drowned Hugh's words as he turned to Nicola, but she had no difficulty in interpreting his response. His grip on her arm, the light in his face told her that Ben Tillett's fervent message had driven straight through the heaving ranks and into Hugh Owen's rebel heart.

Suddenly he was gone, forging his way to the front, heading for the speaker's box. Nicola, jostled and abandoned, scrambled up on to the bench with her back to the wall for support. The crowd seemed to have broken up into milling groups, for and against striking, some demonstrating eagerness to physically convince dissenters. However, the scuffling ceased as Hugh Owen's lilting Welsh voice rang out, praising Ben Tillett, endorsing his views and calling for action now.

A lone man, better turned out than the majority, stood up to Hugh.

'Wait. Listen. We already know what strike action can do. But times are changing. We've got politicians on our side who've promised to fight the conservative stand. They're prepared to appoint a Minimum Wages board in certain industries—'

'Lies to keep us quiet!' shouted Hugh. 'We don't need any milk and water liberals handing us only what they want us to have. We want more. We want Factory Acts defining rigorously the hours and conditions of labour. We want safety regulations, health and sanitary arrangements. And we won't get any of them by going cap in hand and saying "please sir".'

'We won't gain anything with the misery of prolonged strikes and possible police action,' retorted the other man.

Hugh would have none of it. 'Where are your ears, man? What's our comrade Ben Tillett here just been telling us, but how it's possible to win through striking?'

'That's in the Old Country. We're different out here. We've got good men in parliament on our side.'

'Bah. We've got men good at pulling the wool over your eyes. I say we organize a series of rolling strikes, hitting the bosses where it hurts most.Pickets on the gates will stop any scabs getting through. We'll arm our men and take on any opposition.'

His opponent was aghast. 'People could be hurt!'

'If necessary. Isn't the cause worth a few broken heads?'

Back and forth the two men argued, growing more heated by the minute, with those on the floor now well divided into partisan camps. Nicola began to fear a real battle breaking out. Then the sound of a rattle penetrated the voices. Everything stopped. Into the eerie silence the doorman shouted, 'Coppers coming!'

There was an immediate surge towards the door. Someone unbolted double doors in the wall near Nicola, and within a minute she was being swept out in the tide of escaping men. Struggling to keep on her feet, she searched for Hugh, but in the dark it was impossible to make out anything but a sea of bobbing heads. An elbow hit her in the back and she felt herself falling, then an arm went around her waist, supporting her.

'Hold up, lass,' said a gruff voice, as she was swept around a corner into a wider street where the carriage waited. Her rescuer thrust her up the step and inside, then climbed to the driver's seat and whipped the horses into a flying start. Men flung themselves aboard, clinging to the step, and no doubt there were more on top and behind. The carriage bucketed along as the startled horses settled into a gallop, slithering at sharp turns, but held up by the man with the reins.

Behind them, diminishing into the distance, Nicola heard more rattles, accompanied by whistles and shouts. She clung to the strap as the coach bounded over the pitted road, concerned for Hugh's safety, worried that the men clinging on to the coach would be flung off at any minute, yet wildly exhilarated as she had not been in years. All the old Nicola had come to the fore, the minx forever in trouble for thinking up the unthinkable and acting upon it. She was sixteen again and escaping from the riot on the wharves, plotting how to get back into school without being discovered, every nerve alive with the joy of daring.

The coach slowed and turned into a well-lit thoroughfare, then slid to a halt. The hangers-on dropped away and disappeared into the night, leaving just the driver on the box. Nicola put her head out the window.

'Where are we going?'

The gruff voice replied, 'I'm taking you home, miss. Boss's orders.'

'You mean Hugh Owen?'

'That's right. I got told off to watch you and get you back if anything happened. Boss'll be along later.' He flicked his whip and the carriage set off at a decorous pace.

Nicola sat back against the squab, not sure whether to laugh or be angry. Hugh had known what might happen. He'd prepared for the eventuality. Yet, he might have warned her. Or maybe he paid her the compliment of taking her courage for granted. Perhaps he saw through her façade of young-ladyhood to the woman with the itch of curiosity, who occasionally took risks to satisfy that itch.

Alone, in the obscurity of the carriage, she admitted that it *had* been interesting, and she wouldn't have missed discovering for herself just what the union movement was about. It should definitely be taken seriously, divided as its members were on the way to reach their goals. The police raid showed that the authorities treated it as a serious threat to stability.

Yawning with the weariness following on such a huge rush of excitement, she repinned her hair and straightened her hat. It would never do for Josh to see her arriving home looking like a female hanger-on of that notorious larrikin gang, the Rocks Push.

CHAPTER TWENTY-ONE

ROBERT CARRINGTON CALLED again a week later, ostensibly to check on Nicola's protégé. Feeling obliged to invite him in, she kept the conversation neutral, fending off his interest in her activities. She then pointedly requested a progress report on Rose's case, which put him on the defensive, since he had little progress to report. He left soon afterwards, and Nicola did not invite him to return. He'd been kind over Josh, but he looked like developing into as big a problem as Andrew.

The situation wasn't helped when Carrington came face to face with Hugh Owen at the gate. The two men exchanged glares, with Carrington blocking the pathway to the door. To Nicola's vexed amusement they looked like barnyard cocks. Then, with a grin and sweep of the arm, Hugh stepped back. Carrington hesitated, then passed through the gate and on down the street with measured step. Hugh shrugged before looking questioningly at Nicola standing in the doorway.

'Is your reputation going to suffer from so much traffic, Nicola? I only called to apologize for abandoning you at the rally last week. I'd have come earlier, but circumstances forbade.'

Nicola's smile hid her annoyance. After all, he had been her escort and could reasonably be expected to stay by her side. Also, foolishly, she had worried about his safety.

She said, 'I'm glad to see you are still at liberty and unhurt. But if you will excuse me, *circumstances* don't permit me to entertain you this afternoon.'

He cocked an eyebrow. 'You're angry with me. I really am sorry, Nicola. Please tell me what I can do to atone.'

'Why, nothing.' She remained serene. 'There's no need for self-abasement. I found the experience most interesting, although I don't think I shall repeat it. It was just a touch too exhilarating for me.'

'I didn't expect events to turn out quite so exciting. Although the police do like to break us up at every opportunity, that meeting was supposed to be kept secret.' He added ruefully, 'Please let me call again.'

'Why, certainly. Next month will be perfectly suitable. Goodbye, Hugh.' Nicola retired inside with dignity intact, although suspecting that he was laughing at her. It would take more than a rebuff to unsettle the self-sufficient Hugh Owen.

An invitation from Andrew to attend a performance of the play *For the Term of His Natural Life* was promptly declined with the excuse of her work. When further invitations from all three men continued to arrive, she sent each of them a note explaining that she would prefer to be left alone until they had any further information concerning Rose's murder.

While this gave her time to herself, it did not bring peace of mind. Despite all the months gone by, the picture of Rose's brutalized body haunted Nicola, and she despaired of ever knowing real tranquillity again. If an astute detective of police, a huge reward and all Hugh Owen's contacts could make no headway, what hope was there of success?

A miserable spring cold kept her confined for a week, during which time Josh turned himself into a household angel, cleaning and cooking and driving Nicola mad with quarter-hourly enquiries as to her health and offers of tempting titbits. In desperation, she began inventing errands for him. A rabbit hunt kept him away for a morning, and he carried messages explaining her absence to Louisa and the other women she worked with.

A similar note to Eleanor brought a cart to the door laden with flowers, a commiserating letter and a hamper of choice viands, which made Josh's eyes glisten. That night he served a banquet on a tray too heavy for Nicola to handle in bed. So, in house gown and slippers, still sniffling, she went down to the parlour, where Josh had a fire roaring, and joined him in the feast.

With curtains drawn and chairs and table drawn up to the hearth, the room had a cheerfulness that overcame its bareness. Visits to a flea market had provided cushions and curtain fabric of pale blue and lavender, in defiance of the popular taste; while a cream woollen shawl thrown over the sofa hid its worn leather upholstery. The timber mantel remained disgracefully undraped, and the end wall was adorned with a Chinese screen that Nicola had found discarded in the back of a saleroom and mended with glue and backing paper. It now gave her a lot of pleasure to follow the delicate brush-stroked stories of a mysterious world of temples and pagodas, oriental maidens beneath plum trees and men on horseback hunting, all in soft colours faded by time.

This room was the heart of the house. Here Nicola and Josh lived, worked, ate and were as content as it was possible to be without Rose.

In November Nicola accepted a different kind of invitation, to a meeting of representatives of twenty-one women's organizations in New South Wales, all articulate and educated and fitted to fight for the causes they believed in. The object was the formation of a branch of the National Council of Women, a world-wide organization devoted to the wellbeing of women and children.

Staying in the background, Nicola made notes on the perceived value of a unified National Council, able to bring pressure to bear on politicians and other power brokers, nationally and internationally. She came away with a sense of having been a part of a historic moment. She wanted to take part in forming this new world, one that would take women's rights seriously and carry them into the new century.

Anxious to report to Eleanor, she visited her the next day, and was stunned to find herself in the middle of a surprise party organized to celebrate her own twenty-second birthday.

The big upstairs sitting room had been turned into a bower, its centrepiece being a table laden with choice edibles. Josh stood beside it, grinning, his hand engulfing the smaller, grubby hand of a wide-eyed Benny. Mrs Gardiner, Nicola's former landlady, had buttonholed the Foxtons, Daisy's foster parents, seated with their many children at their knees. Andrew stood behind his mother's chair, his hands resting lightly on the back. And next to Eleanor sat Louisa Lawson, quite at home in this assorted society. While flying towards Nicola, like an arrow to its home, sped Daisy, fresh-faced, blooming, her arms outstretched in welcome.

'Happy birthday, Nicola,' she carolled, flinging herself bodily at her friend.

Nicola, her face half-hidden in Daisy's lace collar, felt tears brimming behind her eyelids. She hugged the child to her until she had regained some poise, then straightened to look at Eleanor. Words were unnecessary.

Delighted at her reaction, Eleanor beckoned her forward for a kiss. 'This is to atone for your missed coming-of-age party last year. May you have many more, happier years ahead, dear girl.'

On her knees beside the chair, Nicola asked, 'How did you know, Eleanor?'

'Andrew told me. I expect he had the date from your mother before she left.'

Nicola glanced up involuntarily and met Andrew's gaze.

'Happy birthday, Nicola.' He put out a hand to help her rise. 'Mother has always liked surprises. This one seems to have come off rather well.'

She reclaimed her hand, mumbling about how delighted she was, and gladly turned to the other guests. Andrew was looking entirely too pleased with himself.

Champagne flutes and glasses of cordial were raised in a toast and the guest of honour was enthroned on a high-backed chair. Mrs Peck, the housekeeper, presided over the two fat Shelley teapots and saw that the children had sturdy mugs rather than the frail cups reserved for their elders. Sandwiches and biscuits disappeared at an amazing rate, and young eyes lit with amazement at the sight of a large frosted cake covered in fondant roses being trolleyed in by two maids.

Nicola obediently wielded the carving knife to break the sugared crust and gave a short speech of thanks. Still, the afternoon had a feeling of unreality. Parties were for other people, not for the person she was now, especially a party in her honour initiated, she felt sure, by a man she needed to keep at arm's length.

She listened to Benny's catalogue of successes in his new class, and praised Daisy's pretty frock; she thanked the Foxtons for their good care of the child and admired their offspring; she exchanged notes with Louisa on the latest editorial in *The Dawn* and chided

Josh for stuffing himself with cream cake; and all the while she was conscious of Andrew, attending to his mother's needs and those of the guests, his eyes following Nicola as she moved around the room.

By the time the guests left dusk had fallen. The party debris had been cleared and Andrew closed the shutters and sent for his mother's maid to attend her. Eleanor, while noticeably weary, still had a farewell hug for Nicola and a deaf ear to her insistence that she did not need an escort home in the Dene carriage. Rather than upset her, Nicola agreed.

When Andrew climbed in beside her, she smiled to hide strained nerves and edged as far as possible into her corner. During the journey she strove to keep the conversation on innocuous grounds, while longing for the sight of her own front door.

Eventually Andrew lost patience.

'Look at me, Nicola. You're being deliberately evasive. At the very least you could give me your undivided attention when I'm trying to propose marriage to you.'

Nicola's attention focused with speed. 'Well, you see, I don't want you to propose marriage to me.'

'Why not?' he asked, mildly enough.

It was Nicola who then lost patience. 'For heaven's sake, Andrew. We've hardly been close friends. The moment we met we clashed, and we don't have a thing in common. You must know how I despise your lifestyle, while you treat my aspirations as an amusing game. To even contemplate such a union is to make a mockery of all that marriage should stand for.' She couldn't see his expression in the dark, but she sensed his tension. The hand covering hers, tightened.

'You've left something out of your summation, Nicola, the fact that I love you.'

Feeling ambushed, she said feebly, 'I can't believe that.'

'It's true, nevertheless. You say we clash. I say we are merely two stubborn people who haven't yet worked out a pattern for blending. You are a beautiful woman, Nicola; but believe it or not, it's your vitality and curiosity, and your refusal to bow down to circumstances that first stirred my admiration, which later became love. There's not a moment of the day when I'm not thinking of you. You have captured my heart, my mind, all my energies. I want you, Nicola. I want to be with you and to care for you.'

She rallied, shaking her head and saying, forcefully, 'No. You want to control me. The characteristics you say you admire would be stifled by your need to be in charge. I've seen it too often.' She pulled her hand free, adding, 'But, most important, I don't respect your way of life, and even if I loved you, that would be an insuperable barrier.'

Andrew's voice was low, vibrant with intensity. 'I could change. I could make you love me.'

'I don't want you to change. There's no room in my life for you, or any other man. There's so much to be done, and only a handful of women at present to do it. We have to organize, to train people to. . . .' She clenched her fists, strained with the effort to make him understand. 'I'm needed in my world, Andrew. I don't think I'm really needed in yours.'

'You *are* needed. *I* need you!'

All at once she was in his arms, being kissed breathless. Her struggles were useless. He was stronger by far, and in the grip of something tempestuous that would not be restrained. Whether it was passion, or disappointment, or rage, or perhaps a combination of all three, the result was the same. Her head swam from lack of air. Her back bent under his weight, her neck was held in a tight grip. She knew she was about to lose consciousness. Then she was suddenly free, lying back against the cushion, the air wheezing into her squashed lungs.

Andrew drew away and gripped his hands hard on his thighs. His voice rasped in his throat as if he, too, were breathless. 'I'm sorry. I'm so sorry, Nicola. I've never lost control before in such a way.'

Nicola concentrated on drawing in air, and did not respond.

'Say something. Why won't you at least answer?'

When she did, her voice shook with fury. 'If you had left me any breath I would tell you what I think of your disgusting behaviour.'

'Nicola. . . .'

'Don't touch me. Don't speak to me.' She'd never before been manhandled, and it was a shock, a disturbing reminder of the things she'd so recently learned about the way some men could behave.

Andrew moved back, putting distance between them, while she sat rigidly in her corner until the carriage drew up at Viola Terrace.

Then he leaned towards her. Light from a streetlamp fell on his face, showing it to be strained and unhappy.

'Nicola, whatever you may think of me, you must believe my greatest desire is for your happiness. I know I've gone about this in the wrong way; I've hurt you and angered you. But please don't cut me off entirely. Let me continue to be a friend.'

'We will never be friends. Plainly you don't respect me or you would not have treated me like one of your light women. Please let me get out of the carriage.'

He thrust the door open and sprang down to help her out. 'Nicola. . . .'

'Goodbye, Andrew.' She walked up the path to her door, not caring whether he stayed or went. Only when the door closed behind her did she lean against it, trembling with reaction and inclined to have a good cry.

CHAPTER TWENTY-TWO

NICOLA SOON CAME to terms with the episode, shearing it of drama and admitting that she'd overreacted. It was mostly her dignity smarting. Andrew hadn't harmed her, and he had tried to make amends.

She supposed she should be complimented, although it was hard to believe in his declaration of love. More likely it was an attraction of opposites, the contrast with the women he met socially. He thought he admired spirit and individuality in a female, but these would soon pall in a wife. Without encouragement, the infatuation would pass and he would recover without too much pain.

She repressed the knowledge that if he had approached her more gently and given her the opportunity to respond, she might have surprised them both. That would have been disastrous. Firmly resolved to avoid Andrew if she could, and not be alone with him when they were forced to meet, she told herself that the episode would soon be forgotten.

A temperance march was to be held before Christmas and, in the spirit of female solidarity, Nicola joined the women assembled at the southern end of George Street with banners and placards raised. They were led by a marching band from the Salvation Army, their instruments glittering in the sunlight. It made a brave show, Nicola thought, eyeing the streaming banners with their challenging messages, and the determined faces of the women. She took her place in the rear and the parade began.

Dogs barked and children ran beside the marchers, catcalling. Passers by stopped to watch, some to comment loudly and unfavourably. The women were oblivious. They were out to make a statement and nothing would be allowed to stand in their way.

Up the hill they marched, past the steps of the town hall and on down to King Street, the street of taverns and brothels where the demon drink reigned in undisputed sovereignty. There they met a solid mass of men and women blocking their path. Pelted with obscenities and rotting vegetables, the marchers stood their ground. The band played valiantly on until the speakers had set up their rostrum under a street awning and prepared to face the crowd.

Police had arrived, on foot and on horseback, but they were holding off for the moment.

Then, all at once the mood of the crowd began to turn. Without obvious cause, threatening faces turned jovial. Suddenly there was a holiday atmosphere. The jeers became cockiness; the remarks still drowned out the speakers, but it had turned into a game. Pie-sellers appeared, and vendors of drinks and sweets. Beer mugs were passed through tavern doors and windows to the crowd. Men sat down on the gutter edge or leaned against shop fronts and rolled their cigarettes. Someone brought out a piano accordion and began to play popular airs. The two blocked streets had become a carnival area.

Watching in disbelief, Nicola realized that the marchers had been defeated, not by violence, but by the typically Australian love of a holiday.

Robert Carrington, pushing through the crowd to her side, confirmed her thought. 'It could only happen here. If this were England, you'd have police charges, broken heads, a disorderly mob, all ending in overflowing cells.'

Nicola said, 'I feared we would meet with violence, simply because a certain kind of aggressive passivity does bring out the worst in people. These women are totally in earnest, and they have every justification for fighting the evils caused by drink. Yet, somehow their very righteousness raises hackles.'

'I agree. Sincerity is often mocked and purity derided by the ignorant. Calvary is the great example.' Carrington's dry tone was edged with bitterness. He looked around him at the draggle tail of marchers who had broken ranks and appeared to be setting off home, their proud banners trailing in the dust. 'It's all over for today, I'd say. May I escort you home, Miss Redmond?'

Nicola sighed. 'Thank you, but I have business to attend to down at the offices of *The Dawn*.' She noted the way his lips thinned, and said on impulse, 'You don't approve of women's militancy, do you, Detective Carrington? I don't believe you have a liberal thought in your head.'

'Nicola! I beg pardon. Miss Redmond. . . .'

'You may call me Nicola.'

He flushed. 'Thank you. And my name is Robert.' He drew a deep breath. 'In one way you're right. I like women – ladies – to remember their femininity and behave accordingly. Most men would agree. God knows, I see enough of the other kind of woman in my job.'

She said coolly, 'Do you mean the downtrodden, the poor, the factory slaves?'

'I was speaking of the streetwalkers. I, too deplore the poverty that is a part of any city, and sympathize with the plight of the women you mention.'

'Sympathy doesn't feed children or cut the number of hours of backbreaking toil ageing these women before their time. As for your prostitutes, how many have ended in the gutter through poverty and lack of opportunity? Action is needed, Robert Carrington, and it's "ladies" like myself who will gather the momentum for such action. We at least have the time and energy and the will. And as soon as there's an improvement in their lives, the women we are trying to help will join us. It's too late to stop these changes, whether or not you, and people like you, approve.' She stopped, seeing his eyes narrow in a smile.

'Indignation suits you, Nicola.'

'Have you listened to a word I've said?'

'Of course; and I agree, up to a point. May I walk along with you and continue this discussion? There's another matter I'd like to bring to your attention.'

Her interest piqued, Nicola took his arm and, skirting the crowd, continued down towards the quay. Nicola appreciated the walk on such a day, sunny but not yet hot. Much of her work kept her indoors and it was a treat to be out in the open. Recent rain had laid the dust and dung caught between the wooden blocks underfoot, and the air seemed fresher. Even the building façades looked new-washed. Nicola tilted her head to allow the sun beneath her hat brim and wished, not for the first time, that fashion did not decree such high-collared blouses.

Robert didn't seem anxious to go on with their argument, and she asked idly, 'Where do you come from, Robert? What decided you to join a colonial police force?'

She felt his arm muscles stiffen, and stole a glance at the long, mobile face, still pale under an Australian sun. His eyes, dark as Hugh's, were set deep beneath sleek brows, and his mouth was full-lipped in repose. There was sensuality buried beneath his cool exterior, she thought, and caught herself wondering what he'd be like if his defences were ever breached.

He met her examining gaze. 'I'm ambitious. You may have noticed. I come of a good family, but for private reasons – not questionable, I assure you – I was forced to leave England and make my own way in the world.'

Nicola nodded. 'You're so confident, with the kind of assurance that such a background creates. Hugh Owen has a similar assurance, and yet he's a product of a colliery town in Wales and a struggle for education.' She added, thoughtfully, 'He's every bit as ambitious as you are, but in another direction.'

'In totally the opposite direction from policing! He's a malcontent, stirring up trouble wherever he goes.' Two dents had appeared at the side of Robert's nostrils and those full lips had thinned again. Nicola recognized an indicator to change the subject.

'You haven't yet told me why you chose policing. It seems. . . .'

'Incongruous? Think for a moment. In this land of opportunity it still takes money to set up a business, and I can't see myself going into trade. One can never entirely throw off one's upbringing. However, with a commission in the army beyond my purse and the fact that the police force was once a military organization and is still run on similar lines, I chose it as a career with advancement opportunities.' His cocked eyebrow seemed to say, *Is that all you wish to know?*

Nicola, who now felt she'd been prying, quickly asked what matter he wanted to bring to her attention.

Clearly choosing his words carefully, he said, 'I'm sure your own good sense will guide you, but I should warn you of a proposed union confrontation, if you haven't already learned about it from Owen.' He paused, lips tightened, then began again. 'I am reliably informed of a planned attack by militants on a woollen mill whose management recently fired their staff and put on women operators at a lower rate of pay. The police will attend, and we hope that there will be no violence. However, because of your interest in the union movement, it occurred to me that you might feel obliged to support the female staff.'

Nicola stiffened. 'I suppose the owners have been notified?'

'Of course. But they refuse either to close that night or to deal with the unions, who are demanding reinstatement of their men.'

'Do the women themselves know of the danger?'

'They don't want to lose their jobs. They will stay on the night shift.'

'I see. And you're advising me not to get involved?' Nicola's calmness belied her reaction. Here was another man telling her what she should or should not do.

He nodded. 'I don't want you to be hurt, Nicola. There's no way that you can affect the outcome. It's police business.'

'What about the women workers who might be hurt?'

'Of course we'll do our best to protect them.' His casual tone was not reassuring.

She withdrew her arm. 'Well, thank you for the warning. I'll keep it in mind. Now, here we are at Louisa's offices, so I'll say goodbye.'

He took her hand in both his and gazed at her with sincerity. 'You know your welfare is my deepest concern. Please call on me at any time.'

She smiled non-committally and freed her hand. She could hardly wait to get inside and tell Louisa the whole thing.

Her message to Hugh had him on her doorstep the following evening.

'I'm delighted that you should want to see me, Nicola,' he said, only half-jokingly, 'but you did say next month would be early enough for me to call.'

'Well, it is next month. It's December, almost Christmas. I suddenly felt in a festive mood and I thought you might care to dine out with me on goose and currant pudding. Will you join me as my guest tomorrow night at Dandy's restaurant?'

'No.'

Nicola actually gaped.

'No, Nicola. I'll dine with you if you will be *my* guest.'

'I asked you first, Hugh.'

'Nicola, please don't argue. It will give me great pleasure to entertain you.'

This was awkward. It was one thing to spend her own money while pumping the man for information, but quite another to be beholden to him for an expensive meal to which she had invited herself.

He watched her, smiling quizzically and, with a mental shrug, she capitulated. 'Then, thank you. I accept, with pleasure.'

He sketched a bow. 'Your ladyship's carriage will call at eight o'clock. Goodnight, Nicola.'

She watched him go, admiring the cap of tight black curls that disdained fashion, and the easy gait of a self-sufficient man. It was something she could appreciate in Hugh, his disregard for unimportant conventions. When he chose to dress socially his clothes were reasonable, but not exquisitely cut; his manners were easy but not polished. However, intelligence shone in the dark eyes of the Welsh dreamer, and the discipline that could focus on an ideal to the exclusion of all else. Yes, she respected Hugh, and did not want to use him.

It was unfortunate that, just like Andrew and Robert, he refused to appreciate the needs of one whole sector of society. Andrew thought she was amusing herself, dabbling in charitable works; Hugh disregarded her aims. To him they were unimportant. While Robert Carrington wanted her to be a 'lady', for heaven's sake!

Her decision hardened, and she hurried inside to choose a gown suited to shifting Hugh's focus long enough for her purpose.

Dandy's restaurant, just a stone's throw from Parliament House on the hill, had windows overlooking the finest of harbour views. It also enjoyed a deserved reputation for fine food in an atmosphere of gaiety, with musicians and entertainers. By the time Nicola's nose was being tickled by the bubbles rising in her second glass of champagne, she knew the evening would be a success.

She had brushed and twisted her hair into a blazing crown topped with two white camellias from the garden; and, spurred by the need to captivate Hugh into dropping his guard, she'd been inspired to rip away half the bodice of her best indigo gown, draping her exposed shoulders and bosom to a point just meeting decency. The camellia reposing in her cleavage was no whiter than her skin, and the corset she seldom wore had brought her waist in to a delicious hourglass curve.

Hugh's expression as he handed her into the carriage did make her wonder whether she'd overdone it. It was no part of her plan to have another man mauling her on the way home. But soon she realized he was merely testing the temperature, and would need encouragement.

With the champagne singing in her blood she swayed towards him, raising her glass in a toast, her smile an invitation. Two glasses later he leaned close, his breath playing on her shoulder as she invited him to reveal his latest plans for union expansion. The musicians wove their magic, the air was filled with the aromas of good food and cigars and women's perfume. The wine continued to flow, and Hugh talked.

Nicola didn't like herself much. Her deliberate beguilement of Hugh had been necessary, for the sake of others. She now had the date and place she wanted. Yet, her success had been spoilt by her conscience. Hugh could be forgiven for believing that she would welcome his advances. Now she must deal with the consequences.

Of course, it was Hugh's own fault that she'd been reduced to such tactics. He should not encourage violent confrontation in the work force; fire must be fought with fire; the end justified the means; and all the other clichés people use to excuse their behaviour. She still didn't feel any better about her own role.

Unhappy at being made to feel that way, she pleaded a sudden headache and asked Hugh to take her home.

He was obviously disappointed. But he paid the bill and escorted her to the street.

'Perhaps the cool night air will help,' he suggested.

They walked for several blocks before Hugh hailed a hansom and handed Nicola up. Tucked in beside him with the apron closed over their knees, she was aware of their intimacy. No one, including the cab driver, could see them.

Hugh's hand stole over hers. 'Are you feeling better now, Nicola?'

'Yes, thank you. But I'm quite tired. I think I must have drunk more champagne than is good for me.'

He laughed indulgently, then bent to kiss her. It was an experienced kiss, not impassioned, as Andrew's had been, but seductive, exploratory, setting up warning nerve signals all over her body. She made herself sit still, holding herself rigid until at last her lips were free. She felt his gaze trying to penetrate the darkness in the cab.

'You're not very encouraging. Are you a complete innocent, Nicola?' He sounded more puzzled than annoyed.

She adopted an affronted tone. 'I'm not accustomed to being manhandled by my escort.'

'Well, my dear, you have every chance of it if you encourage a man as you did me over dinner.'

'Did . . . Did you think I was encouraging you?'

He sighed. Playing idly with her hand, he said, 'You *are* an innocent. I must put it down to the unaccustomed champagne.'

Relieved that his amorousness had subsided for the moment, Nicola felt irrationally annoyed by his assumption that she lacked sophistication – she who had danced with ambassadors and curtsied before Her Majesty, the Queen! She pulled herself together and decided to play the innocent in earnest.

'I'm sorry, Hugh. I didn't mean to be provocative. I was enjoying myself so much, and I suppose the wine did go to my head a little. I do feel terribly drowsy.' She lowered her eyelids and stifled a yawn with her free hand. She didn't dare try to pull the other away just yet.

If she were honest, she'd admit that his kiss had not been unpleasant. In fact, it had produced quite enjoyable sensations in the oddest places. Nevertheless, dalliance would be highly dangerous. Hugh wasn't the man to be led into any May games. She held her breath as Hugh shifted and sat back, releasing her hand.

His voice held its usual half-jesting undertone. 'Nicola, you must develop a protective instinct where men are concerned. If they see a weakness, they just naturally take advantage, and your sexual naïveté is a most enticing weakness.'

'What do you advise me to do?' Nicola sounded deceptively meek, but he wasn't in the least deceived.

'Minx. In plain words, control your mischievous desire for flirtation. It will get you into trouble.'

'It already has. Hugh, thank you for being understanding. You're a good friend.'

'A friend. Yes, for the moment, if you like. There'll be time enough in the future.'

CHAPTER TWENTY-THREE

M EMBERS OF *THE Dawn* club convened at Louisa's offices the following evening after work, when they could slip in unnoticed and have the doors locked behind them. Nicola was torn between amusement at the secrecy and disappointment that it was really necessary. The very fact that they met to discuss a male union attack on female workers should prove the point, she thought. Unhappily, many men did resent women having jobs when men did not. But did they have to be militant about it?

'Yes, they do,' Louisa answered when Nicola put the question. 'Some folk are so insecure they must forever be proving themselves superior, and the male psyche is the more fragile of the sexes. Still, we can hope that a show of solidarity on our part with the women workers at this factory will have an effect. I don't believe they will be physically assaulted, but there'll be a confrontation of some kind. The men have a point to make.'

The factory in question was a large woollen mill in the inner city, and twenty of the younger, stronger women were chosen to group around the entry with placards supporting women's right to work. They were not to enter the building, since the management had proved unsympathetic and would be ready to eject demonstrators of either sex. There would be no incitement, and the pickets' behaviour would at all times be lawful and dignified.

'No shouting slogans,' Louisa directed. 'Remember, when people are keyed up it takes little to start a conflagration. We want a peaceful rally stating our position, without a disturbance.'

As a volunteer, Nicola was provided with a placard nailed to a pole and told to meet the others outside the Town Hall at six o'clock on Friday evening. Her dress was to be sober and of little value. The older hands didn't put it past the unionists to come armed with vegetables. Also, a headscarf was suggested, instead of a hat. Nicola went home brimming with zeal.

On the evening in question she began her preparations, which Josh watched with growing anxiety. After quickly braiding her hair, she pinned it high beneath a covering scarf, nodding with satisfaction at the stranger in her mirror. She added her oldest jacket, then trotted downstairs for her placard, followed by a limping, protesting Josh.

Persuasion was wasted on him. She couldn't seem to make him understand that the women's greatest strength lay in their solidarity; that by standing together they would change situations in the workplace and in society generally. Only concerted effort would force through the laws to protect and enforce these changes. Josh blocked her passage to the front door.

'Oh, Josh, don't be silly. Stand aside please and let me pass.'

'I won't!' Josh almost sobbed, and Nicola saw that his distress was far greater than she'd realized.

'Josh—'

'I won't let you go. Something dreadful will happen and I'll lose you, too.'

Nicola dropped the placard and took him by the shoulders, gazing into his eyes. 'Listen to me. Nothing dreadful will happen. This has all been planned carefully as a peaceful rally.' Searching his too-old face on the thin, young shoulders, she felt a stab of compassion. He'd borne so much in his short life.

'Ho, yes.' Josh attempted irony. 'Like the union meeting you went to and nine men ended in the hospital with broken heads and their ribs stove in.'

'The circumstances were different. The police attacked them. And clever speakers had already inflamed the men. They were ready for trouble.'

'They're always ready for trouble,' Josh said morosely. 'You're the one who doesn't understand. Don't go. I've got a feeling about this, and it's bad.'

Nicola shook her head pityingly. 'Dear Josh, I do understand. You've lost everyone you loved so your fear for me has grown out of all proportion to the event. I promise I'll be safe and back home with you before midnight. Now, do the history questions I've set you and have supper ready for me. Please?'

He stared mutely at her, his whole body a silent plea that she forced herself to ignore. Picking up her placard she waited until he stepped aside, his head hanging. When she would have kissed his cheek, he pulled away and hobbled off to the back of the house. With a sigh, she called out 'goodbye' and closed the door firmly behind her.

The twenty women convened at the town hall steps under the leadership of Molly Jensen, a hardy, experienced campaigner for women's suffrage. They then proceeded quietly to their destination.

Their placards and freshly painted banners sported the one message, *Women, too, support families. Let them work!* People in the street stopped to read and comment as the silent band went by. There were a few ribald comments, but just as many shouts of 'Good on yer, girls!', and Nicola's spirits rose high. It was thrilling, this feeling of mission, of involvement in important matters. The Temperance March fiasco had been a gesture of solidarity on her part. But this was different.

She hadn't realized how depressed she'd become after visiting so many poor homes and seeing so many families in destitution. Tonight she would be striking a blow for the other half of the human race, the half with few rights. The right to work should belong to all people. Given the chance, she would shout it from the rooftops. Now she understood how Hugh Owen felt when he went into battle for his unions – almost exalted by the rightness of the cause.

Quietly the little band filtered down the industrial back streets to arrive at their target, the Great Southern Knitting Mills, a bleak, bare-fronted block several storeys high, with few windows for daylight and ventilation. Through the locked doors the women could hear machines humming, the crash of a hundred huge mechanical shuttles working non-stop.

Nicola pictured the scene inside, with rows and rows of these tireless monsters, floors of them, all attended by their female acolytes, all working like machines themselves. It was a form of slavery. For an instant she doubted the purpose that had brought her to this place. But, wasn't this just the first step on the path to decent, just, humane employment for women. There had to be jobs to go to before the job conditions could be changed.

A wind had risen, gusting uncomfortably in the women's faces. Overhead a block and tackle swung from a girder at right angles to a gap high in the wall. In the meagre light of a streetlamp the women deployed into a semicircle, their backs to the building. They were only just in time. In the distance boots clattered on pavement.

As the marching feet drew closer, Molly Jensen called, 'Banners up!', and the forest of poles rose with their mute protest, white against the sooty bricks. Lanterns were lit, and now the words stood out, clear and unmistakable.

Nicola's heart beat uncomfortably against her bodice and her sweating hands would have slipped from the pole if she hadn't worn gloves. The marching feet crashed on, closer and closer, like the approach of some huge mechanical creature, drowning out the mill machinery. Lights flickered at the end of the street, growing brighter, throwing monstrous moving shadows on a wall. Nicola's teeth clenched, biting her inner cheek, the momentary agony flooding her eyes with tears so that she saw through a watery haze an army of men carrying torches and batons wheeling into the street.

They saw the waiting women and stopped, those at the rear cannoning into the front ranks. Voices rose in surprise.

'Holy hell! What's going on?'

'Who told them we were coming?'

For an instant the two groups faced one another, fifty yards apart, like armies across a battlefield. Then the men moved forward, their step broken, but the boots still setting up a clatter that played on Nicola's nerves and, she suspected, set up the same reaction in the other women. Hobnailed boots were an unfair advantage, she thought. Their side should have brought rattles and whistles. But the idea had been to remain silent in their protest and not to provoke. Now she had her first misgivings. There were more than twice as many men, armed with cudgels, and their expressions as they surveyed the banners were anything but conciliatory.

A rough-looking type whose muscular frame would be at home in a forge, stepped out of the crowd and thrust a huge finger in

Molly Jensen's face.

'What're you lot doing here? Get out of our way. We're going inside.'

Molly ignored the finger and the words, saying, 'Please listen to us. We're not here to cause trouble.'

'No. That's our job,' someone called from the ranks of men, causing laughter.

Molly continued, unperturbed. 'Read what our banners are saying. Women need to work, as well as men. Many are widowed or deserted, supporting large families.'

The leader shrugged. 'There's charities for such as them. They're taking the work from good men with mouths to feed.'

'That's not true. Women don't take carpenters' jobs, or labourers'. They are employed in areas which are traditionally regarded as women's work.'

The leader held up an impatient hand. 'Enough jawing. We've come to do a job, and by God we're going to do it. Out of the way, or you'll get hurt.'

When nobody moved, he looked surprised. His face reddened and he wheeled about. 'Come on, let's move 'em.'

Before she realized it, Nicola had been swept off her feet and deposited in the gutter, along with the rest of the band, amidst outraged female shrieks and a few male oaths as unladylike kicks connected with shins. Nicola, landing hard on her bottom, felt her placard crack beneath her. She watched in distress as a group emerged from the crowd clutching a heavy pole. They lowered it horizontally and took a good grip.

A woman said disbelievingly, 'They're going to ram in the doors!'

Molly Jensen staggered back on her feet. 'Come along, ladies. We can't let them break in and terrify those poor women. Link arms and we'll form a line across the entrance.'

Clutching at the women on either side of her, Nicola joined the line straggling across the front of the building. The men with the ram hesitated, but a furious order from their leader sent them shuffling forward. Encouraged by their fellows, all yelling and waving their torches, they picked up their pace, and Nicola saw in one horrified instant that they would not stop. She felt the tremor in her companions. The linked arms dropped and, at the last possible moment, the women broke and scattered. Those slow to get out of the way were thrown aside as the men heaved their ram at the doors, hitting them so hard that the hinges shivered.

As they drew back for another run, Nicola dragged herself up from the pavement on scraped hands. Her hip ached and she knew she'd be black and blue by the following day. But she was better off than Molly, who lay moaning and clutching her wrist. Two women went to her aid as a small window overhead was thrown up.

'What's going on down there?' a male voice enquired. 'You'd better not try anything or you'll end up in gaol.'

The leader raised his voice. 'We're coming in. Stand away from the door or you'll be sorry.'

The man at the window sounded querulous. 'I've sent for the police.'

His answer was a resounding crash as the ram hit the doors again.

'Stop! Stop!' he shrieked. 'What is it you want?'

'You know what we want. Stop the machines. Send the women packing and employ men, at men's wages.'

'I can't. I'm only the night-shift manager. I don't have the authority.'

The leader snorted. 'That'd be right. The owner heard we were coming and made sure he wasn't here. Well, he had his chance.'

In the ensuing silence the ram hit the doors with an ominous splitting sound. It was followed by shrill feminine shrieks from within the building. The machinery had stopped, and in the relative quiet other sounds seemed magnified – voices, the hissing of the torches, hobnails on the pavement as the ram was readied again.

The leader nodded and, for the last time, the ram thudded into the doors, splintering wood and tearing the leaves away from their hinges to fall flat. Light poured out into the street, illumining the faces of the waiting men.

They didn't wait for long. With a roar of victory they surged inside, waving batons and iron rods. Those in front raced upstairs, while others, ignoring the women operators cowering back against the walls, proceeded to attack the machines. They moved quickly and methodically, inflicting the maximum damage, as if aware of a time limit.

The noise was appalling. Nicola thought it must be like this in a foundry. But unlike most of her companions, she didn't cover her ears and run. She was struggling with an urge to pick up her battered placard and attack any one of these men. The blood raced in her veins so fast that she was almost dizzy with it, and her jaw had clamped hard enough to hurt. How dared these men behave like brutes? What gave them the right to terrorize and destroy?

Hardly knowing what she intended, she marched across the broken doors, oblivious of jagged spars catching at her skirt and unmindful of the danger within. Pieces of broken loom shot past her head and hit the wall. The floor had become an obstacle course, a tangle of torn fabric and snapped threads, broken spindles and unused reels of yarn. She could hear cries from above and the crash of overturned machinery. A man clutching two bolts of cloth slipped at the top of the stairs and came tumbling down, limbs windmilling, to land unconscious at the bottom.

Looting as well, thought Nicola, as more men negotiated the stairs with their arms full of cloth, leaping over their fallen comrade and racing for the door. Where were the police? Robert Carrington had known this would happen. Why hadn't he stopped it?

Hearing a child's scream, she turned swiftly to see a girl not yet in her teens struggling and being dragged backwards towards the door by two men.

'Throw the bitches out,' a man shouted, and pandemonium ensued.

Women huddled in corners shrieking, others picked up their skirts and ran, only to be grabbed and thrown over a shoulder and raced outside. A few of the braver ones joined Nicola, who had picked up the nearest dropped baton and prepared to defend her person. She'd collided with the pavement once too often that night, with bruises to prove it. No one was going to throw her out in the street. Rage and excitement were a heady mix. She felt ready to take on the world.

CHAPTER TWENTY-FOUR

Now ANOTHER ELEMENT had been added to the fray – fire. Most of the attackers had thrown down their torches outside, but not all, and the building contained floors of flammable yarns and fabrics. There came a sudden whoosh of flame at the end of the long room, and within seconds a whole wall was enveloped. Fiery rivulets raced across the floor, pausing to feed on the torn piles, crisping the yarns to blackened webs, then falling hungrily on oil from the broken machinery.

In the immediate stampede that followed the doorway quickly jammed with struggling bodies. Windows above the door were smashed, creating a draught to suck the flames higher. Smoke, thick and oily, filled the air. The whole ground floor was ready to explode into an inferno.

Nicola grasped the nearest woman by the arm and shouted above the din, 'Upstairs. We'll never get through the door. Tell the others to pass it on.'

Terror shone in the woman's eyes, but she controlled it. Swiftly she turned to a workmate and the word was passed along. Following Nicola's example, they flung their skirts over their heads, tearing a gap in a seam to see through; then, clutching petticoats about their ankles, they ran for the stairs, dodging the flaming rivulets, tripping over bits of broken machinery, helping to pick each other up.

Twice they had to stop their headlong dash, once when smoke blinded them, and again when something heavy crashed to the floor just in front of Nicola, throwing up sparks in her face. Beating them away from her woollen skirt, she sidestepped and reached for the banister rail. More smoke enveloped her. She couldn't see more than twelve inches ahead. Shouting to the woman behind to grab hold of her petticoats and tell the others to follow suit, she scrambled around the stair post and fell on her knees, coughing.

Near the floor the air was clearer. On hands and knees she crawled up the steps, feeling the tug on her waistband and hoping the other women were still with her. Her eyes streamed and her throat stung as if she'd swallowed hot vinegar. But now she could see ahead to the bottleneck of bodies at the top, their faces registering horror as they saw their escape cut off.

Near the top step Nicola turned and looked down. Below her seethed a sea of black billows, underlit with orange. Strangely, the fire made little sound. Whatever crackling or munching it did was drowned by the cries of people trapped below and the keening of those equally trapped on the upper floor. When she turned back, the bottleneck had dissolved into individuals rushing to another stairway to the next floor.

One glance at the impossibly small windows and the flammable mess in the room convinced Nicola, too, that she should make for these stairs. The destruction on the floor above had been minor. There hadn't been time for more. Yet, she could still see no way out. The windows matched those below – hardly big enough to allow a head through. A commotion in the far corner drew her notice. Men were dragging ladders and throwing them up against the wall to reach a trapdoor in the ceiling.

'The storeroom. The storeroom. The loading bay.' It had become a chant, taken up by the two-score men and women, all scrambling to be first on a ladder. It was the leader of the unionists who reached the top and flung back the trapdoor to the topmost floor. He scrambled through and gave a great shout.

'It's open!'

A bomb blast exploded beneath Nicola's feet and the building rocked. Suddenly the fire had a voice. It roared its way up the well created by the disintegrating first floor. Machines crashed down through the gap, their ear-splitting cacophony an added terror for the band of men and women crouched above, with just one more floor between them and the holocaust. The scramble for the ladders became a fight.

Nicola knelt and pressed a hand to the floor. It felt hot. Now she knew the touch of real fear. She'd been too keyed up to think beyond a blind rush to escape from below. But there was no safety here. And if they all made it up the ladder before the floor went, what then? Presumably the storeroom had an outlet – four floors above the street. If they jumped, they'd break their necks on the pavement.

Her thoughts must have shown in her face, for the woman who had been right behind her, who had been prepared to fight rather than run, now shook her roughly by the shoulders and screeched above the din,

'Come on, missy. We've got this far. Don't give up yet.' The oil-smeared face was grim with determination. The woman jerked her head. 'They've all gone up. It's our turn, now.'

Nicola blinked, and saw that they were the last two on the floor, which had begun to smoke. She rushed to the ladders with her companion and climbed.

It was cooler up here, with the wind gusting through the open doors of the loading bay. Nicola shivered in the sudden change of temperature. In the darkness of the crowded storeroom people stumbled over crates and bales, lamenting, cursing and praying. It seemed as though, having fought their way this far only to discover a dead end, they'd given up.

But not one man, who lay on his stomach and leaned out on the girder high above the street.

Watching him edge his way back inside, his bulky silhouette rising to his feet as he bellowed for silence, Nicola recognized the union leader.

'Listen. There's still a chance. I can let you down on the pulley rope, if you've the stomach for it. There's not much time. Who's for trying it?' He added, with irony, 'O'course, there's the slight problem of landing in the arms of the police. I can hear them coming.'

'Bugger that.' It was a man's voice. 'I'd sooner cool me heels in a cell than fry. I'll go first and take one o' the women.'

Nicola shook her head, marvelling at the inconsistency of men who could be attacking women one minute and saving them the next.

A clamour rose as people fought to be the next in line, except that no one wanted to stand in line. Shoving and cursing, they struggled to the opening, not heeding the union leader's warning to stand back from the brink. The inevitable happened. Someone at the back pushed hard, and the man nearest the edge lost his footing. He went over, frantically clutching at the air, his scream tearing the night. It was echoed from below, where the lucky ones who had escaped were gathering to watch the drama overhead.

'Now will you bloody stand back?' the union leader shouted, as people shrank away from the opening.

Satisfied at last that he had control, he beckoned forward the man who had offered to go first, and helped one of the women to climb upon his back and take hold without strangling him. The arm was brought in and, with it, the hook. As Nicola watched, the burdened man put his foot in it, grasped the cable, and was swung out into space. Taking hold of the big cogged wheel, the union leader began to turn. Gears meshed, and the two passengers on the hook dropped from sight. A cheer from below soon afterward announced their safe arrival. The wheel spun, the hook reappeared and the process was repeated.

But time had almost run out. People had grown quiet. Faces craned upward, gripped by the race to save lives. There was a flurry of activity in the street as police arrived in force with their wagons and handcuffs, too late to help. The fire had such a hold, the building had to be doomed. In the distance a bell clamoured – the fire engine. It, also, would be too late.

Shivering with reaction, Nicola huddled against the wall, her arms around a young girl who was quietly sobbing into her pinafore. She watched the man who was their enemy hastily pairing off partners and sending them to safety, controlling the wheel, controlling incipient panic in the waiting crowd, and knew she was witnessing true leadership. He was a stranger, an enemy and a saviour all in one. She found it easier to ponder his nature than to dwell on her own peril. Utter terror lurked so close, ready to take her over if she let it.

Now this floor had become uncomfortably hot. And it moved. Out of every cranny poured a tide of rats, foaming across the boards in waves, their eyes red pinpricks in the darkness. The sound of scrabbling claws and squeals brought Nicola to her feet. She felt them running across her boots, one even clawing up her leg. With a shudder, she threw it off, but not before it sank its teeth into her hand. Then within a minute they'd gone, over the edge of the loft opening, like lemmings into the sea. A few of the creatures made it across the girder, most tumbling off the end, although some tried to scramble over the pulley and down the rope. But in the end they died.

As we will probably die, Nicola thought. Still, she urged the young girl beside her into the line, which had grown much shorter. The fire's menacing voice thundered in her ears, punctuated with the noise of falling timbers. She took off her coat, which was stifling her anyway, and wrapped it around the girl, whose thin wrapper would be no protection from flying sparks, if and when she rode the hook to the ground.

Now it was a race between the fire and the remaining few men and women crouched around the opening in the wall. Below her Nicola saw a shifting mass of upturned faces. The fire engine had arrived, the horses steaming and blown, and water was being hand-pumped into the ground floor, achieving little. Fortunately, the wind blew against the face of the building, keeping the reaching flames within, and increasing the chance of negotiating the distance between girder and pavement without being burned.

Voices shouted encouragement as the hook travelled slowly down and up, limited by the speed of the gears. Nicola wanted to urge the union leader to hurry, yet knew he could not. She found herself praying to a God whose existence she had ignored for most of her life: an incoherent prayer mainly consisting of the word 'please'. She prayed for help and for courage, but mostly her prayer was involuntary, a call for something greater than herself to intervene and save them all.

The atmosphere had thickened until it was barely breathable. Sweat ran down her face and body as she removed her scarf and bound it around the head of the young girl. She'd seen one woman's hair burst alight in a tangle of sparks on the way down. Already two others had been unable to maintain their grip on their partner and had fallen, sustaining shocking injury. It was ironic that there had been enough fleece and cloth in this building to soften the landing of any number of people jumping, but it had all been burned or looted.

A sudden flare up brought a roar from the helpless spectators. A spurt of fire burst through the trapdoor to hit the roof.

'Jump. Jump for your lives!' screamed a dozen voices.

The last four people crouched on the sill saw the tongues of flame reaching out to them. The hook swung tantalizingly a few feet below, but far out on its arm. And there it would stay. The gears had seized in the heat and the cogwheel would not move. The union leader was forced to drop the red-hot handle and retreat.

'I can't operate it. It's locked tight,' he panted.

'We'll be roasted alive!' The last man, a scrawny fellow already twitching with nerves, flung past him and propelled himself through the opening, aiming to catch the rope passing through the pulleys. But the arm was beyond reach. Grasping futilely at the air, the man crashed to the pavement. An 'ohhh' of horror rose from the crowd as people scattered to avoid being hit. The two plump little machinists huddling against Nicola looked at one another, looked back at the approaching flames, then held hands and jumped.

Fire belched across the room to lick at Nicola's back. She screamed, and would have followed the women, but the union leader grasped her by the waist and flung her out on to the girder. On her hands and knees she clung there like a monkey, rigid with fear, her grip enough to bend the steel. Behind her she heard the death cry of the man who had saved her – for the moment.

Now the spectators were numbed into silence, their collective gaze fixed on the lonely figure crouched above on the girder, lit by the unearthly orange glow behind her. The wind plucked at her skirts, flapping them like flags against the backdrop of fire.

Then a voice from the crowd bellowed, 'Hold on, Nicola. I'm coming to help you.'

Nicola heard, but she didn't take in the words. Her whole mind was concentrated in her fingers, clamped about the girder. She was a part of it. Eyes tightly shut, she balanced her weight on her bruised hands and knees and became one with that metal beam. Time disappeared. She'd been there for aeons, perched high above the pavement. The fire would soon consume the building and bring her down with it.

Andrew! It was a cry from her heart. Not for rescue, just . . .

a farewell to the love she had denied for so long. Now she could acknowledge its depth and meaning for her – now that all impediments were about to be destroyed, along with life itself.

In an agony of despair she called out to him again. Her voice spiralled away into the smoke-filled sky.

A flurry of sparks like tiny stars exploded around her as something hit the girder. She flinched, fingers slipping, and a great sigh went up from the crowd as she fell forward, her cheek to the metal, her arms and legs wrapped around it.

Then, through the fog of terror she heard a voice.

'Catch hold of it, Nicola!'

Her mind drifted towards awareness. That was Andrew's voice. He was calling to her. He wanted her to do something.

'Nicola! Catch hold of the rope! Don't let it slip off.'

It *was* Andrew. He was there. Suddenly she was wide awake. A rope. Something about a rope. She looked up and saw it, miraculously looped around the metal arm. And it was about to slip off the end.

Panic tore through her. She couldn't let go. If she let go she would fall. Her fingers would not relax their grip on the girder. The wind was stronger. Her plaits had come undone and now her hair blew in her face, veiling the terrible depths.

'Nicola! It's your only chance. Catch the rope.' Andrew's voice had such urgency. She wanted to obey. Slowly, stiffly, the fingers of her left hand relaxed. She reached out, peering through a mesh of hair. It was too far. She couldn't.

'Yes, you can. Do it, Nicola. Do it now.'

Blindly she clutched and found the rope. She dragged it towards her, securing the loop beneath the weight of her body. But she could do no more. She couldn't climb down the rope. It was the end.

The rope tightened and the knot pulled against the underside of the girder. She felt the movement in the metal as it took a weight. It was coming loose from the building. She knew it would go any minute. The wind plucked at her, the pulley swung and clashed, the night began to swirl around her, moving ever faster.

And then Andrew was there, his arms over the girder, panting from his climb.

'Hold on just a little longer. You've been wonderfully brave.' He hauled himself up, sitting astride, steadying himself before unloosing more rope from around his shoulders. 'Sit up, Nicola. I'll help you. I won't let you fall.'

The stars stopped whirling in the wind; the night steadied. Nicola slowly sat up, clutching Andrew's rocklike arm. She didn't move as he placed a loop of rope over her head and under her arms, then drew her to him, lashing the rope around his own body. Numbly she listened as he explained how he'd take her down the knotted rope with him, promising not to let her fall. She knew he could be trusted. Even an explosion behind her and a definite movement in the girder failed to bring back panic. She wound her arms around Andrew's neck and let him tip her off into space.

Nicola would never forget that climb down the rope in darkness shot with flame, or the heat radiating from the brick walls, bulging ready to burst; the monstrous bellowing from within; the pain of the rope cutting into her body; the strain in Andrew's face, so close to hers, as he drew on all his strength to bring them safely to earth.

And when they were down, the hands grasping them, dragging them away from the burning building; the race along the street to the corner and falling flat as the night was rocked by explosions. Bricks raining down, and Andrew protecting her with his body; screams as glass shards and bits of machinery turned to missiles scything down anyone still standing; and when the deadly hail had ceased, looking back to see a brilliant, glittering gold fountain reaching for the sky, at its centre the girder that had held just long enough, now plunging into the heart of the fire.

CHAPTER TWENTY-FIVE

EXPLANATIONS WERE SAVED until later. Nicola, sooty, singed and exhausted to the point of tears, was glad to be taken to the Dene home, where Eleanor and her maids fussed over her and tucked her up to sleep for the next twelve hours.

She woke to bright sunlight pouring in through the balcony doors and a gentle breeze stirring the muslin bed-hangings. A bowl of violets on the bedside table scented the air, and beside them sat a tumbler of iced lemonade, its sides invitingly beaded with droplets. Nicola, with a groan for her bruises, propped herself up on her elbow and reached for the glass. The juice slid down her parched throat like wine to a connoisseur in a temperance desert and she lay back against lace-edged pillows and realized that she was truly alive.

There had been a moment when, balanced on the girder, she had wanted to surrender – a knife-edged second when she could have let go and fallen, thus ending her pain and terror. But when courage was no longer enough and fear had taken over, she had been given a blinding revelation of what life might be, and she had held on. And by holding on she had been saved.

Now came the reckoning. That vision of total love had been the most remarkable experience. It would stay with her for ever. But how could she be sure that it was shared by Andrew? Wealthy, popular, indulged, he had his choice of companions, and had known many women. Newspaper reports kept readers apprised of his activities, and there would surely be conquests among them. She had already decided that he viewed her as a challenge, a different sort of quarry. And in the enjoyment of the pursuit he had trapped himself. How long would it have taken for him to realize his terrible mistake, had she accepted his offer of marriage?

That was her fear.

She tried to talk herself out of such a conclusion, but honesty prevailed, as always, reinforcing her earlier decision; the barrier of commitment to lifestyle was insuperable. If they wed, he would inevitably want her to conform, and she knew she could not. Their love would inevitably die – if Andrew had not already discovered that she was not the woman of his dreams. She could not bear such a scenario.

Pain lanced through her, a thousand times worse than any physical torment. She clasped her shoulders and rode out the storm until it became bearable.

The smell of coffee and sounds of a spirited altercation in the doorway brought her out of her horrible trance. The door opened wide and Josh tumbled into the room, followed by a maid bearing a tray, scolding and apologizing at the same time.

'Missus said no visitors, but he *would* come in,' she complained, setting the tray down on a table near the window.

Sunlight gleamed on silver cutlery and on the bud vase holding a luscious red rose. Nicola's eyes were drawn to the coffee pot and her mouth watered. But Josh had descended on her with a bear hug that woke a dozen bruises, and she yelled, 'Ouch! Get off me, Josh. I must be black, blue and purple all over.'

'Sorry, Nicola.' Josh released her, but refused to move further away than the end of the bed. He sat there while the maid plumped Nicola's pillows and tenderly deposited the tray across her legs, poured the coffee, then left, threatening to tell the mistress of Josh's impertinence. He poked out his tongue at her retreating back and grinned at Nicola.

She eyed him measuringly. 'I know what you're going to say.'

'I told you so. And I did tell you it was dangerous. If I'd known *how* dangerous, I'd have tripped you up and sat on you to stop you going.' His freckled face was solemn with remembered fear, and Nicola reached out to him.

'You were right and I was wrong, and I apologize, most sincerely.'

'So you should,' said Andrew, from the doorway. 'May I come in? Maggie says you're respectable and able to receive visitors.'

Although he was impeccably turned out, as usual, Andrew

showed signs of last night's adventure. His hair had been badly singed on one side, along with one cheek, and Nicola stifled a gasp at the sight of his bandaged hands.

Josh slid off the bed and, to Nicola's great astonishment, gave a little bow in Andrew's direction. Andrew laid one bound hand on the boy's shoulder.

'How are you, Josh? Did you sleep at all?'

The boy shrugged and looked sheepish.

'Josh insisted on staying near you last night,' Andrew explained, 'so we gave him a bed next door. I doubt whether he used it. He seemed very concerned about you.'

'Dear Josh. He's so protective. I owe him a good deal.'

'Perhaps more than you know. Josh was responsible for saving your life last night.'

'But I thought you. . . .'

'Who, do you suppose, took it upon himself to warn me of your intentions? Fortunately, he knew where you'd gone. I saddled up Saracen and arrived in time, thank God. I don't suppose there's another man in this city as experienced in roping cattle. It's not a skill that's easily forgotten. I got the loop over the girder on the second try.'

Josh broke in. 'You should have seen him, Nicola, whirling the rope around his head and throwing it up into the sky to land just where he wanted it. And then he shinned up it like, like . . . I don't know what.'

'Like a monkey up a coconut palm?' Andrew suggested.

Nicola inspected her own palms, which were scraped and slightly blistered, but they would heal easily. A shudder passed through her. She looked up at Andrew. 'Then you brought me down. You hurt your hands and burned your face. You took the most appalling risk for me. I don't know how to thank you.'

'Don't try. Others took risks, also. One brave fellow gave his life in saving at least a score of people, including you.'

Nicola shivered, again. 'I know,' she whispered. 'I'll never forget him. And I'll not repeat the mistake of judging a person by one action. I dismissed him for a brutal enemy and he proved to be a hero.' There was a moment of silence when both looked back, wishing that the past could be changed. 'How many perished in the fire, Andrew?'

'Too many. The exact number isn't yet known; but I can tell you that all your lady demonstrators are safe. It seems you were the only one to go dashing into the building like some kind of crusading knight. What did you think you could accomplish, for heaven's sake, against all those men?'

His asperity was welcome to Nicola, who had been feeling almost crushed by her huge debt to him, and by the need to maintain a calm façade. She started to argue about the need to physically demonstrate support, conveniently forgetting that fury alone had carried her through the broken door into the midst of the uproar. Too late, she recognized Andrew's ploy. His deliberate provocation had worked as a method of distracting her from remembered horrors. Feeling a little foolish, she fell silent.

He said, 'Your coffee's getting cold. I'll leave you to your meal and take this young rascal down for his lunch. Josh, how does veal and chicken pie sound to you? And if I'm not mistaken, Mrs Peck has ordered a jam roly-poly pudding to be served.'

Josh shot to the door, only then remembering to reassure Nicola that he'd be within call for the rest of the day.

Andrew lingered for a moment and Nicola asked, 'How bad are your hands? Has a doctor seen them?'

'Simple rope burns. They'll heal quickly. Our Mrs Peck was trained by Mother, who is as experienced as any doctor. She would like to see you, by the way, when you feel you can rise.'

She nodded. 'Andrew, I'm truly grateful—'

'Don't! No gratitude, please. No obligation.' He smiled. 'However, you must promise that you will never again take part in such a dangerous activity. That climb up the rope damn near killed me.'

'Not to mention the climb down. Very well. I'll try not to be grateful, and you have my promise never, never to do anything so foolish again. It's my temper, you see. It sometimes overwhelms me, and I dash off without thinking.'

'I should never have guessed.' He paused. 'Nicola, about my recent unmannerly declaration. . . . Will you forgive me? You can't know how much I have regretted that scene. I'm still astonished at my ineptness.'

She stopped him with a raised hand. 'I blush when I recall my excessive response. But Andrew, nothing has changed. I must decline your flattering offer in the knowledge that such a marriage would be disastrous for us both. You know why.'

'You don't believe me, do you? You don't really believe in my love for you.'

She said, carefully, 'I believe you think that you love me. Whether such love could withstand the tests it would undergo in a relationship between two such dissimilar people. . . .'

'I believe it could. But only if you truly care for me. Do you, Nicola? Give me an honest answer, I beg you.'

She quailed before the intensity of his gaze. Dear God, what a dilemma. She either lied, denied her love, and endured the consequent agony; or she gave him unwarranted hope. In that case he would continue to pursue her and eventually overcome her resistance, with all the possibility of an even greater agony to come when their love failed. It was a hopeless choice.

He must have seen the struggle in her face. Crossing the room swiftly he bent to take her hands in his.

'No. I was wrong to ask you now. You must be sure before you give me that answer. Last night was a tremendous emotional shock. You need time to recover.' He dropped a swift kiss on her fingers and stood back. 'Now I'll be off, or a certain young villain will have snabbled the whole pie.'

When the door closed, Nicola lay back and thought about the gift of her life, about friendship and love and obligation, and let the tears rise and slide silently down her cheeks.

She recovered quickly and spent the afternoon with Eleanor, who needed reassurance that Nicola had not been hurt. Of course, at a very deep level she had, but she kept this knowledge to herself.

Eleanor had dwindled after a bout of arthritic pain, yet she refused to discuss her health. It was to keep her company that Nicola agreed to stay on for a few days, endorsed by Josh, who had tried to leave the grounds and found himself the centre of unwanted attention.

'Newspaper reporters and photographers, Nicola. They're all around the place, thick as fleas on a dog. We can't get out,' Josh reported.

Andrew, who had run the gauntlet on the way home from the city, looked grim. 'A more felicitous description could be found, Josh. They're more like barbarians at the gates. I resent having to fight my way into my own home.' All the wrath of the master of a besieged domain throbbed in his voice.

'But why are they there?' Nicola was genuinely puzzled.

Josh grinned mischievously. 'Don't you know you're a heroine, Nicola? You helped people to escape from the burning building; then Andrew made his daring rescue on the girder. He's a hero, too.'

Andrew said disgustedly, 'There's even a photograph being circulated of the pair of us coming down the rope. Some fire engine chaser got his camera there in time to immortalize us both.'

'Oh, no!' Nicola's dismay amused Josh, who went off cheerfully to offer his help to the gardeners in defending the barricades.

By the end of the week the reporters had given up the siege, and Nicola was ready to go home. There were things to be done. She wanted to meet the other women involved in the rally and discuss the outcome. She needed to put certain pertinent questions to a smug police detective and a single-minded union activist. And she simply had to get away before Andrew decided it was time to demand her answer.

CHAPTER TWENTY-SIX

A CALL INTO detective headquarters on the following morning found Robert Carrington in his office, immersed in a report on M. Bertillon's system of anthropometry. He rose and greeted Nicola with enthusiasm.

'Just think. No two persons possess the exact same combinations of width of head, length of face, of middle finger, of lower limbs from knee to foot. Now properly catalogued criminals can be recognized and identified in any country where this system is used. What an advance in criminal detection!'

Nicola swept this aside. 'I want an answer from you, Robert Carrington. You knew of the proposed attack on the Great Southern Knitting Mills. Why didn't you send men to stop it?'

'Oh, you've heard about the fiasco. I was most annoyed, I may tell you. The information received turned out to be false, and our men were sent to another address miles away. It wasn't my duty to be involved, but I'd like to have seen a better outcome.'

'So would the people who were burnt to death, I should imagine.'

He looked surprised. 'It was a bad business, I agree. Why are you taking it so much to heart?'

'Because I *was* involved. I was there and I heard those people screaming in terror and agony. I saw them die. It was the most horrible experience of my life. And it could have been prevented.' She began to tremble and sat down hurriedly on the hard, government-issue chair provided.

'Nicola! How could you place yourself in such a dangerous situation? You might have been killed. I warned you not to take part in any such demonstrations.'

'So you did. I chose to help the unfortunate women who were

159

about to be terrorized. If your police force had done their job there would have been no attack, and no fire and no loss of life. You call it a fiasco. I call it murder of innocents.' She whisked out a handkerchief and blew her nose fiercely.

Visibly upset, Robert rushed to fetch his usual panacea, a glass of water, while releasing a torrent of apologies for something she knew was not his fault. Still, she couldn't forgive his lack of compassion. He cared only that the culprits should be punished for flouting authority. She soon realized that her visit had been a waste of time. She left as abruptly as she had come, dissatisfied with herself and with Robert.

Her words with Hugh, when she found him declaiming on a street corner, were just as unsatisfactory; and her accusation of responsibility for the disaster was met with raised brows and another disclaimer.

'I was at a council meeting in Rockdale. In fact, they threw me out for objecting to the proceedings. You know the sort of thing – the usual farcical local government scheme for lining the pockets of the fat men while nothing gets done. Why are you so interested in the fire? It was a tragedy. It should never have happened. Sometimes the best-laid plans do go wrong.' He tucked her arm in his and led her to a nearby tea room. 'Let me get you a cup of tea.'

Nicola freed herself and, oblivious of the fact that she blocked the doorway, said, 'So you did plan the attack?'

'No. I don't run all the union activities in this town. Look, please will you sit down and I'll get you a cup of tea.'

'No! I don't want any tea, thank you.' She did move aside, however. 'Don't hedge, Hugh. I think you know everything that goes on. You knew about this demonstration. You could have stopped it.'

'Why should I want to?'

'Because people were killed. *I* was nearly killed.'

He looked startled. 'What were you doing there? I know one of your meddling women's groups tried to stop the demonstration—'

'It was no demonstration.' Nicola's voice had risen sharply. People were looking at her. 'Those men came armed and ready to destroy. It's little wonder things got out of hand. You and your unions are fine ones to talk of meddling.'

Hugh spread his hands resignedly. 'You never will understand our reasoning. You don't want to understand. All you can see is the needs of women.'

'I'm no more single-minded than you are, Hugh. But I can at least claim not to use violence to attain my ends.' Nicola delivered this as a parting shot and swept out, intending to meet her friends at Louisa's print works.

She found herself intercepted by a posse of newspaper reporters who had tracked her down and had listened with enjoyment to her impassioned speech. Forced to hire a cab to escape, she had the humiliating experience of taking part in a race, with other cabs hurtling after her down the street, the bribed drivers willingly whipping up their horses and joining in the fun.

Upon arriving at her destination, Nicola abandoned dignity and jumped out, throwing money to the driver. Furious and panting, she flew through the doorway and slammed it behind her, just ahead of the pursuit.

The women meeting inside ignored the hammering and shouting to gather around Nicola protectively, asking whether she'd fully recovered from her ordeal. Yet, despite their kindness, they could barely disguise their curiosity and speculation. Only Louisa's quelling expression kept them from bombarding her for details.

The investigation into the previous Friday night's fracas was painful for all concerned. The whole thing had been detailed in the newspapers, with the *Bulletin* taking a particularly scathing attitude.

Louisa read the banner headlines grimly, aloud: "Women Agitators Involved in Fire Disaster. Who is Responsible?" Who, indeed? The union men who marched on the mill are here depicted as rescuing heroes. *We* are cast as the villains of the piece.

'Listen to this: "These women are nothing but a public nuisance and, as in this case, can prove to be an actual danger." There's even a sketch showing a bunch of old maids in pince-nez and ridiculously pointed boots, brandishing umbrellas as they attack the building. The inmates are crowded at the windows and jibing at the attackers. And directly opposite is a sketch of the building burning and the umbrella brigade scuttling away up the street.'

She laid the paper down. 'Not one word is there about the real reason for our presence at the mill. This is misrepresentation at its worst.'

Someone asked what could be done to remedy the situation, and Louisa snorted. 'Nothing at all. Newspapers are free to print anything they like.'

As they went on to discuss the frightening death toll of factory workers and union men trapped in the fire, some members were inclined to accept part of the blame, but Louisa would have none of it.

'I don't think our group can in any way be held accountable for what happened. However, it would be unwise to repeat the experiment. Other measures must be devised to protect women workers under threat.' She glanced meaningly at Nicola. 'Nor should we ever take matters into our own hands. It's essential to work as a team under good leadership. Molly Jensen was your leader and you should have awaited her orders before dashing headlong into danger.'

Nicola hung her head. 'I know. I behaved foolishly.'

'You almost paid with your life.' Louisa softened. 'I do understand why you plunged into the fray. I'm no stranger to overwhelming rage at injustice.'

There wasn't much more to be said, thought Nicola. It had all been thoroughly rehashed in every city paper, each horrifying detail, drawn out, embellished, picked over until she longed to run away. It had become an epic of sacrifice and survival to be dished up day after day at the breakfast tables of middle class Sydney, carried in buses and trams to offices and factories and discussed endlessly over dinner breaks. Her name and Andrew's, not to mention their faces, had been blazoned from one end of the city to the other, and Nicola felt as naked as a crab without its shell.

When the women applauded her courage she shook her head.

'I was terrified. Alone out on that girder, all I could think was that I would die without having yet lived. All those years still owing to me were being snatched away from me, and it was bitterly unfair.'

Heads nodded in understanding and commiseration. When the meeting resumed, no one opposed Louisa's motion ruling against any similar confrontations with the unions.

Nicola returned home that night, unutterably weary. She knew she had been cowardly in denying Andrew his answer. It felt terrible. But she would feel much worse when she finally brought herself to lie to him. That was her decision. There could be no other. In denying her love she'd be hurting them both, but he would recover.

She was looking forward to her bed when a carriage drew up at the door bringing a message from Andrew that electrified her. Rushing for her hat and coat she called to Josh that she had to go out.

'What is it! What's happened?' Josh appeared in the doorway of the scullery, a dripping dishcloth in his hands. His strained expression stopped her in mid stride.

He needed reassurance, but this news was not for Josh to deal with just yet. It might even turn out to be a colossal disappointment. 'It's nothing for you to worry about, just something I have to talk over with Andrew. You can see his carriage waiting for me. I'll be perfectly safe.'

Josh dropped the cloth and headed out the door to check that it was Andrew's carriage and coachman waiting.

'Well, all right. But you're as pale as a turnip, Nicola. You should be in bed.'

She kissed his cheek. 'Stop fussing, godmother. I'll be home in my pumpkin carriage before midnight.'

'What?'

'Never mind. I'm just being silly. Josh, I must fly. Don't wait up for me.' With her coat unbuttoned and her hat pinned on crookedly, she rushed down the path and clambered into the carriage.

All the way across the city she struggled to contain her excitement. Could it be true? Had there been a breakthrough at last? Who *was* this mysterious person offering information for Andrew's reward? His note had been maddeningly brief, just asking her to come to a meeting of their small investigative group. Someone had information to sell, but who, or what information, had not been said. All she knew was that the offer had come through a third party.

Tantalized and desperately hopeful, she willed the horses to move faster through the traffic, hardly aware of the bright lights and crowds promenading the streets. Her thoughts were all of Rose. It had taken a long time, but now it seemed that on this night she would be close to the answer. She would know the monster who had taken Rose's life.

The thought of her cruel death still made Nicola ill. She still questioned how it had all come about. How had that dear, gentle girl started on the downward slope to degradation, ending in a vile death? How could it have happened to someone as true and loving as her dear Rose?

The general answer was always the same. Poverty and want were at the root of the evil that fed upon the innocent and brought them to ruin.

Hastening through the night to a rendezvous that could lead to justice for a murderer, Nicola swore that it would happen. He would not be allowed to escape. Tears overwhelmed her, dissolving some of the pain and guilt that had lingered for so long. By the time the carriage turned in to the gates of the Dene property and started up the drive, she had wiped away all traces of the emotional storm and felt ready to face whatever came.

CHAPTER TWENTY-SEVEN

THE HOUSE SEEMED quiet to Nicola as she stepped inside, past the maid who relieved her of her coat. The marble paving of the entrance hall echoed under her feet as she was led towards Andrew's book room. The maid announced her and, unsure of what awaited, she took a deep breath and went in.

It was an anticlimax. The three men sprang to their feet to greet her with the sort of anxious care usually accorded to an invalid. Hugh reached her first, guiding her to a chair near one of the French windows. The shutters had been folded back to let in the breeze and the last of the evening light.

'Don't be too disappointed if this turns out to be a mare's nest,' he warned. 'We only have the word of this newspaper fellow that he has anything to offer.'

Before Nicola could respond Robert had come up to greet her and Andrew was offering her refreshment. She shook her head quickly, nauseated at the thought of food and drink. 'Tell me what's happened. What "newspaper fellow" are you talking about? What has he said?'

Robert answered her. Standing close enough to edge Hugh Owen aside, he said repressively, 'He comes from the *Sydney Morning Herald*, a most reputable organ. As you know, we advertised the reward for information concerning the death of Rose Basevi in every major newspaper, using the chief editor as our link. However, up until now there has been no response whatever.'

Nicola could have shaken him. 'What response have you got? Tell me.'

Andrew, standing silently regarding the others, now said, 'Someone anonymous has contacted a certain journalist named Leach, offering information in exchange for the reward. This unknown person is being very cautious. Obviously there's some danger attached. However, he has agreed to pass on the information to Leach and, in accordance with our agreement, his editor is sending him here tonight to tell us what he's learned. Leach still doesn't know who is behind the reward offer.'

Feeling rather let down, Nicola sank into her seat. She'd developed a severe headache and felt as though her skull was being systematically beaten like a gong.

'I'd hoped for more,' she said. 'I expected . . . I don't know what I expected. To see the monster in chains, I suppose. To confront him and tell him what I thought of him.'

Three faces looked compassionately at her as Andrew said, 'That day will come. I truly think this man Leach has important information for us; we must hope it will be enough for us to identify the killer.'

'And arrest him,' Robert added. 'I want to put the cuffs on him, personally.'

Hugh's beautiful voice held an ugly note. 'After we've given him a little lesson in keeping his murdering hands to himself.'

'Oh, don't!' Nicola covered her face. 'I've been thinking terrible thoughts of vengeance all the way over here. But I don't want to be like him. Hatred is soul-destroying.'

'"Vengeance is mine, saith the Lord,"' Robert suddenly intoned, surprising everyone. 'We must all live by God's law as well as man's, and I'd never be guilty of injuring a prisoner, whatever he'd done. But I would see him prosecuted to the fullest extent. If he breaks the law he pays the price.'

Nicola studied him curiously. Was he really so bloodless, or did his apparently rigid sense of justice hide a man as capable of violence as any other? She'd seen the flame of passion flare in him. It might have been desire rather than fury, but the two could go together. She rather thought that Robert was as capable as anyone of hot-headed behaviour. She hoped so. His coolness could be daunting at times.

Hugh was surveying the detective with a sardonic expression. He strolled over to the mantelpiece and picked up a matchbox, looking a query at Andrew, who said, 'Go ahead and smoke if you wish, and if Nicola has no objection.'

Nicola shook her head and Hugh drew a cigarillo from his breast pocket. When he had it alight he remarked, 'I'm all in favour of a little corporal punishment, myself. There's nothing like letting the other fellow know how it feels to be on the receiving end. He frequently decides to mend his ways.'

'I suppose you'd still have men lashed at the triangle,' Robert scoffed.

Hugh merely smiled.

Shifting impatiently, Nicola asked when Mr Leach was expected.

'At any minute.' Andrew pulled out his watch and compared it with the clock on the mantelshelf. This had just chimed the first of eight strokes when wheels sounded on the gravel outside.

Nicola turned to the windows, although it had grown too dark for her to see beyond the open shutters. Despite the balmy evening, she felt suffocated. She struggled to draw breath into her lungs. Was this it, the breakthrough she'd anticipated for so long? Would this Leach name the killer? She heard the doorbell ring and the maid's footsteps crossing the tiled hall. It seemed an hour before the door was thrown open and Maggie announced, 'Mr Clarence Leach'.

A spare, dapper man with thinning grey hair advanced confidently towards Andrew, his hand outstretched.

''Evening, all. Pleased to make your acquaintance, sir. Had no idea you were behind this until our editor told me. May say I've heard a lot about you.'

Andrew, looking non-committal, introduced Nicola and the other two men. Nicola stared at Leach as if mesmerized, waiting for him to continue. However, the journalist would not be hurried. He surveyed the room for the most comfortable chair and sank into it. When Andrew offered him whisky he assented with alacrity, and waited in silence while the drink was poured and brought to him. He raised the crystal glass to the light and examined the prisms formed by its pattern. Nicola set her teeth.

After many moments, the man took a large gulp of whisky and carefully placed the glass on a side table. He caught Robert's eye and said, 'Won't keep you in suspense. Got the information you want, or, rather, got the informant. Like an oyster. Won't talk to *me*.'

'Where?' Hugh asked.

'Tell you in a minute. First, the reward's got to be up front. Won't talk to anyone, otherwise.'

Nicola tried not to shout. 'Who won't talk? Who *is* this informant?'

Leach smiled mechanically and switched his gaze to Andrew. 'Didn't know *you* were offering the money or I'd've been able to reassure her. She's afraid, see? No names, no pack-drill.'

'She?' all four listeners chorused.

Leach shrugged his narrow shoulders. 'Not unusual, a female informer.'

Andrew said, 'Get to the point, man. The reward's genuine if the information's good. We want to hear from this woman. Where is she?'

'Outside.' The laconic Leach jerked his thumb.

'What?' Andrew strode to the door and flung it open. 'Where is she?'

'I'll fetch her. Told her to wait in the garden while I sniffed the air. Told you. She's afraid.' Leach tossed off his whisky and went to the nearest window. 'Be back in two shakes.'

Andrew's face would have amused Nicola if she hadn't been so frustrated herself. And both Hugh and Robert mirrored his annoyance. Now footsteps approached along the gravel path beneath the windows and a woman appeared framed between the fold-back shutters. Small, dressed in soiled and bedraggled finery, she looked what she was, a citizen of the gutters, half-starved, opportunistic, ready to leap like a cat to safety. Suspicious eyes gleamed under a broken hat brim, taking in the room.

'Lizzie!' Nicola sprang up.

For a moment the tableau held, each person immobile. Then Lizzie dropped the purse clutched in her hand. Her reddened mouth stretched wide in a scream that pierced Nicola's aching head like a hot wire, making her reel. When she opened her eyes, only a bewildered Clarence Leach hovered in the window, his head turned towards the darkened garden.

'What the devil. . . ?'

'What happened?'

'Stop her!'

'Lizzie, come back!'

There was a concerted rush for the window. Leach was mown down as the three men pushed through, followed closely by Nicola. She tripped on the sill and stopped to pick up the purse that Lizzie had dropped. She put it in her pocket, then rushed out on to the path. But it was dark of the moon and she could see nothing except the vague silhouette of trees against the night sky.

A moan at her feet recalled her to the journalist's presence. She helped him up and guided him back inside to his chair. He sank into it, holding a handkerchief to his bloody nose and muttering words that she judged it better not to hear. Obviously he wasn't badly hurt, and she was about to resume the pursuit when she heard the men's voices, then the crunch of gravel underfoot.

Andrew strode in through the window, pale and furious. He headed for the decanter and poured himself a generous tot, then tossed it straight down.

'I'll have one of those.' Hugh, looking as if he'd collided head-on with a prickly bush, dropped into the nearest chair. He said to no one in particular, 'It's as dark as a black cat in a coalhole. Hopeless.'

Robert was longer in returning, but eventually he came in, straightening his coat and brushing dirt from his shoes. He refused a drink and made straight for the dazed Leach, hunched over his bloodied handkerchief.

'What's going on, Leach? Why did your precious witness flee the moment she got here? What's your scheme?'

Leach muttered through the cloth that he was as baffled as they were.

'Thought she was the genuine article. Promised she had proof. Must've been spooked somehow.' He stared hopefully at the decanter, but when no one responded he struggled to his feet, saying disgustedly, 'What a waste of time. Might've saved myself the trouble. Silly bitch.' He picked up his hat. 'Sorry, Mr Dene. I'll be off and tell the boss it was a wash out.' Sniffing and wiping, he nodded to Nicola and the others and followed Andrew to the door.

Nicola, feeling sick with the pain in her head, struggled to make sense of what had happened. As Andrew returned she said, 'I knew Lizzie when she was a maid in our house. She told me that Rose was on the streets, and I didn't believe her.' She delved in her pocket and brought out the purse that Lizzie had dropped. 'Maybe there's a clue to her behaviour in this.'

'Let me look.' Andrew stretched out his hand, but for some reason that she couldn't name, Nicola held back.

Upending the purse on the desk, she stared at its pathetic contents, searching for an answer. There was a broken-toothed comb choked with hair; a jar of lip rouge, well-worn; some hairpins; the greasy remains of a bun wrapped in newspaper, all fusty from the bottom of the bag. A rusty medal depicting St Patrick and two unused matches completed the list, except for a piece of knotted rag the size of a thimble.

Nicola picked it up. There was something hard inside. She carefully teased the knots apart until the piece of fabric lay open on her palm. At the centre lay a ring composed of a few slivers of turquoise and two seed pearls. A small thing, of little value. But Nicola had last seen it on Rose's hand on the day she had announced her engagement.

For a long moment she simply stared at the ring. Then she started to shake. Her hand trembled so violently that the ring dropped to the floor.

'What is it, Nicola?' Andrew supported her, guiding her into a chair.

Nicola's teeth chattered. At length she forced the words out. 'It's hers. It's Rose's ring. *He* gave it to her.'

'Who gave it? What man?'

'He promised to marry her, then he slowly destroyed her. She died long before the night when he took her life.' She was struck by a sudden thought. 'How did Lizzie get the ring?' Looking up at the three men regarding her with varying degrees of concern, she felt the first touch of disquiet.

It was Robert, in detective mode, who gave her the answer. 'She must have stolen it, either from the body, or from the actual killer who had taken back the ring himself.'

Hugh looked sombre. 'The poor creature's a scarecrow. No man would attempt to buy her favours with jewellery. Yet, clearly the ring is a clue to the killer's identity, or why would she have thought it worth the reward?'

'She must be found,' Andrew said abruptly.

'Of course. It's certain that she knows this man.' Hugh bent over Nicola. 'I'll start the search at once.'

Robert bustled up. 'I'll get men straight on to it, Nicola.'

Nicola shrank back in her chair. Suddenly she was surrounded, hemmed in on all sides. The disquiet tapping at her subconscious now flared into full life. The impact was so awful that she frantically tried to blank it out, but it would not be denied. Panic ripped through her. She had to get out of here. She had to get away.

'Let me up!' She pushed frantically at the two men leaning over her, thrusting them aside as she stooped for the ring, then quickly rose. They stepped back, clearly puzzled by her reaction. But when Nicola turned to face Andrew she had another shock. He knew what was in her mind. The cool grey eyes were ablaze.

'No, Nicola! It's not true. It can't be true.'

She said through dry lips, 'But it is. Why else would Lizzie have been so terrified? She was so afraid that she dropped the one piece of evidence that might have bought her out of her sordid, miserable existence. Lizzie ran because she saw the killer in this room.'

The utter silence following these words was just the calm before a storm. When it came it broke over Nicola like high seas over a rock. She knew she was right, and all the expostulations in the world would not change her. But as the three men closed around her, vehement, horrified and angry, she backed away towards the door, her eyes flashing defiance as they tried to bar her way.

'Nicola. You can't believe this nonsense. You're upset.' White-faced, Robert stretched out his hand, and she backed another step.

Hugh stood, arms akimbo, a half-smile on his face. 'It's ludicrous. You must know me better than that. I'd never harm a woman, let alone drag one down in the way this bastard did.'

It was Andrew who brought back reality, saying coolly, 'She's right, I'm afraid. It's got to be one of us.' He held up a hand against any protest. 'Nicola saw it first because she's so emotionally attuned at this time. But it doesn't take genius to recognize that the woman in the window was shocked out of her mind. She knew Leach, and while she hadn't expected to see Nicola, that would hardly bring on the terror we all witnessed.' His gaze went slowly from face to face as he repeated, 'It was one of us.'

But which?

171

Again there was silence. And while the men gathered their thoughts, Nicola moved. Whirling through the doorway, she raced across the tiled entrance hall, wrenched the front door open and sped down the steps. With wings of fear on her heels, she dived into the shrubbery and headed for the fence adjoining next door's property.

She heard shouts and running footsteps on the gravel, and crouched down behind a large rhododendron shrub, waiting for the pursuit to pass. When she judged that the men were well on the way to the front gate, she gathered up her skirts and climbed over the fence. This garden was more open, and she raced across the lawn, dodging an ornamental fountain that loomed up in the darkness, then into the shelter of a stand of trees. Here in the pitch dark she had to feel her way to the next fence, stumbling over roots, grazing her knees, but picking herself up as soon as she fell, hastening on to the next fence, and the next, scrambling across them without regard for her clothes, scraping her hands and her stockings, until she reached another road.

It took her two hours to reach Viola Terrace, and another half-hour of waiting in the shadows until she saw the watchers leave. They, too were only shadows. But there had been three of them, which reassured her. No single killer had been lying in wait. She hadn't stopped to ask herself why she should be in any danger. She simply felt threatened and, like a hunted animal, she longed to go to ground in her own place, with the rest of the world locked out.

When certain that there was no one watching, she crept to the door and let herself in.

Josh was waiting for her, teapot at the ready. He took one look at her and dropped the teapot. With a sigh, Nicola stretched out her arms to him, and subsided into the broken shards in a dead faint.

CHAPTER TWENTY-EIGHT

NICOLA WAS ENDURING a nightmare.
The road was narrow and rutted. She knew she must not stumble, must hurry, hurry. They were coming, the wolves with their eyes dripping blood, and saliva drooling from their saw-toothed jaws. They ran on huge padded paws that skimmed the ruts, and they saw their way easily in the dark. Oh, the darkness of that moonless night, the enclosing trees, the endless road strewn with stones. Her long skirts wound around her ankles. Her chest hurt. Every breath was a furnace blast, searing lungs and throat. She dared not look behind. They were so close. She could smell their rank odour.

Was that a light ahead? Branches were outlined against a soft glow. Light meant people, safety. But the wolves were so near. The fiery agony burned in her breast. She knew she must hurry. Faster. Faster. Padding steps behind, closer. The smell of rotting carrion between those hideous teeth. Hot panting breath on her neck. The jaws. No! No!

Falling, down, down into darkness and nothingness.

'She's still burning up. Nurse, more wet sheets and a saline draught if she wakes. I want her watched carefully.'

'Yes doctor.'

The dream had changed to a vision. It was Rose. It was really her. But so icy and remote. She was there, and yet she was not ... drifting, unaware of Nicola's hands reaching out to her. Why wouldn't she respond? Was it because of that great wound in her breast? Had she lost her heart? It would have meant so much if she'd recognized Nicola, even just smiled. But no. She simply faded off like an old photographic print, until there was only blankness where she'd stood. Rose! Rose!

'Doctor, I'm worried about the haemorrhaging from the stomach and lungs. The patient is unable to keep down fluids.'

'Do what you can with the fluids, Sister. But I confess I'm more concerned about liver damage. She's very tender in the area and I detect some jaundice in the corneas. I shall consult with Dr. Ferris when he comes in.'

'Yes doctor.'

It was so still. Nicola wondered where she was. Pale beams of light filtered from overhead. High windows, perhaps? She was lying down. At least, she thought she was. Her body felt . . . insubstantial, but her head was there. Too heavy to lift. Thank heaven it had stopped aching. The pain had been a great gong pounding in her skull. Now she could move her eyes. The place looked like a large cave with its roof lost somewhere up in the darkness. Perhaps the light filtered through cracks in rocks – moonlight or starlight. She'd find out later, when she wasn't so tired. She'd rest for a while.

'Praise be, the fever has gone. Nurse, when she wakes we'll give her chicken broth and start to build up her strength. The poor lass is just worn to skin and bone.'

'Yes, Sister. What about the visitors. They've been clamouring for a week to get in and see the patient.'

'No visitors until Dr. Parsons gives permission. He has been worried about her mental condition. She seems to be afraid of something or someone, and I won't be responsible for having her upset. So, nurse, we draw the screens during visiting hours and see that no one approaches this patient.'

'Yes, Sister.'

She knew where she was: in a hospital ward. She lay there, neatly tucked in a narrow bed in a row of narrow beds. They'd all been tidied like drawers in a cabinet. Or like a row of matchboxes positioned exactly so far apart. What would happen if one of the matchboxes got pushed out of place? She was parched. She could drink the harbour dry, if only it was made of lemonade. Her body had come back. It felt like a heavy lump of clay that wouldn't move. But she could move her head, even raise it to see down the end of the room.

How had she got here? She must have been ill, but couldn't remember. She felt as though time had passed her by and she'd somehow been abandoned amongst the matchboxes. Why? Surely someone would come soon to answer her questions. She was so tired, so very tired.

'Well, young lady, you're back with us at last. I'm Doctor Parsons and I've been treating you.'

Nicola stared up at the round face with its pouched cheeks and fluffy sideburns and thought that he resembled a benevolent owl. He wore an old-fashioned frock-coat that stuck out at the back and a rumpled cravat above a waistcoat bearing evidence of his latest meal. But he raised her wrist with gentle fingers as he asked how she felt.

'I'm not quite sure,' she replied. 'My muscles won't obey me. I can barely lift a hand.'

'That's normal enough. Your body has been so busy fighting off the fever that it has exhausted itself.'

'Have I had a fever? I seem to recall terrible dreams.' She shifted her gaze to the starch-fronted sister at the other side of the bed. 'You were there, sometimes. You were trying to calm me.'

The woman smiled. 'You've been extremely ill, my dear, but now, thanks to our excellent doctors and nurses, you are on the road to recovery.'

'Thank you. Please thank them all.' She still felt too languid for conversation, but she needed to know what had happened to her. She looked questioningly at the doctor. 'Please tell me how I came to be in the hospital.'

His expression was grave. 'I'm sorry to say that you have fallen victim to one of our fair city's scourges. Can you remember having recently been bitten by a rat, say within the past three or four weeks?'

It all came flooding back, the fire, the terror of being trapped, and the rats' suicidal rush to destruction over the edge of the loft.

'Yes,' she whispered. 'They were running, dozens of them, trying to escape the flames. One ran up my leg and I pulled it off. And it bit me.'

The doctor nodded. 'It left you a legacy of parasitic infection, which attacked your liver and brought on a febrile condition of some severity. However, happily, you are now convalescent and, if you obey Sister, you'll soon be on your feet again.' He turned away to give instructions in an undertone, while Nicola thought over his information.

Judging by her lack of control over her body, she would take time to recover. This worried her. She knew there was something she must do, but couldn't remember it. Oddments of information came to mind, but nothing she could grasp and pin down. She had a sense of urgency, which had to do with the frightening dreams. Perhaps, if she could remember them. . . ?

She raised her voice a little. 'Sister, do you know anything about my bad dreams? Did I call out anything you can remember?'

The nurse replied brightly, 'Oh, you don't want to remember all that. It's best to look forward and think of happy things, don't you think?'

'No. I must remember. There's something I have to do.' She heard the rising agitation in her voice.

Doctor Parsons's bushy brows met like caterpillars in conversation above the bridge of his nose. He studied Nicola and evidently came to a conclusion. 'I think, Sister, we should humour our patient, if we can.'

'If you say so, Doctor,' she answered stiffly. Then, to Nicola, 'You did call upon someone named Rose, several times. At other times it was obvious that something or someone you feared was chasing you. You kept saying "one of three" or "one of the three". That's as much as I can recall.'

'"One of the three". Oh, my God, now I remember! It's one of *them*. One of them killed Rose. I've got to get out of here!' Making a supreme effort, Nicola managed to raise head and shoulders before falling back again, the sweat popping out on her forehead.

Both doctor and nurse rushed to restrain her, exclaiming. Sister's eyes held an accusatory gleam, and Doctor Parsons said ruefully, 'Perhaps that wasn't a good idea.'

'Help me up! Help me to get away. They mustn't find me here. Don't you understand? One of them is the murderer.' Nicola, imprisoned in her helpless body, grew increasingly hysterical.

Doctor Parsons sent for laudanum and administered a dose, and gradually she began to quieten. Tears of frustration overflowed to trickle down into her hair while the sister tried to comfort her and the doctor left, shaking his head. Nicola felt vaguely that she'd somehow let him down, that her path of steady convalescence had suffered a setback.

Even as the opium wreathed about her brain she clung to her knowledge. She remembered the fateful meeting in Andrew's book room and the revelation that one of the men in her life, the men she'd trusted and liked and who professed to love her, was a cold-hearted killer. It couldn't be Andrew. Of course not. She felt close to despair.

At her urgent request all visitors continued to be refused admission and the screens were kept around her bed during visiting hours. She knew the other patients whispered about her and speculated on her demand for privacy at those times, but she needed security.

Andrew, Hugh and Robert were all determined men, accustomed to getting what they wanted. They'd seek her out, and would not scruple to use underhand methods to get into the wards. And at the moment she couldn't withstand them. Anxious to prove their individual innocence, they'd try to bully her, in a kindly way, and it would all be too much for her at present.

Although the new wing of Sydney hospital was luxurious by comparison with the old, and the staff could not have been kinder, she longed to get out and discover what had been happening while she was incapacitated. It infuriated her, having to lie there fuming over her weakness, knowing that only time could cure it.

She did, however, relax her rule of 'no visitors' on the day when a young nurse pleaded Josh's case. She was glad she'd relented when she saw him bound through the screen with a bunch of flowers in his hand, hair slicked down and clothes so neat that she barely recognized him.

'Josh, you look the complete gentleman.' She held out her arms, and he rushed into them, although first checking for observers.

The bedraggled daisies were crushed to Nicola's bosom.

'Holy H . . . I mean, gosh, Nicola, you gave me a terrible fright, swooning into the broken crockery like that.'

Nicola picked the daisies off her and thrust them into a water jug beside the bed. 'Is it any use saying *sorry*? I didn't mean to do it, you know.'

A grin split his freckled face. 'Well, you don't need any more bruises, for sure. And I've got another teapot, a tin one. Are you better now, Nicola? What happened?'

'It was a rat bite. I remember having a tussle with one during the fire. And, yes, I'm a lot better. I should be able to leave here at the end of the week. Josh, did you tell anyone where I am?'

He said anxiously, 'Didn't you want people to know? I'm sorry, but I told everyone who asked me. They're not happy at being kept out, Nicola. In fact, there've been some pretty good rows in the matron's office. Why won't you let visitors come?'

She returned a light answer. Josh would be better left in ignorance for as long as possible. He liked all three men. He'd be devastated that she could even include Andrew, his hero, among the suspects. But she had to. No one could know the full workings of another's mind, and she could not eliminate any one of the three. No matter that the cost to her was unthinkable. This was for Rose, who had no one else.

The most important thing was to find Lizzie and extract whatever information she had on Rose's killer before he tried to silence her. He would be out there searching. She hoped poor frightened Lizzie had a safe burrow to hide in.

Each day Nicola grew stronger, and soon she could get out of bed and practise walking. A few days later she had another visitor, this time one who could not be refused admittance on any grounds.

A deferential sister wheeled Eleanor's Bath chair in beside the bed. She looked reproachfully at Nicola.

'I thought I was your friend, Nicola.'

'You are. You're my dearest friend.' Nicola sought for words. 'I had good reasons for staying away. Oh, Eleanor, you must be in agony. I know every movement cuts you like a knife. You shouldn't have come.'

Eleanor clasped thin gloved hands in her lap and looked as though the word pain had no meaning for her. 'How could I not? The first time I came you were too ill for a visitor, so I waited until you were convalescent.'

She paused, then said carefully, 'Andrew has told me what happened at your meeting.'

'Did he tell you what conclusion we have drawn?'

A look of sorrow crossed Eleanor's face. 'It's barely credible. Needless to say, I refuse to believe that my son could ever be responsible for the deliberate degradation and murder of a young girl! Surely you can't think so, Nicola.'

'I don't know what I think. But I'm afraid, Eleanor. Because it has to be one of those men whom I've admired and looked to for support.'

'Not Andrew.'

'I don't – He's your son. You have to believe in him.'

Eleanor said heavily, 'But you don't.'

'I daren't.'

Eleanor remained silent. Beyond the screens muffled voices filled the air with a vigorous humming; but in Nicola's little enclosure it was like the eye of a storm, waiting for the worst to come. She couldn't bear to face the woman who was so precious to her, knowing how much she'd hurt her.

At length, Eleanor said, 'I cannot believe it. Your intuition should tell you that my son is innocent. But I realize that only time will reveal the truth. How can I help you, Nicola? You say you are afraid, but of what? Of physical attack?'

'No. I'm afraid for Lizzie. She's the one who can bring down the killer. I've got to find her first. But there's great danger of my leading him to his prey.'

'I see. Of course you realize that if you do find this woman, and the killer thinks she has already passed on her knowledge to you, then you, too, will be at terrible risk.'

Nicola shivered. 'I'll just have to be careful. You can't help me, dear Eleanor. Nor can I come to your house any more. I think Andrew and the others will try to stop me if they know what I'm doing, two of them with the most benevolent of motives. I ask you not to tell anyone. Please, Eleanor?'

'I won't betray you. I can only pray for you and for the success of your quest. Then one day you will realize that you have nothing to fear from my son.' Eleanor leaned forward painfully to offer her hand.

Nicola gently took the crippled fingers between hers and kissed her friend's cheek.

'I'm so sorry, Eleanor.'

Eleanor picked up a small silver bell in her lap and rang it, and Sister appeared like a starched genie between the folds of the screens. All but genuflecting to the stately doyenne of Australian nursing, she wheeled her out of the ward.

Thoroughly miserable, Nicola hunched down in her bedclothes and tried to forget the last quarter-hour.

Two days later she was discharged and, in accordance with her plan with Josh, was met by him at the back of the hospital with a hired buggy containing two packed bags of books and clothing. They drove through the Domain, down the hill to Woolloomooloo and plunged into the back streets leading to Sydney's underworld.

They established themselves in a one-room tumbledown shanty reminiscent of the Basevi house in Upper Kent Street. Here the earth closet had not yet been dreamed of, and tenants emptied their chamber pots into a cesspool adjacent to the back fence. The lanes were so foul that Nicola wore only her heaviest boots and turned up the hems of her garments well clear of the ground.

She'd purchased plenty of disinfectant powder, and the first thing Josh did was to scrub down walls and floors and dust these liberally to discourage the livestock. They kept no food in the house, and slept with the legs of their beds stuck in jam tins filled with kerosene. Their only pretensions to comfort were an oil lamp and table and chairs for reading and study purposes.

Nicola at last told Josh what had happened that night at the Dene home, and the conclusion she'd drawn.

As she'd feared, Josh was agonized. 'It can't be true! Are you sure, Nicola? It couldn't be Andrew.'

'I just don't know. But there's no other explanation for Lizzie's flight. I was there. I saw her face. She was literally in terror for her life. Which is why I must find her, before *he* does.'

Josh said, impetuously. 'It's got to be that Hugh Owen.'

'Oh, Josh. You say that because you're fond of Andrew and his mother, and because Robert Carrington has helped you out of trouble. You know very little about Hugh.' She sighed. 'I'm beginning to wonder how much I know about any of them.'

They talked until late in the night, discussing ways of searching for Lizzie Perkins without alerting the killer. Josh elected to go amongst his old street cronies and discover what he could, while Nicola decided upon a visit to Rose Scott, whose wide knowledge of so-called fallen women might be useful.

Obviously, to find one particular prostitute amongst the thousands plying in Sydney it would be necessary to go where they congregated. Nicola doubted whether Lizzie had the money to flee the city. Her only hope was to bury herself in one of its warrens and try to escape notice; and it was there that they must dig to find her.

When they'd exhausted all possibilities Josh rose, white-faced and determined. 'We're going to get him, Nicola. No matter what we've got to do, we'll see him hanged for what he did to Rose.'

'Yes.' Nicola fought back a surge of emotion. 'No matter what we have to do. This is for Rose, and for all the other women like her.'

CHAPTER TWENTY-NINE

'LIZZIE PERKINS? No, don't know 'er.' The young woman with the old eyes leaned her elbows on the bar and shouted into Nicola's ear above the noise in the saloon.

A dozen battered iron tables were packed about with the usual Saturday night crowd, men and women eager to shrug off the grinding week by drinking and merrymaking, and driving themselves into a forgetful stupor. Nicola couldn't blame them, but the racket they made worked on her nerves. Her errand was so serious that she could think of nothing else.

The cap, coat and pants she wore as a male disguise, already past their prime, had become impregnated with smoke, sweat and the odd beer stain, since she'd hardly been out of them for the past fortnight. Her eyes ached from the glaring gaslight and smoke-filled atmosphere of stuffy rooms packed with people, and she was tired. The taverns and bars had begun to merge in her mind, a composite of sights and sounds and smells that had ground themselves into her soul. For she'd seen the misery that went along with the merrymaking, seen the pitiful grasping for something more than a life of drudgery or shame.

The women, in particular, wrung her heart – their smiles stretching lined, unhealthy skin, the painted, laughing mouths wryly twisted at the corners, the eyes so bright with alcohol, holding a depth of experience that saddened Nicola. She turned her back to the scene, leaned towards the barmaid and raised her voice.

'I was told this was a resting place off the street, and I know Lizzie is partial to gin.'

The barmaid laughed. 'Do you know how many grog shops there are like this in Sydney? Your Lizzie might take her tipple in any one of hundreds, from the waterfront to Redfern railway. Why, there's twenty-six pubs in King Street alone.'

'I know it. I've been into them all, and more, in the past few weeks.'

An elbow hit Nicola in the ribs, almost displacing her from the bar. Voices called for Sal to get a move on and serve, and the woman leaned closer, displaying a full bosom straining the buttons of her blouse.

'If your friend's on the game, why don't you try some of the fancy houses? They've got rooms upstairs in passages like warrens, leading into more houses. A person could stay hid there for a twelvemonth.'

'I've an idea that such places would be a bit too up-market for Lizzie.' Nicola sighed. 'It seems I've tried everywhere, but no one's even heard her name.' She looked about her anxiously, driven by the sense of time rushing by and each passing day a lost opportunity. Lizzie could stay hidden for just so long, before the monster seeking her would dig her out. He probably had all the right connections, which Nicola and Josh lacked.

A male voice rose above the hubbub. 'Stir yer stumps, Sal, or I'll come back of the bar and light a fire under yer arse.'

Sal reluctantly straightened. Perhaps Nicola's weariness and disappointment evoked some sympathy, because Sal winked and held up an admonitory finger before turning away. In a screech that shook the glassware she replied, 'You try it, Ted Tyson, and I'll peg yer crown jewels out on the clothes-line.' Under cover of the responsive laughter she said to Nicola, 'I can't talk now, but if you'll wait 'til I knock off I'll meet you at the back door. There might be something I can do.'

Nicola smiled tiredly. 'You're very kind. I wonder . . . is there somewhere I might wait, away from the saloon?'

Sal jerked a thumb behind her. 'Down the passage there's an office. Wait there.'

Deftly sidestepping a pretty ankle stretched out to trip her, and taking care to avoid eye contact with anyone, Nicola threaded her way between the tables and hurried down the passage indicated by Sal. The dingy office was a refuge from the bedlam of bar and street. Nicola lit the gas and sank thankfully into the chair at the desk. She propped up her feet on a pile of newspapers, removed her plain glass spectacles and pocketed them carefully, then she waited.

Her experience had recently been considerably widened. She now knew the differences between the tenants of the twelve-pound-per-day luxury apartments in Elizabeth Street and the footpath strollers offering themselves for a shilling in a dark alley – as well as all the levels between the two. She hadn't wasted her time on the notorious 'saddling paddocks' of the various theatres. Lizzie would never have got through the door. But neither did she think that Lizzie would be plying her trade in the open street where she could be recognized by the killer. No, Lizzie would be found, if ever she were found, in some dark den where faces were unimportant and business was transacted with maximum speed.

Sal, when eventually released from the bar, listened as Nicola described her efforts of the past week, then shook her head. 'Your Lizzie's more likely to be down some place like the Rocks. Still, I wouldn't go there, if I was you.'

'I might have to.'

'Hmm. There's one other way, if you'll take it.'

'Anything. Tell me.'

'There's a sort of clinic where the prossies go when they've broken a leg, or even just when they're sick. You could ask there if anyone knows your friend.'

'Thank you, Sal. I'll go tomorrow.' Nicola made a note of the address. 'Er, do the women often break their legs?' It seemed a curious sort of danger to find attached to their profession.

Sal smiled grimly. 'You really are green, aren't you? It means a baby on the way. Now, watch yourself. It's not the best address in town.'

Nicola held out her hand, and after a moment of hesitation, the barmaid took it in her own red, chapped fingers.

'Thank you for trying to help, Sal.'

Sal flushed. 'The likes of you shouldn't be in a place like this.'

'Nor should you. How many hours have you worked today – sixteen, eighteen? On your feet the whole time, at everyone's beck, taking the rudeness and the odd knock. Whatever you're paid, it's not enough.'

Sal laughed, although her mouth twisted in irony. 'You're right

184

there. But it's a living, and I'd rather make it on my feet than on my back. No broken legs for me, or a slow death from the pox.' She stretched and yawned, showing gapped yellow teeth. 'I'm for bed. Come on. I'll lock up when you've gone.'

Back in the street, Nicola headed for the slum room which could hardly be called a home, and reported to a cold-ridden Josh on her lack of success. While he coughed and protested, she renewed the mustard poultice on his chest and made him inhale eucalyptus steam. Tucking him up in his blankets, she promised to let him accompany her if she decided to penetrate the dangerous Rocks area in her search. She didn't mention the clinic.

Finding the address proved difficult, and once admitted to the dingy slum block she found her errand to be next to useless. Records were sketchy and too many women resembled the description Nicola gave.

The doctor in charge, while possibly quite altruistic at heart, displayed little empathy with his patients. He lectured Nicola on the subject of 'diseased magnetism of the nerves', which the harlot might impart to men, along with venereal disorders; he then enlarged on the danger of mental degradation, not to the woman, but to her partners. Nicola bit her tongue and instead sought cooperation from some of his patients.

The shabby room where they waited was cold and stuffy and lined with two battered wooden benches, all fully occupied. They seemed a surprisingly cheerful crowd, swapping gossip and local news or enquiring after family members, just like housewives going to market. Here were women like Sal, often coarse-grained, but with a strong survival instinct and a sense of sisterhood that appealed to Nicola. But the moment they noticed her, conversation ceased. A wave of hostility laced with cynicism hit her.

Nicola swept off her cap and spectacles, and let her hair fall down.

'Good evening, ladies,' she greeted them nervously.

'Ghost! What's this crawled out from under a rock!'

'What you got in them trousers, love? A half a walnut shell?'

Nicola hurriedly explained that she was neither seeking a sexual partner nor was she on a voyeuristic expedition, but was the friend of a murdered prostitute. This brought her instant attention.

The women gathered around, listening to her tell of the quest for the one person who could name the killer.

Offers of help came from all sides. Two women in particular admitted to knowing Lizzie, although she seemed to have disappeared lately from her usual haunts. Heartened by even this tenuous link to her quarry, Nicola invited the two, along with anyone else who cared to come, to take a cup of tea with her.

Relaxed in familiar surroundings, they gladly exchanged information and ideas that might help Nicola, and incidentally gave her a further insight into their lifestyle.

She discovered how varied were the types of 'fallen Angelicas' commonly clumped together in prim minds as social pariahs. She discovered their mordant humour, and the fact that they sometimes supplemented their income with lawless activities, like the pickpocket who worked the buses with a false hand on her knee while a real one emptied someone's wallet.

Lydia, one of the two women claiming friendship with Lizzie, proudly displayed her Russian blouse with its inbuilt pouch for lifting goods from shops, and a glove with a pocket in the palm for smaller items.

Shocked and amused, Nicola was grateful for the group's easy acceptance of her, and was touched by their real desire to help. An instance of this was the offer to spread the word carefully that Lizzie was sought by two very different hunters. Methods of contact were arranged, and Nicola went home in a far more optimistic frame of mind.

She carried with her a strong warning from Lydia about the dangers of the world she now frequented, not least of which were the informers. The killer was a denizen of the under class, with a network of spies who would be on the watch for Nicola. She should keep moving, not settle in any one spot, Lydia warned, and be wary of betrayal. Money and favour could buy loyalty, even to a murderer – perhaps more particularly to the powerful predator in question.

Nicola took the warning to heart. She knew she had, in fact, three hunters on her trail, all authoritative, determined men with great organizational ability, and she feared she might be found before accomplishing her task.

*

A few nights later, she rendezvoused with Lydia and her friend Josie, who had known Rose when she was on the streets. Josie, sparrow thin, with bleached hair let down to her waist in pathetic imitation of youth, seemed nervous, and needed some prodding by her friend. Eventually she admitted to having seen Rose coming from a house of assignation, bruised and battered from an encounter. When pressed, Rose had admitted that her lover had beaten her and left her half-fainting. She had only just recovered sufficiently to move.

Bile rose in Nicola's throat but she swallowed it to question Josie about the man. No, Josie didn't know his name, had never seen him, although his reputation in her circle was wide. No, no one seemed to be able to describe him. It was thought that he wore a wig and a beard as disguise, that he led another life in a different stratum of society. He was powerful and feared, even by the most hardened and brutal criminals.

Could he be a member of the police force? Some people thought it likely. He seemed to know a lot about the wrong side of the law. Or could he be a man of means playing out his more vicious instincts in a world where he could get away with it? It was possible. Might he be a well-known leader amongst the workers? He might. No one knew. It was safer not to speculate. And now she must go, or her man would tan her hide for wasting working time.

Nicola thanked both women and pressed a coin on Josie to spare her a beating. Her thoughts were bitter. What a world she'd entered, full of sharks and victims. On impulse, she leaned over and kissed Josie's sunken cheek, and looked up to see Robert Carrington standing on the opposite pavement. With a squeak, Josie disappeared into a doorway. Lydia, following Nicola's gaze, gave the detective a saucy smile and swing of the hips before sauntering off. Nicola simply took to her heels.

The following day, just on sunrise, she and Josh moved from their tumbledown premises, piling their few bits of furniture on to a cart and stealing away to a filthy room two miles across the city. Once settled in they reviewed what information they had.

Nicola ticked off points on her fingers: 'Number one. This man is known in criminal circles, although his identity is a well-kept secret. Number two. It's believed that he leads another, separate life altogether and steps between each one whenever he chooses to do so. Number three. He knows the law, can pass for a gentleman, and he has contacts in every stratum of society. Which adds up to a man who is powerful and feared.'

Josh looked at her hopefully, and she continued.

'I've been thinking about his disguise. Hair and beard are easy enough. What of his stature, his walk, his voice? These things are not easy to change. I know!'

'He's practised, that's all. Different boots, or a pebble in one foot. And he could whisper a lot. He could change the way he talks.'

'That's hard to maintain for long periods. If I were he, I'd adopt an accent of some kind, especially if he's familiar with another language. Robert Carrington had an English gentleman's education. He'd speak French. I don't know about the other two. It does seem unlikely.'

Josh fidgeted. 'This isn't getting us anywhere. It could still be any one of them.'

'Oh, I believe we're getting closer each day. We're bound to make a connection sooner or later. But I wish we were nearer to Lizzie. She's managed to bury herself really deep.' Nicola was thoughtful. 'Josh, I think we're going to have to brave the larrikins and go down to the Rocks.'

He grimaced. 'It's the gangs you've got to watch, though they're cowards out on their own. The girls are as bad as the blokes, you know. I've seen them pull a fellow down like a pack of wolves.'

'Are you trying to frighten me, Josh?'

'Yes. You don't know what you're taking on. The police won't even go down there alone.'

'Hmmm. I suppose I could hire a guard to go with us. I'd better give this more thought.'

Josh got up and stretched. Then he started. 'Gosh, Nicola, I forgot to give you this. Someone pushed it under the door late last night when we were asleep.' He drew a crumpled bit of paper from his pocket and handed it to her.

The note, scrawled in badly formed letters, said: 'Before you do anything else, lissen to what Big Ruby says. She wants to see you, and if you know what's good for you, you'll go. She's got her ear to the ground, that one, and more eyes than a centapeed's got legs, and what she doesn't know about this city isn't worth the knowing. She runs a high-toned house in Darlinghurst. Anyone can point it out to you.'

It was signed by Lydia, and with an addendum: 'Don't cross Big Ruby.'

Nicola didn't hesitate. 'Let's go, Josh.'

CHAPTER THIRTY

BIG RUBY'S ESTABLISHMENT turned out to be a narrow-fronted building down behind the city's main gaol. Its inconspicuous entrance led into a palatial set of rooms lit by dozens of flaring gas jets. Crimson and gilt abounded, enhanced by the stiff, elaborate gowns and coiffures of the women displaying themselves on the many sofas and chaises-longues placed at strategic intervals. Mirrored walls reflected a blindingly harsh light on faces masked in paint and powder. They looked like dolls, thought Nicola, animated Olympias ready to be wound up by clockwork and set in motion.

Standing in the doorway between two iron-faced henchmen, she felt a few qualms. This house was far too sophisticated for Lizzie to be known here. It was a planet's distance from the back alleys and cellar dens that were her lot.

An enormous blimp of a woman encased in black appeared at the head of the stairs and began a majestic progress downwards, assisted by two children, one under each arm. Nicola saw with some surprise that they were painted to resemble Africans and wore pages' costumes, complete down to the snowy wigs and buckled shoes. Even at a distance, the woman's black eyes bored like gimlets out of a doughy face. Nicola had no doubt that she was in the presence of Big Ruby herself.

Arriving eventually at the bottom of the stairs, the woman dismissed her panting attendants and inspected Nicola as if she were a doubtful purchase. Then, nodding to the henchmen crowding Josh, she said, 'Keep him here.' To Nicola she was equally economical with words. 'Follow me.'

She sailed away in a trail of black crêpe, through a doorway and down a passage to a workmanlike office. She closed the door behind Nicola and carried out a further penetrating inspection. Despite her coat and trousers, Nicola felt as naked as a slave on an auction block.

'I hear you're in the market for some lost property.' The voice was pleasant and low-toned, in total contrast with those eyes. 'I might be able to help you.'

Nicola reminded herself that she was not a schoolgirl in trouble with a headmistress, although anyone less like the proper Miss Jephson could hardly be imagined. She said politely, 'That would be very kind. What would you want from me in payment?'

The woman chortled and lowered her bulk into a huge chair obviously designed to support her weight. 'You're no fool, dearie. Yes, normally I'd want a substantial payment for my services. But in this case, my reward would be the removal of a beast who fouls my pond.' She nodded. 'I want to know the identity of this murdering scoundrel. He's giving the business a bad name, scaring the girls.

'It was all right while he preyed on silly innocents and those who won't be missed; but lately he's taken to poaching his game from my preserves. Some of them are useless when he's finished with them. I won't have it. It's costing me. He's got to be stopped.'

Nicola kept her reactions to herself. 'What do you want me to do?' she asked.

Big Ruby frowned. 'Use your head, dearie. I want you to find this Lizzie, and when you get the name from her, I want you to give it to me. I've got the contacts. I'll do the necessary.'

The sudden malevolence in her tone made Nicola shiver.

She said, 'I haven't been able to find Lizzie. You said you could help me.'

'You'll get nowhere on your own. However, with my connections it might be possible. She'll have sewn up her lips, and I need you to undo them – to get the name out of her before it's too late and he stops her mouth for ever. If I can find her, he can. It only takes a whisper in the right quarter. It might already be too late. Did you know your place is being watched at this moment?'

Startled, Nicola said, 'My home at Viola Terrace?'

Big Ruby shook her head. 'The place you moved to last night. Someone's on to you, dearie, and you might not want to meet him.'

She heaved her bulk out of the chair. 'Don't look so shocked. It had to happen some time. Now, I've got a proposition for you. You and the lad can stay here, hidden in the back, while I put out the word for this Lizzie. Oh, no need to colour up, my girl. You won't be meeting any of the clients in the front of the house. And they wouldn't give you a second look in that garb.'

Nicola forced a laugh. 'It's good of you, Mrs . . . Miss. . . ?'

'Big Ruby will do. You know quite well I'm doing this for myself. But I like a girl with some gumption. I don't want to see you fall victim to this hellhound. And he'll get you as sure as daylight if you go back to your room.'

Nicola looked at Big Ruby appraisingly and decided to accept the offer, with reservations, and understanding perfectly that Big Ruby would help just as long as it suited her.

Josh, who hadn't liked his treatment by the bullying guards downstairs, wanted to leave. Nicola hushed his protests, bundling him upstairs to the attics before his outspokenness got him into trouble. She explained her bargain with Big Ruby.

'I don't like the place any more than you do, but this is a good opportunity for us. Big Ruby has the means to find Lizzie. And if what she says is true, we daren't go back to our room again.' She thought about walking through the dark doorway into the waiting arms of the strangler with a knife, and swallowed.

'Well, I still don't like it,' grumbled Josh.

Josh and Nicola had been given a tiny room overlooking a court-yard strewn with rubbish and visited by whole families of cats. A maid brought them food and nightwear, and Nicola, conscious of the guards on each stairway, went to bed trying to stifle her misgivings. It seemed they'd exchanged their freedom of movement for a more than dubious protection and a promise that might not be fulfilled. Josh, still highly suspicious, lay on top of the coverlet fully dressed, his cudgel handy beside him.

A knock on her door shortly before dawn awakened Nicola. She sat up as one of Big Ruby's girls put a tousled head around the jamb, then entered cautiously.

Clutching her wrapper around her, she whispered, 'I've got a message for you. It's from Josie. She got someone to slip it to me, but you mustn't let on. If you want to leave, the back gate's unlocked and the guard's out to it.' She gave Nicola a folded note and glided to the door, where she paused. 'You know Big Ruby's got your clothes.'

'What!' Nicola looked at the door, which she distinctly remembered locking.

The girl shrugged. 'I'll bring you some of mine, if you like. But be very quiet.' She slipped away like a wraith.

Nicola unfolded the note and read: *Annie Jones can help you. She clears the slops at the Jolly Waterman off Cumberland Lane.* Josie had not signed it. Blessing the little tart's good heart, which had overcome her timidity, Nicola hurriedly and quietly wakened Josh, who had slept through the episode.

'We've got to try it, Josh. It'll be daylight soon, so we should be safe enough.'

Muttering that the 'Push' would all be sleeping off their night's rampages, Josh turned his back while Nicola scrambled into the kind of dress she'd never imagined herself wearing, then accompanied her on tiptoe down the backstairs to pick a path through the jumbled mess in the courtyard.

No one tried to stop them. The watchman guarding an iron gate into the alley snored peacefully, a quart pot overturned beside him. More of Josie's good work, Nicola supposed. On reaching the main street they hired a cab with the money fortunately still in Josh's pocket, paying an exorbitant fee to be taken into the fastnesses of the Rocks.

They drove past the docks with the sun rising over a sparkling harbour and a refreshing breeze snapping the flags on the rows of ships moored for loading. Nicola could hardly believe they were about to enter the most notorious slum in the city.

Placed in such a beautiful position on a rocky promontory surrounded by water, the area was a leprous blight. The collection of brick and rubble-stone hovels tumbled downhill from the crest, joined by steep and narrow passages that acted as drains and sewers. Filthy water accumulated against the walls of the houses, some of which abutted rock walls with various spouts and drains and privies discharging over them. So steep was the fall that the eaves of some cottages were level with the foundations of the ones above.

Paying off the cabbie, Nicola reluctantly eyed the glutinous track weaving up to Cumberland Lane. Then, with Josh treading on her heels, she started the climb, watched by slovenly, dull-eyed women leaning in their doorways. A pack of mongrel dogs ran at them with bared teeth but were soon routed by Josh's cudgel. Stepping over evidence of goats and other roaming beasts, with her skirts held high, Nicola was not surprised that this place had become the breeding-ground for the city's criminals.

Cumberland Lane was as damp and dark as a well, with the light cut out by rows of tenements sprung up like mushrooms in the unhealthy soil. Its atmosphere of decay and despair enveloped them like a fog. The inn sign swinging above the entrance was almost indecipherable, and the Jolly Waterman itself turned out to be a collection of foul rooms joined by a rickety outside staircase.

Nicola felt like holding her nose as she pushed aside the splintered door and entered the taproom. When no one answered her call, Josh pushed through another doorway and immediately backed out again, followed by an enormously fat man only half-clothed in undershirt and trousers, rubbing his face sleepily.

'What you want, eh?' His eyes crawled all over Nicola, making her shudder and wish for a heavier dress with a higher neckline.

'I'm looking for Annie Jones. Is she here?'

He scrubbed his unshaven chin. 'Lazy bitch. She don' come up yet.' Gazing around the dirty room at the slop-stained bar, the floor thick with mud, tobacco juice and other unnameable substances, he seemed surprised.

Maybe he thought a good fairy would wave a wand and turn the pigsty into something resembling a fit habitation, thought Nicola. She said, 'Tell me where she sleeps and I'll get her up for you.'

The man yawned grossly then stepped closer, leering. Josh leapt in front of Nicola, his cudgel raised.

'Ho. The bantam cock tries his spurs.' The man's expression changed to amusement. He pointed to the floor. 'Down there. In the coal hole.' Suddenly losing interest, he turned and disappeared through the doorway behind.

Nicola looked at Josh. 'In the coal hole?'

He shrugged. 'It couldn't be any dirtier than this place.' He led the way outside to a flight of steps going down the outside of the building. Nicola negotiated the slimy surfaces with care, stopping at the bottom before a recessed doorway.

'This seems like it.' Josh gave the door a tentative push and it moved on rusty hinges.

Standing ankle deep in mud and drainage, Nicola found she was reluctant to go in. It could just have been the atmosphere of this horrible place, or even simply the idea of entering a window-less, lightless cave. She had to force herself to move.

'Stay outside will you, Josh, and don't let anyone in, or try to shut the door on us.' The bare thought was enough to give her goose bumps. Taking a deep breath she pushed the door right back, calling 'Annie. Annie Jones,' and stepped inside.

She waited, letting her sight adjust, hoping for an answer, even for a snore. But there was no sound. Nor was there much light; but she could smell the coal, and something else that she couldn't quite name. Her nostrils wrinkled at the coppery taint. She called Annie's name again. She could hear her own quickened breathing. Why couldn't she hear Annie's, if she were here? Something whitish on the floor caught her eye and she moved forward and bent to touch a stockinged leg. She froze.

'Annie?' The word strangled in her throat.

Josh called anxiously, 'What is it, Nicola?'

She couldn't answer. Still doubled over, she felt for the other leg, lying crooked under a heap of ragged petticoat. Both legs were cool, but not rigidly cold. Suddenly she couldn't bear the uncertainty any longer. Going on her knees she felt for where the girl's shoulders would be, lifted and dragged her sideways into the light from the doorway.

Annie wasn't ever going to be warm again. She gazed fixedly at the roof of the coal hole and her head dangled impossibly. Where her throat should have been a great hole gaped, with the white of bone and cartilage showing through. She lay in her own blood, her hair clotted and drowned in it, her chemise and petticoats wine dark and glistening.

Nicola looked blankly at her cuffs, rapidly absorbing the red stain.

'Christ!' Joshua dropped his cudgel and fell against the doorjamb. 'Somebody got to her. Somebody knew she could tell us where to find Lizzie.'

Nicola said through wooden lips. 'We're too late, Josh. This is Lizzie.'

CHAPTER THIRTY-ONE

Nicola didn't know how long she knelt beside Lizzie's body. Her mind had stopped working, waiting for shock to subside.

It was Josh who broke the tomblike silence in the coalhole. 'Come on, Nicola. We've got to get out of here.'

She stared at him.

'Nicola!' He dropped his cudgel and, stepping gingerly around Lizzie's body, pulled Nicola to her feet. He tore off his shirt tail and scrubbed at her hands until the bloodstain lightened to an unhealthy pink. 'Let's go, please, Nicola.'

She looked down at the remains of a once vital young woman and bent to close the staring eyes. Not long ago Lizzie had been happy polishing Nicola's grand piano and dreaming, like any other girl, of a future husband and a home and children. The wreckage at her feet was all that was left of that girl, destroyed by life long before it had been taken from her. Nicola could have wept for pity. Instead, she clamped down on emotion and tried to think.

'Josh, she's barely cold. Her killer was only just ahead of us.'

Josh glanced nervously over his shoulder. 'He'll be long gone. He wouldn't hang around after this.'

'We were so close. How did he find Lizzie? Did someone betray her? If only we'd known where to come just one day earlier.' And what about Josie, the obvious author of the note? Was she, too, in danger? This killer had the hundred eyes of an Argus. Nothing escaped him.

With gentle hands she straightened Lizzie's limbs. Then, at last obeying Josh's urgent tugging, she went with him out into the passage, feeling as though she abandoned the girl, knowing there was nothing more to be done for her. She'd be sought soon enough when her services were wanted in the tavern, and her body would be given a pauper's burial. But her memory would live on in Nicola's mind.

Filled with immense sadness she plodded up the steps. At the top she let Josh lead her swiftly along Cumberland Lane and downhill through the maze of alleys to the shore. There she stopped to catch her breath.

The early morning bustle of loading, the cry of the gulls wheeling and diving, the sight of fishermen sorting their catch, slippery silver in the pale sunlight, were breathtaking in their normality. Nicola turned her face to the breeze and took in great breaths of salty air. She didn't know where to go from here. She needed time to think.

'Josh, I don't think our place is safe. Let's find the pieman and take our breakfast down into the botanical gardens.'

Josh agreed with alacrity. Soon they were walking along the sea wall to Nicola's favourite spot, the point known as Mrs Macquarie's Chair. It was deserted at this hour, except for a fisherman down on the rocks below. There the two sat under a Moreton Bay fig tree while Josh munched both pies and Nicola decided to eat later. Her stomach had definitely rejected the idea of food. She did share Josh's bottle of ginger beer, purchased along with the pies.

Faces turned to the sun, eyes following the soothing passage of small boats and ferries criss-crossing the harbour, by unspoken agreement they avoided anything to do with death and disaster. In fact, they didn't speak at all. Instead, being emotionally exhausted, and knowing she was guarded, Nicola fell asleep on the grass. If she dreamed, she didn't remember it when she awoke. What she did have in her mind was a fully developed plan.

While Josh climbed down on to the rocks to see if the fisherman would part with some of his catch, Nicola took a mental stroll around the borders of her plan, testing it for weaknesses. She knew it was risky but it was the only thing left to her. Somehow, things must come to a head. She felt the killer breathing down their necks. His net reached out across the city, and it would only be a matter of time before she and Josh were caught in it. In fact there was no time left. The hunter could not be sure that Lizzie had kept her fatal knowledge to herself.

There was another factor. His love of brutality had been fed until he'd come to believe that he could kill with impunity. Why would he give up now? Had he found that a knife gave him more pleasure than his bare hands? Or had he been pressed for time and decided that one slice across the throat was all that Lizzie merited? Poor, fated Lizzie. She'd never had a chance.

Nicola would have liked to keep Josh out of her plan. Still, he was already endangered by his association with her, and he would say that, as Rose's brother, he had a right to be included. Certainly it was a comfort to have his reassuring presence at her back. How would she have felt, going alone to face the proprietor of the Jolly Waterman, and discovering Lizzie in the coalhole in a lake of blood? It didn't bear thinking about.

Yet, she'd have gone ahead, even without Josh's support, driven by her overwhelming sense of outrage. How dared this creature take upon himself the power of life and death over another human being? The brute was a coward, preying on the weak. His deliberate debasement of Rose was unforgivable; her death, and that of Lizzie, and perhaps many others, unknown and unregretted, branded him cruel and degenerate. He had to be stopped.

When Josh clambered back up from the rocks, brandishing the dinner he'd wheedled out of the fisherman, Nicola beckoned him to sit beside her while she unfolded her plan.

He didn't like it. He said so as vehemently and in as many ways as he could, but Nicola would not be swayed.

'It's the only way, Josh. It will finish this whole dreadful business one way or another. It's got to be finished, you know.'

'It'll finish *you*, Nicola. The risk is . . . is . . . gigantic.' Josh's freckles stood out against his pallor like a virulent case of measles. 'Look what happened last time I warned you about going into danger. You nearly got burned to death, that's what. You were lucky that time. But you're no match for this killer.'

'Not physically, I know. However, I can match him in guile.' Nicola grasped his hands in her earnestness. 'Josh, I can't do it without your help. Please, Josh. I need you to be with me, heart and soul. Together, we need to avenge Rose.'

Josh, the undemonstrative, put his arm around her shoulders.

'Come on. I know a place where we can build a fire and cook this fish. And afterwards you can explain your plan to me again. I don't think I took it all in the first time.'

CHAPTER THIRTY-TWO

THAT NIGHT NICOLA stood at the mouth of an alley running off Sussex Street. It was an unfrequented area bounded by warehouses. The only light came from a single streetlamp, making the surroundings all the darker.

She felt exposed. The light revealed the full glory of her costume, which had been supplied by a giggling Lydia and friends earlier in the night. Examination in a mirror had convinced Nicola that she was unrecognizable. Determined to do the job properly, she had modelled herself on a lithograph by Toulouse-Lautrec, which hung in Eleanor's room. It was the portrait of a dancer in a Paris nightbox, extravagant, lively and utterly unlike the sort of artwork to be found in the average home.

Now, like the dancer, she showed a painted face beneath a frizzed bang of hair, and the addition of a most opulent hat. Feathers drifted around her head like clouds about a mountain peak; her skirts were short enough to expose the tops of her boots at mid calf, and the expanse of bosom protruding above a boned corset made her blush whenever she thought of it. Long net gloves covered her bare arms and a band of velvet encircled her throat. She looked, and felt, like an adventuress.

She also shivered in the night air, partly with cold, more likely with nervous tension. It comforted her to know she wasn't alone, that support lurked behind her in the dark laneway.

She wondered when he'd come. Her note enticing him with the promise of information about Rose's murderer had stipulated one hour after midnight. She had been in place much earlier, in case he decided to set a trap. There was no trap. Yet the half-hour after one had struck on the town hall clock, and he hadn't come. Nicola clamped her chattering teeth and resumed what she hoped resembled a provocative stroll beneath the lamp.

Ten minutes later she heard footsteps approaching. Quickly arranging herself against a wall, with her face just beyond the circle of light, she searched for the man materializing out of the dark. He was in no hurry, but walked towards her at an unbroken pace until he reached the lamp. There he stopped and looked her over.

'I thought it'd be someone like you,' said Robert Carrington. His scornful tone stung. 'What new information could you possibly have on the case?'

Nicola swallowed and said in a false high tone, 'What's it worth to know the man what did it?' She stared at his hands, long, pale, sinewy, with dark hairs at the knuckle. Were these the hands that had closed around Rose's throat and choked the life out of her?

Frowning, Robert took a step forward. 'Who are you? How do you know the killer?'

Nicola shaded her face from the light and thrust her bosom forward as a distraction. 'Never you mind my name. I know what I know, and it's worth good money.'

He smiled unpleasantly. 'Not to me. I won't have to pay a penny. You'll come with me to the nearest lock-up, you two-bob tart, and there you'll tell me what you know, if anything.' His hand shot out and grasped her wrist, dragging her up to the lamppost.

She gazed up at him with a sinking heart. He wasn't the one. He wanted to interrogate her, not kill her. It was either Hugh . . . or Andrew.

Robert's utter amazement should have been funny. But within an instant it had turned to outrage. He dropped her wrist as if it had burnt him.

'Nicola? It is you, Nicola?'

'Yes,' she said, in her normal voice. 'I'm sorry to have put you through this charade. It was necessary.'

He brushed this aside. 'I've had men searching for you for weeks. Do you know I've been almost out of my mind with worry, picturing you ill, helpless, in dire need? And all the time . . . All the time you've . . . I can't believe it!' His voice quivered with rage, underlaid with an incredulous contempt that made her wince. 'You couldn't wait, could you? You weren't getting results so you forgot who and what you are, and where you come from, and lowered yourself to the level of your dead friend. What did you think you would achieve in the company of street drabs? Did you even pause to consider the awful risks of such a . . . a disgraceful masquerade?'

Weighted by fury, his words struck her like hammer blows, deliberately wounding. 'Or was I completely mistaken in you? Have you been leading a double life all along? Were you seeking some sort of perverted thrill? There must be bad blood in you, Nicola. I should congratulate myself upon a lucky escape.' He turned, as if about to leave, then spun around again. Fists clenched at his sides, he stared down at her painted face, his own taut with misery. In a pain-filled voice he said. 'Why did you do this? I loved you so much. And now . . . I could just strangle you!'

Nicola's gulp of laughter was not mockery, but an involuntary reaction to the awful irony, the stupidity of his words. More laughter, cruel and taunting, came from the laneway as Lydia and a half-dozen friends pranced out, clearly relishing his discomfiture. Josh followed, looking both embarrassed and disappointed.

As the women circled around their victim, he covered his face. A moment later he wheeled and rushed away up the street towards the city.

Nicola slid down the lamppost until she crouched on the gutter's edge, her head drooping. Josh squatted beside her, patting her awkwardly.

'Never mind, Nicola. Never mind,' he crooned.

She said in a muffled voice, 'I'm all right, Josh. It was just a bit more confronting than I'd bargained for. I've hurt Robert badly, and he's a good man.' She suddenly flung off the ridiculous hat and turned to Josh. 'It's awful, Josh. I'd hoped it was him, not one of the others.'

The boy said grimly, 'So, we go on?'

She could only nod.

It occurred to her that when Robert Carrington had regained his poise, he would see past his first furious and hurt response to her ploy. Realizing that he had witnessed an orchestrated performance, he would start looking for reasons behind it. His search would be much more specific now. What if he were under observation by the killer, and led him straight to her? She decided she'd better carry out the next stage of her plan at once.

But Josh seemed more than ever reluctant.

After a quick visit to Mr Montague Pritchard's pawnshop, Nicola took the calculated risk of returning to Viola Terrace with Josh for just a few hours' rest in safety, sneaking in through the back entrance while it was still dark. Now, in the late afternoon Nicola sat at her desk, ready to implement stage two.

'What's wrong, Josh? All you have to do is deliver a note to Hugh and make sure he doesn't catch sight of you.'

'Why does it have to be him first? Why not Andrew?'

It was a fair question, for which Nicola had no answer. Of course, it might have had to do with facing an innocent Andrew and having to explain herself. But if he were the killer. . . ? She would not, could not think of that.

'I just know it's best to do it this way. Don't argue with me, Josh. My head's splitting.' Nicola dipped her pen in the ink, then sat nibbling the end. The bait had to be the same yet subtly altered for a mind like Hugh's. His weakness, as with Robert, was vanity. Both men wanted to be seen to excel in their field. However, Robert's was a class-conscious need for superiority, whereas Hugh desired power over other men. He would enjoy the acclaim for capturing a brutal killer and delivering him to justice, having first adminis-tered some rough justice of his own. Yes, that would be the lure for him. She began to write.

Later, when Josh had returned from his errand, she questioned him eagerly.

'Did you find him easily? I hope he didn't catch sight of you.'

Josh just grinned.

'And how did he react?' She knew it would be no guide to Hugh's guilt or innocence, but she had to ask.

'I couldn't see from behind the door. He just screwed the note up and put it in his pocket. Then he went on drinking with his pals. So I cut off home.' He hesitated. 'Nicola, this is getting too dangerous. This meeting place down on the wharves – there's rats of all kinds there, including human ones. There's only one of me, and I can't see Lydia and her lot being much use if you're attacked by a couple of bullies, let alone a murderer.'

Nicola reassured him as well as she could, while hiding her own misgivings. The pawnshop pistol gave her some protection, although admittedly she knew nothing about firearms and doubted her ability to shoot point blank at anyone. She had already refused further help from Lydia and her friends, deciding that they might prove more of a hindrance.. But Josh was right. The meeting place down on the waterfront was necessarily lonely. The killer would not be lured into attacking her in a public place. She had to have back-up.

Her solution was to have Josh hire two men willing to hide near by in case of need. As a guarantee of their loyalty, the second half of their payment would be made only after the meeting took place. Josh argued, but she knew she could rely on him.

That night she dressed carefully in her harlot's outfit and again painted her face. It gave her a feeling of anonymity, spurious, maybe, yet a definite boost to her courage. She was frightened, yet fully committed. The weight of the pistol in the bag on her arm helped, as did the knowledge that Josh was out there in the darkness with his hired bravos in place.

The driver of the cab she hailed needed an inducement to take someone of her sort as a fare, and he grew even more dubious when told the destination. But Nicola didn't jib at bribing the cabbie to drop her at the top of a street leading down to the Pyrmont docks.

However, the walk down that street, alone in the windy dark, was the longest, hardest walk she'd ever taken. She crept along, hugging the walls of factories and yards, cringing at the sound of her boots on the pavement, trying to walk on tiptoe. This time she felt even more exposed, the tethered goat about to enter the trap as bait for a tiger.

The wind whipped at her skirts and tugged at her hat, and a thin crescent moon did little to light her way. Sometimes she stumbled on rough stones. Once she tripped and fell, shredding the net gloves and grazing her hands. Her bag had flown half across the street, and she picked it up with trepidation. She withdrew the pistol and examined it for damage. It seemed all right. Now she trembled so violently that she feared she might drop the weapon, or even fire it by accident.

Holding it carefully in both hands she leaned back against a brick wall and drew a few deep breaths. She had to calm herself or she'd never be able to sustain her role. A part of her mind, the part she'd been quelling for two days, told her that she was crazy to be where she was. It rapidly reviewed all the reasons why she should be somewhere else. Her teeth chattered in a mouth as dry as the desert, and every nerve in her body seemed to be leaping, eager to get her out of there.

It needed all her willpower, but she overcame the nerves, admitted to the fear, then locked it away. She stood up and carefully wiped the dirt from her hands and clothes. She was ready now. With the pistol concealed in the folds of her skirt, she set off down towards the wharves.

The harbour was dark and oily, the water sucking up against the piles and receding like the breath of a sleeping animal. Strips of cloud banded across the crescent moon, creating false shadows that flickered and went, hiding any real movement amongst the warehouses and crates stored on the wharves. Large cranes raised their antennae overhead and hooks and wires clinked, stirred by the wind off the water.

Rotating slowly, Nicola strained eyes and ears, seeking reassurance that her back-up was there. Only the creak of metal joints rewarded her, and the cry of a night bird swooping out towards the harbour mouth.

When he came it was with the stealthy rush of a panther, straight out of an alley, springing for her throat. Hands gripped, tightened, cutting off her air.

The pistol dropped to the ground as she swayed back, clutching at those murderous hands. Her mouth opened in a choked scream. Her eyes were wide, staring into the soulless eyes of a killer. Lungs straining, throat burning, she saw the night light up with coruscating stars. She knew she was going to die.

The pressure eased and a familiar voice said, 'Clever Nicola. You hunted in men's clothing. No wonder you were so hard to find.'

She struggled to force words through her mangled larynx, but no sound emerged.

'I loved you – would have spared you if I could; but I know you too well to believe you might ever forgive me. Goodbye, Nicola.'

The hands tightened inexorably. Her nails tore at them. Then quite suddenly she was free, and Hugh went staggering back. For a moment he teetered off balance. Then a whirlwind rushed by and fell upon him.

Nicola lay collapsed in the spinning darkness, but she heard Josh calling her, felt him dragging at her shoulders.

'Get up, Nicola. Are you all right? Speak to me!'

'Yes,' she croaked, opening her eyes. But she made no attempt to rise. Her attention was riveted to the battle going on just a few yards away.

The two men were equally matched in size, and each seemed determined to overcome the other at any cost. It was brutal to watch. Nicola winced at every crack of bone on bone, horrified at the gouging, kicking and clawing as the opponents left human decency behind and fought for life itself. Even Josh loosened his clutch on her and watched, transfixed, as the men grappled, tripped and fell heavily against a crane. One hit his head an almighty crack, then rolled aside as the other threw himself bodily after him. Now they were on the ground, punching and tearing at each other's eyes. Then one man broke away, staggered upright and peered around.

Nicola knew why. Her pistol lay half in the shadow of a timber baulk, its metal dully reflecting the moonlight. He saw it at the same time as she did. Their eyes met. Instantly Nicola sprang, clutching at the weapon, twisting aside as Hugh reached out and swept her legs from under her, pinning her with his weight. The pistol flew out of her hand and over the edge of the wharf. She heard it splash and saw the blind fury in Hugh's face as he raised a hand to smash hers.

The hand was arrested. She thought she heard a whisper, 'Ah, no. . . .'

And then his opponent was upon him. Hugh, dragged upright, arms flailing, met with a terrific blow to the jaw that lifted him right off his feet, to fall, a dead weight, across an iron bollard. Nicola heard bones crack, followed by a groan.

Her rescuer stood waiting, feet astride her body, fists clenched, ready. All three waited as slowly, painfully, Hugh dragged himself on to his knees, then on to his feet, crouching, weaving his head as if trying to clear it. It was obvious that only his clutch on the bollard was keeping him upright. His eyes burned like those of a trapped animal, and the beautiful voice was hoarse, defeated.

'I should have known better. There's no place for sentiment in my world. And now it's brought me down.'

Without another word he threw himself backwards over the wharf edge.

Josh dashed forward, and Nicola heard another, familiar voice call harshly, 'Leave him! Let him take that way out.'

Then Andrew knelt and gathered her into his arms.

CHAPTER THIRTY-THREE

A NDREW PEERED CLOSELY and gave a crack of laughter. 'My God, you've really got yourself up for the role.' He produced a handkerchief and began wiping the paint from Nicola's face. But his levity was an obvious mask for anxiety as he examined her in the half-light for damage. 'What in Hades have you got around your neck?'

Nicola put up a hand and winced. 'It's a dog collar. I thought it might save me if he went for my throat, and it did – for a few vital moments.'

Shaking his head, Andrew sought for the buckle at the back of her neck and carefully removed the collar. He examined the bruising it had left and said unemotionally, 'Little fool. I've never known anyone like you for taking risks.' And seeing nothing seriously wrong with her, he proceeded to cover her face with kisses.

Nicola flung her arms around his neck and said fervently in his ear, 'I'm so glad it wasn't you.'

He drew back to look at her. 'Should I thank you for the compliment? It's not exactly pleasant to be suspected of being a murderous deviant.'

'You knew I had to include you among the suspects. I had to. My intuition told me to trust you, but I couldn't afford a mistake.'

He kissed her gently. 'Rogue! I understand, and I love you for your loyalty to your friend. Oh, Nicola, I died fifty times over on the way here, fearing I would be too late.'

She saw the sheen of tears in his eyes and was swept by a sudden surge of emotion. 'Oh, my dear love,' she whispered, and buried her face in his shoulder.

They stayed clasped in each other's arms for a long moment, until Nicola said, 'Could we get up off the ground?'

Smiling, Andrew raised her to her feet. 'Can you stand?'

'Of course I can.' All the same, reaction had set in, and she wobbled, glad of his supporting arm.

'You're out on your feet. Let's get you home and leave the post mortem discussion until tomorrow. Josh, will you fetch the horses?'

Now that Nicola had time to really look at Andrew, she exclaimed distressfully at the blood caked in his hair and streaking down one cheek. Even in the poor light she could see cuts and grazes down the side of his face. She touched the wounds gently.

'Don't look like that.' Andrew grasped her hand and held it to his mouth, mumbling through her fingers, 'It's nothing. Don't you know I'd walk through hellfire to save you a moment's pain?'

'I wish you wouldn't say such things,' she whispered.

'Why not? You are my heart, all my life, Nicola. Without you it's a wasteland, without savour or excitement. I've wanted you since the day we met in the solicitor's office and I could see exactly what you thought of me. You have led me a dance ever since, but now I've got you. If nothing else, you are mine by right of conquest, so resign yourself, woman.'

His mouth came down on hers firmly, his arms tightened around her, holding her where he wanted her. And Nicola began to melt. His tongue did extraordinary, magic things, wakening undreamt-of feelings, while her body had taken on a life of its own, straining against his with an urgency that astonished her.

When released after an eternity, she leaned back in his arms and gazed at him, bewildered and disturbed.

'Andrew. . . .'

'Hush, now, my darling. You suffered an ordeal tonight and I've selfishly kept you standing here in the cold.' He let his eyes glide appreciatively across her bare bosom. 'Fetching as your gown is, it was not designed for the wharves on a windy night.' He let her go and whipped off his coat to wrap it around her. 'I wonder whether Josh has . . . Ah, yes. Here he comes now. '

Hoofs rang on stone, then clattered on to the wharf as Josh appeared out of the darkness leading Andrew's Saracen and a smaller mare. Andrew swung stiffly into his saddle, and Nicola realized that he must be suffering the results of his battle with Hugh. Hugh! Memory hit her sickeningly, like a blow to the stomach, and she turned back to scan the oily water sucking against the piles. She shuddered.

Josh said bracingly, 'He deserved to die, Nicola. I hope the sharks make a meal of him.' Obeying Andrew's order, he bent and cupped his hands for her foot.

An immense wave of weariness washed through her, and without argument, she stepped forward and allowed him to launch her up before Andrew.

He quickly enfolded her, tucking her against his chest and murmuring into her hair, 'Owen wanted it this way, my darling. He could never have lived with defeat. And the water was quicker and kinder than hanging.'

'I know. I still regret such an ending. Vengeance is a cruel thing.'

'Justice, not vengeance. Even though he hesitated at the end, he would still have killed you, and gone on killing. The man was a misfit. He couldn't be contained within the rules of normal society.'

'Yet he did care about others. He fought like a demon for the rights of working men. It's as though he were two people in the one skin, one single-minded in his devotion to a cause, the other brutally self-indulgent. No wonder he didn't fit into society. He had no hope of it.'

Andrew's grip tightened. 'Soft-heart. There's nothing anyone could have done to help Owen or to change his nature. Try to forget him.' He headed Saracen towards home, with Josh following on the mare.

Under cover of the horses' movements Andrew whispered many things to Nicola, things that both delighted and dismayed her; but she was too worn out to do more than listen and snuggle against his protective warmth and let the words of love flow over her.

Only after she was tucked up once again in the guestroom next door to Eleanor did Nicola sleepily recall the gaps in the story. How had Andrew appeared so opportunely? What had happened to the hired guards? What had caused Hugh to release her and stagger back, just before Andrew attacked him? Puzzling over these points she fell asleep and didn't wake until late the next morning.

*

It was a bright cold day, with sunlight streaming in to pool on the timber floor and capture the colours in the rug beside her bed. Nicola lay drowsily watching shadow leaves dance against the wall. When the maid brought her breakfast, then water for her bath, she dawdled, putting off what was to come. At last the moment arrived when she could no longer procrastinate. Dressed, and with no further excuse possible, she knocked on the door of Eleanor's room.

It was a tentative knock, but Eleanor's response took her over the threshold and straight into her friend's open arms. Kneeling, Nicola laid her head in Eleanor's lap and began to sob.

'What's this? The heroine of the hour dissolving just when she is celebrating victory?' Eleanor stroked the smooth, coppery head, her twisted hands as soothing as a mother's.

Nicola continued to sob. So Eleanor waited. After long moments Nicola sat back on her heels and mopped her face.

'I'm sorry, Eleanor. I don't know what came over me.'

'It's quite simple, my dear. Your nerves have been strung tight for a long time, and this is their way of releasing. I was always the same, stalwart in emergency, and quietly collapsing afterwards, in secret if I could manage it.' Eleanor raised the damp face and kissed both cheeks. 'Do you feel better now?'

'Yes, I do. Oh, Eleanor, I do apologize for ever having suspected your son.'

'I understood. I also knew that you had to discover the truth for yourself.' She saw Josh standing in the doorway, looking tentative, and her bright smile lit. 'Dear Josh. Now here's a young man who trusts his instincts.'

'Oh, yes, indeed.' Nicola rose, her expression non-committal as she greeted him. 'A most instinctive person, I'd say. Josh even decided for himself that Andrew could not be the killer, so he enlisted his help. I suppose the hired guards never existed.'

Josh fidgeted with his buttons. 'That's right. I'm sorry I disobeyed you, Nicola, but I'm not sorry – if you know what I mean.' His anxious eyes belied his assertiveness.

Nicola softened. 'Well young man, I suppose I'll have to forgive you. In fact, you should be praised for trusting your own intuition when I could not. Come here, Josh.'

He came eagerly, even submitting to a fierce hug. Eleanor reached out and demanded her morning kiss, which he gave her with no sign of embarrassment. Josh was growing up rapidly, Nicola thought. Yet, when she tried to thank him, he wriggled like a small child and cut her short. So she ended by questioning him on one point.

'About that moment just before . . . before the fight began. Something happened to make Hugh release me.'

Josh's cheeky grin appeared. He dug in his back pocket and dragged out his shanghai. 'I brought along some good pebbles and got him square between the eyes. If he'd been a rabbit he'd've dropped on the spot.' He seemed to take her amazement as sufficient tribute. 'By the way, Andrew wants to talk to you. He's waiting in the book room.' Having delivered his message, he left hurriedly, most likely to try his wheedling tactics in the kitchen, thought Nicola.

Feeling more troubled than eager over Andrew's request, she turned back to Eleanor, who said gently, 'Go to him, my dear. He cares for you very much, you know.'

'I do know. And I'm conscious of how much I owe him.'

Eleanor shook her head. 'No, no. This is not the time for obligation. Come here and let me tell you something.' She took Nicola's hands in her own frail ones. 'You have probably wondered why I wear these rings, when my hands are distorted and the weight of the jewels is almost too much for them. I wear them for memory of the man who gave them to me and who loved me with all his heart.'

Puzzled, Nicola had a vision of some madly dashing affair, then as quickly dismissed this. 'Your husband.'

'Yes, Geoffrey, my husband and lover. Each day when I look at these rings I am reminded of the man he was before guilt and self-recrimination destroyed him. Even in the darkest hours we never ceased to care for one another.'

'Yet you leave his portrait downstairs. Andrew says you can't bear to have it with you,' Nicola said, more confused than ever over this curious relationship.

Eleanor's eyes held a far away expression. 'I left it there hanging in Andrew's book room in the hope that he would one day forgive his father. The portrait is of the true and loving man I married and who loved his son, whatever he may think. One day, perhaps Andrew will realize it.'

But it's not in the book room any longer, Nicola thought. Eleanor's scheme had failed. Her heart ached for her friend, adding to the sorrow already there.

Eleanor was saying, 'Andrew has the same capacity for lifelong devotion. He needs your love, and you do love him, don't you?'

'Yes, I love him.' She spoke so sadly that Eleanor was silenced. 'I'll go to him now.'

Nicola trod down the grand staircase slowly, dreading the coming meeting. Eventually she arrived at the book room door, knocked and went in. Andrew awaited her by the fireplace. His face still showed the marks of battle, but nothing could mar his eager expression. He came forward, took her hands and drew her to the hearth, gazing down at her face, drinking it in as if securing it for ever in his memory.

'Did you sleep well?' he asked.

She nodded, not trusting her voice.

'And your throat?'

She heard the anxious note, and forced herself to say, 'Quite all right, thank you.'

Still holding her gaze, he raised her hands to his lips, holding them there for a long minute. 'What is it, Nicola? Something is troubling you.'

She avoided a direct answer and asked if they could sit down. Andrew led her to a chesterfield and seated himself beside her, half-turned in order to study her expression. He also retained hold of her hands. 'Tell me, Nicola.'

'It's so difficult. I owe you my life, twice over, Andrew. I'm so grateful. . . .'

He pulled her into his arms and kissed her until she stopped resisting and lay pliant against him. But she did not return his kiss.

'I don't want to hear about gratitude, my darling,' he said. 'And I warn you, whenever you begin to talk nonsense I'll have to kiss you until you regain your senses.' His tone was teasing but he was watchful, waiting.

She sighed. "I can't marry you, Andrew.' The bald statement hung in the air, sharp and clear.

Eventually he asked, 'Why not? I adore you and would do all in my power to make you happy. And I think you love me. I've waited a long time for your answer. Tell me honestly, Nicola, *do* you love me?'

'Yes.' She drew back, her fists clenched in her lap. 'But marriage would be disastrous for us both. How can I make you see?'

'I can't, unless you explain.' Andrew sounded reasonable, although she sensed his strain. It showed in the set of his shoulders and his absolute stillness.

Frustrated, she burst out, 'We've been over this before, but you just will not listen. I told you once that I couldn't respect your way of life. I know how pompous and priggish I must have sounded, but there's a core of truth in it. My own ideals, the principles by which I live my life are important to me. I can't live in idleness as a rich man's wife. I have to be involved in all the sorts of schemes that would only embarrass you amongst your friends and colleagues. I'd be an oddity, a burden, a subject of mirth.

'Nor would you want to be dragged into the circle of my friends, amongst suffragettes, preachers of temperance, women fighting for recognition at every level of society. Many of my days are spent in factories and hovels and I come home weary, dirty, and often sick at heart. I'm called to meetings at odd hours, and whatever time is left to me is spent in studying. There'd be nothing left over for you, Andrew, don't you see? You love gaiety and high living. You are a kind man, when you choose to be. But you're a business man, not interested in politics or in bettering the lot of people less fortunate than yourself. In short, you lead the life of a pleasure-loving member of upper society. I can't and won't lead such a life at your side.'

When she paused, he waited politely, then said, 'Have you finished?'

'Yes.' Nicola felt wretched. She hadn't wanted to say such things, but he'd forced them out of her. He had to realize that there was no hope whatever of their being compatible, and her love for him would have to be stifled, somehow, whatever it cost her. She couldn't bring herself to look at him, to see what damage she'd done.

Andrew still spoke mildly. 'Is it any use my pointing out how little you know about my way of life, only what is reported?'

'I know enough. The whole world knows. It's hardly any secret. Don't make this any more difficult for me, Andrew.' Something was threatening to clog up her throat. She rose hurriedly. 'I have to go home. There's so much neglected work waiting for me.'

Andrew rose and caught her to him. 'Don't leave just yet. Let me try to prove that there is hope for us together. You can't turn your back on this kind of love, my darling. It's too strong.'

She pulled away. 'I can. I must.' Her voice broke. 'I can't take any more just now, Andrew. So much has happened. I need time alone. Let me go before I make a complete fool of myself.' There was such a pain in her heart. She had to get away.

'I understand. I won't press you any more just now. But promise to talk to me again soon. I'm not letting you run away to bury yourself, refusing to see me.'

'Yes. Yes. I promise.' Nicola would have promised him just about anything to enable her to escape. A part of her, a very strong part, wanted her to throw herself into his arms, to feel his mouth on hers, stirring her to passionate abandon. But that would be a betrayal of her innermost needs and beliefs. She had to remain her own woman, with all that that meant. If she surrendered now, she would be denying everything she'd fought for and, in the long run, she would despise herself.

Back upstairs she said an awkward goodbye to Eleanor, who was clearly baffled and unhappy at the way events were turning out. However, she had the wisdom not to interfere when Nicola announced her intention of returning home immediately. Nicola did agree to visit later, after she'd reorganized her routine and reported back to the various organizations depending upon her support. Then having extracted Josh from the kitchen, where he filled the role of culinary critic and taster in chief, she accepted the offer of the Dene carriage back to Viola Terrace.

Andrew saw them off, acting the impeccable host, his manner covering the hurt and disappointment he must feel. Nicola carried her guilt with her all the way home. She wished she could be angry with him, but all she felt was the agony that she had inflicted on them both. It would be a relief to throw herself back into work.

CHAPTER THIRTY-FOUR

A
FTER A SLEEPLESS night, Nicola sat at her desk, opening the correspondence accumulated over the time she had been away. She tried to ignore her sore heart for the moment and take a real interest in the successes achieved by various political groups. There were exciting things happening with the push for the female franchise. It did seem as though things were coming to a head.

Near the bottom of the pile she found a surprisingly formal note from Andrew. In it he advised her that he did not intend notifying the police about their activities at the wharf two nights ago. Whether or not Hugh Owen's body was ever recovered from the depths of the harbour, there would be nothing to connect Nicola with his death. Robert Carrington might guess at her involvement, but he could never prove it, and it was highly unlikely that Lydia and her friends would feel impelled to visit a police station with information.

Nicola smiled. A vision of Lydia's pert face, and Josie's half-fearful one, and Sal, the barmaid's assertive stance when dealing with her customers, caused a sudden rush of warm feeling towards these women who were forced to live such quietly desperate lives yet could still give so generously to a stranger.

However, she did not agree that Robert should be kept in total ignorance, unable to close his case. It needed only a whisper to be circulated in the right quarters, giving the name of Rose's murderer and planting the rumour that he'd fled the country. Robert would hear and draw his own conclusions.

She wrote a carefully couched note for Josh to deliver to Lydia. Nicola did not intend to lose touch with the women who had helped her. Already she had an idea for a refuge hostel, which she intended to put forward to Rose Scott at the first opportunity.

But something more immediate waited for her amongst the pile of letters. This was an invitation to attend a public meeting at the Sydney town hall, which would mark the founding of the first Australian chapter of the National Council of Women.

At last! Recognition of the part to be played by Australian women in politics, in the work place, in each facet of public life. The members of this new council would represent every women's organization in New South Wales, and be joined to the worldwide sisterhood of powerful women lobbyists. And this was just the beginning.

When Josh heard Nicola's triumphal shout, he left his breakfast and rushed into the sitting room. Nicola stood with a flushed face and shining eyes, brandishing a letter.

'Josh, we've done it. Raise the bright banners and sing in joyful praise. We've done it! There'll be no going back. Women are on the march, thousands of women all over the country – an untapped source of power that will make our society sit up and take notice.'

Josh blinked and relaxed his taut stance. 'That's good, Nicola. Do you want a pie for supper or will I go out for a rabbit?'

The scene on that twenty-sixth day of June in the year 1896, was unprecedented. Long inured to political rallies, the city opened its eyes to the sight of a flood of women converging on the wide hub of George Street, that space dividing the sandstone Cathedral of St Andrews and the flamboyant cross between Italian Renaissance and ponderous Gothic known affectionately as the Wedding Cake, or otherwise, the Town Hall.

Carriage after carriage drew in under the great square portico to disgorge the female passengers, all dressed with importance. George Street itself was awash with enormous hats, some as wide as serving platters and flat as mushrooms, some with high winged brims supporting whole stuffed birds or piles of artificial fruit. There were flowing veils and tiny squashed caps tied under the chin, à la Queen Victoria; there were feathers, flowers, velvet scrolls and satin bows; there were straws, velours and toques, large and small, of every age, shape and variety.

The hats streamed into the town hall's ornate vestibule, their owners chattering excitedly, and Nicola lamented that there'd been no time to fashion silk banners to wave on this auspicious day. She would personally see to it that they were ready for the next conference.

The scene inside was impressive. There must have been 200 women squeezed into the huge decorative vestibule, while others waited beyond the doors to hear the outcome of proceedings.

Nicola found herself a place squashed into a corner with her notebook at the ready. Once again she was experiencing the great surge of triumph that had swept through her at news of this event. There would be no going back from this day. For so long the women had struggled in isolated groups, each dedicated to a worthy cause but, because of this fragmentation, unable to exert sufficient pressure to bring about change. Now they would have a united voice. After today, every organization dedicated to the betterment of women and children would be gathered in under the worldwide canopy of one council.

She could see Rose Scott up front, her lovely face joyful under the brim of a magnificent leghorn straw. Louisa and other co-workers were lost somewhere in the sea of hats. As the initial excitement quietened to expectancy, proceedings got under way.

The pivotal moment arrived with the second resolution: 'that the Constitution drafted by the Provisional Committee be adopted'. The meeting voted in an executive committee and the National Council of Women of New South Wales was officially born.

Looking around her, Nicola saw the hope in women's faces. It was not so much the actual proceedings that she would remember about this day, but the atmosphere of shared optimism and pride rising above class and culture to join this disparate group.

By the time it had all finished and the women began surging out towards the main entrance, Nicola was exhausted. Success could be every bit as tiring as failure, she thought as she joined the departing crowd, edging her way towards the flight of marble steps. She was annoyed with herself for feeling depressed. Surely this day was a triumphant pinnacle reached. But a cloud clung to this peak, reminding her of the price she was paying for independence and a part in the successful climb.

Then an arm came out of nowhere and plucked her from the crowd. She found herself whisked behind one of the stone pillars of the portico gazing up at Andrew. His bruised face was alight with satisfaction.

'So you've done it, Nicola. Congratulations! You and your fellow workers have taken a remarkable leap forward. The next decade will see a revolution in the status of women.'

Nicola, with legs unaccountably weakened, rested back against the pillar, welcoming its support. She wished Andrew had not come. How could she cut him out of her life if he refused to stay in the background?

She hunted for the right reply. 'Thank you, Andrew. We know there's a long road ahead of us, but this is, as you say, the first huge step.' She shied away from the expression in his eyes. How had she once thought them cool? A tremor ran through her, plucking at her nerves.

Andrew moved a little closer, his hands now resting on the pillar, enclosing her. His conversational tone belied his manner, encroaching on her space by fractions of an inch. 'You know, of course, that the Australian Workers' Union is seeking better conditions for women. There's a select committee of inquiry looking into the need for old age pensions and invalid pensions; and by next year there will be an employers' liability act to deal with workplace injuries and compensation for these.' He was now almost pressed against Nicola, who could move back no further.

'Indeed? How . . . How interesting.' Her heart beat suffocatingly fast. She had to tilt her head back to meet his gaze. This was so burningly intense that her own eyes quickly fell. 'Andrew, I have to go—'

'Give me just ten minutes. You promised, remember?' The heat of his body so close to hers, the tremor in his limbs communicated an unbearable excitement. She felt her body's treacherous response, and was swept with longing to feel his hands, his mouth, all of him.

'Andrew, you're not fair!' It was a despairing wail. 'You know why I can't give way to you.'

'I know why you *think* you can't.'

'It's the same thing. I won't be coerced into changing my mind.'

'I? Coerce?'

He was laughing at her; almost, but not quite touching her, and

ringing to bear all the power of his considerable personality. She
elt her energy draining away in its gravitational pull. Eyes closed,
he grabbed desperately at her resolution.

'Nicola. Look at me.'

His mouth was an inch from hers. Such a beautiful mouth, so
irm, so gently insistent, so . . . She pulled herself up with a jerk.

'Now, Andrew . . .' she began.

'I agree. This is the moment. However, it's entirely too public
here for our discussion. Come with me. I know a place where we
can be private.'

'No!' The protest was useless. Nicola found herself whisked
hrough the lobby and up a side staircase, along a passage lined
with solid timber doors. When she pulled back it was like trying
o stop a runaway tram. Dragged remorselessly onward, she struggled to keep her feet and her dignity.

When eventually she had been towed into a capacious office,
clutching at her hat, she turned in a rage to see Andrew locking
the door and advancing upon her. She retreated behind a huge
mahogany desk, her cheeks ablaze, prepared to rend him asunder.

He halted on the other side of the desk, and said admiringly,
'You look like an infuriated tigress. Quite magnificent. But your
claws are unnecessary. You're not in any danger.'

She sputtered wordlessly, eventually managed to say, 'Kindly
unlock the door at once.'

'All in good time. How do you like my office?'

Nicola blinked at the sudden change in topic. 'I'm not interested
in your office. I just want to be let out of it.'

'Tsk. I'd hoped to impress you with my new dignity, but I see
my hopes are vain.'

Nicola stopped seething. What did he mean, his office? She
gazed around her at the elegant appointments of the room, at the
magnificent gilded and coffered ceiling, at the portraits of former
Lord Mayors on the wall . . . Former Lord Mayors!

Andrew grinned. 'Wait until you see me in all the glory of my
robes of office.'

'You! Lord Mayor of Sydney? I don't believe it.'

He threw back his head and laughed. 'It's worth the wait to see
your face, my darling. It's quite true. My election is very recent,

and you've had other things on your mind.'

Nicola's mind at this moment was confused. 'Then you are interested in politics?'

'Oh, in far more. I care about this city and its people. I've worked towards this day for a long time. As head of the city council I'll have the kind of influence that can't be achieved anywhere else, including parliament.'

'Then it was all a sham,' Nicola said slowly. 'Your pretence at being an idle, pleasure-loving man about town was a fraud.'

'I'm afraid so. Or rather more of a veil over another purpose. You see, I wanted the support and friendship of men who had not already committed to work for the community. In my underhanded way I've managed to convert quite a number of hard-headed businessmen to improving conditions for their employees, male and female, as well as taking an interest in civic works. I've nurtured connections in taverns, clubs, workshops, racecourses and parliamentary back rooms – wherever men gather to talk business or to socialize.

'My pet project is federalism. I've toured country areas with Henry Parkes, stirring up interest in the formation of a true, cohesive nation.' He paused and cleared his throat. 'Now that great heart has gone to rest, but others are carrying the flame. We've been slowed by the effects of the Depression, but a new federal convention will be held next year to draft an Australian constitution.' Again he paused, awaiting Nicola's reaction.

This was so divided that she hardly knew whether to be angry, humiliated or sheerly delighted. 'I don't know what to say. You lied to me by implication.'

'I had a number of delicate operations in hand at the time when I first realized you were important to me. Then my two rivals came on the scene, and you seemed to favour Owen, who stood for all that I opposed. He aimed to destroy relations between worker and employer with militant unionism.'

Nicola sighed. 'And I was bowled over with enthusiasm for "the cause". Naturally you wouldn't have confided in me.' And privately she smarted at the remembrance of pride in her judgement of character. How much more wrong could she have been over Hugh Owen?

Then she rallied. 'But you have been low and sneaky, Andrew Dene. Once Hugh had . . . gone, you could have told me and not let me rant on about the nobility of my own precious aims.'

'It was the wrong moment. You were overwrought by your recent experiences, and I thought it would be better to leave weighty matters until you had recovered. It was too soon for other things, as well, but I couldn't help myself.' His smile crept back. 'And from previous experience, I knew you responded deliciously to my lovemaking.'

'Andrew!'

'Speaking of which, I believe we have some unfinished business, and what better place to discuss business than my office?' In two strides he was around the desk and holding her.

She looked up at him steadily. 'Blind I may have been, and unfair in my judgement of you; but you deliberately deceived me, and for that reason the balance is restored. Yet nothing has changed, Andrew. I refuse to live as a wealthy and idle woman. There is too much that needs to be done. I intend to go on fighting for women's causes. I want to finish my degree and perhaps to teach. I want to establish a refuge as a memorial to Rose.'

'Nicola, I—'

'No. Hear me out, please. I love you, but I will not be dictated to, and it's in your nature to take charge. We should both become frustrated, and unhappy. It's best to end our relationship before we bring such misery upon ourselves.'

His grip tightened.

'Do you think I don't understand all this? There is always the possibility of difficulties in any marriage; and I'm aware of the need to curb my somewhat dictatorial nature. Mother has been working on that for some years.' His voice grew tender. 'My own dear love, you will do as you please. I swear I'll not stand in your way. Yet, my hope is that you will join me in my work, too. As Lady Mayoress of this city, your influence for change could be immense. Just as queen of my heart you will always reign supreme.' His expression held such a depth of love that she was transfixed.

Nicola clasped her hands behind his neck, drawing him down to meet her kiss. As the now familiar flame of passion rushed to engulf her, she had time for one brief thought. *This* was why she'd held on through her pain and terror on the night of the fire. This was why, even without reason to hope, she had never given up on the promise of a future worth having.

When Andrew released her she murmured a protest, but he hushed her.

'I want to give you something – just the first of many gifts of love.' He opened her palm and into it dropped the fire opal heart. 'This is a reminder of a man who loved you in the past, and a promise that you hold my own heart for evermore.'